USA Today Bestselling Author

DALE MAYER

Yipped in the Yams

Lovely Lethal Gardens
REWIND 02

YIPPED IN THE YAMS: LOVELY LETHAL GARDENS RE-WIND, BOOK 2
Beverly Dale Mayer
Valley Publishing Ltd.

ISBN-13: 978-1-778866-66-1
Print Edition

Books in This Series:

About This Book

When the Captain suggests that Doreen might want to break her boredom spell by looking into an old case, she jumps at the chance. Anything new is always great, and anything that the Captain gives her means she has his permission—which gives her a lot of leeway in getting the information she needs.

However, when she realizes the case is about the long-forgotten and unidentified bones of a baby, ... she knows this case will hurt in so many ways. Still, the thought of this case remaining unsolved for so many years makes her all that more determined to solve it.

However, the more digging she does, the more people try to clamp down on talking to her, as she learns that family members of that little girl are still alive. No one is willing to talk, except one—who dies the morning after ...

When her case dovetails with another case and an old big-business local family, the gloves are off, and Doreen wades into the mix as always ...

Sign up to be notified of all Dale's releases here!
https://geni.us/DaleNews

Chapter 1

A Couple Days Later ...

DOREEN POURED A cup of coffee and stepped out onto her deck. It was not quite mid-January and still too freaking cold. She didn't know what she was thinking, but she continued to hold on to that misplaced hope that it would warm up at least a little bit, so she could sit out here comfortably. Still, she couldn't stop smiling as she'd heard from Nate, who'd given Gavin the best New Year's gift ever—he could keep the puppy. The two had a serious talk and had come to a compromise where Gavin would be responsible for looking after the puppy, as well as keeping his nose out of trouble and his marks up as his part of the bargain. Nate would cover the cost of keeping the puppy as his part of the bargain. It seemed like both were happy with the deal. She was thrilled.

Mack stepped up behind her. "Why are you out here in the cold?"

"I don't know," she muttered. "It's just funny that I still want to sit out by the river right now. The only reason I like winter is because I know that very quickly it'll be spring, and we can enjoy being outside again."

"And by then you'll have a huge appreciation for the nice weather too."

She smiled and nodded. "Good point." She leaned back against him.

"My brother's been trying to get a hold of you."

"Of course he has," she replied noncommittally.

"And is there a reason why you haven't responded?"

She shrugged. "No. No reason other than the usual, which is that I'm busy," she replied. "It's been a crazy ten days, you know? And I haven't told him about this case."

"Ah," Mack said, with a note of amusement in his tone. "Even he will be impressed. I think you solved, what, three cold cases all at once? Plus, my current murder case. Believe me that the captain is just crowing."

She sighed. "At least then maybe he won't argue so much about the cost of DNA testing in the future."

"I wouldn't count on that. He likes to argue. Besides, you've solved so many of the cold cases already, so how many more DNA tests could you ask for? Although … another one bothers all of us. Maybe one day we can get there."

"What is it?" she asked.

"A case of bones in a box. A baby's bones," he began. "We have the box, and we have the skeleton, but not much else. They're still on a shelf at the coroner's office."

"Oh my," she muttered, twisting around to look up at him. "Seriously?"

He nodded. "Yes, they were found in a patch of yams, a very long time ago. I don't even have the details, but the captain brought it up, wondering if maybe it was time for that poor case to be resolved. Just rehashing that one case hit all of us pretty hard."

"And yet you don't remember much."

"No, I don't. My mom might have more answers about it than I do. But, if you're interested, the captain told me to give you the file and to let you run wild."

She looked at him in delight. "Seriously? You're not joking?"

"No, I'm not joking. I would say the captain is a happy camper and must be if he's willing to invite you to rummage around, settling these cold cases."

"I do cost him money though."

"You do, indeed," he agreed, with a laugh, "but that's okay."

"A baby? That's sad," she muttered.

"Yes, and"—he winced—"it sounds terrible, but there are definitely bite marks on the bones."

"Of course," she said. "Anytime bones are left out in the wild, that could happen. And yams? Those grow really well here. So could have been in anyone's garden."

"Do they?" he asked.

She nodded. "Yes, they do, especially in these parts. I'll take a look at the case, though the thought of a baby dying is just heartbreaking."

"I know," he muttered.

Then she giggled and quickly stifled it.

"What?" he asked suspiciously.

"Nothing, nothing at all," she said. "I'm going to the burial this weekend. Are you coming?"

"You mean for Rose to have a proper funeral? Yes, and I guess we'll have one for Jack too."

"Yes, now that he's been dug up from Milford's zucchini bed," she muttered. "Who would have thought that Poppy could do that?"

"They had farm equipment at the time, remember? A

tractor. She just used the bucket and worked away at it, I presume, all in Milford's absence. It's what I would do." He nodded. "I guess it's what all of us would do, and, being out in the middle of nowhere like that, there was a certain level of privacy."

"But what about Jack's vehicle?" she asked Mack. "He had to get there somehow, right?"

He frowned at her. "I have no idea."

Doreen suggested, "I bet Poppy drove it off in the middle of nowhere and just left it parked there or maybe drove it into the lake and sunk it there."

"Maybe. I can check to see if we've got any abandoned vehicles found in that area."

"Oh, you keep track of those things too?" she asked, her eyebrows raised.

"No, not always, it depends on the circumstances," he replied. "Much more can be done now with the advances in technology, but, back then, not so much. Yet, if we find a vehicle, and it's in the way, we'll tow it in. Often they are held for the legal owner. ... Poppy was smart and devious. I guess we'll never really know the whole truth about Rose's sister."

"Maybe not, but I'm guessing that, if nothing else, Poppy walked away when her pregnant sister needed help."

"Maybe," Mack agreed. "It sure sounded as if there was absolutely no love lost between them."

"No, not at that stage," Doreen pointed out sadly. "It seems there's only so much love when it comes to jealousy between siblings, and, once somebody crosses the line, well, it's all over."

"Yet I'm not sure what it would take to cross that line."

"I don't know," she said, "but I can guarantee you that

Rose did it."

"And what would that have been?"

Doreen sighed. "I would assume Rose seduced Milford, the man Poppy loved."

"So, Poppy gets rid of her sister and took over Rose's identity, in order to have the man Poppy loved?" he asked, with a headshake.

"Yeah, and that just deepens the mystery about Rose. Nobody really knew what happened to her because they didn't need to know. Poppy took over Rose's identity, and she could say that her sister *Poppy* had moved to Alberta or Vancouver or wherever, and nobody would be any the wiser."

"Smart," he repeated, with a nod, "but also devious."

"Poppy didn't always choose wisely, but I guess it worked because she got Milford, and she got to die in peace in the arms of the man she loved. She sure left him a heck of a mess to clean up afterward."

"And yet I wonder if he was ever intended to find out the truth. She probably assumed he would stay there on his own farm and maybe never would even find that journal."

"I would like to think that she meant for him to know something at some point in time. Otherwise why bring up the zucchini patch? Why press him to find out about the blood there? Why even write out her confession?"

"Maybe so, but I suspect that she couldn't stand the thought of having him hating her, even then, even after her death. Or finding out the truth beforehand because, what if, when she needed him the most, he found out the truth and left her?"

"That may have been Poppy's greatest fear," Doreen whispered.

He wrapped his arms around Doreen and asked, "What was that laugh about earlier?"

She smirked and looked up at him. "Well, I just closed out the *Zonked in the Zucchinis* case."

He rolled his eyes. "You don't know he was *zonked*."

"I'll bet you that the autopsy will prove he was hit with a shovel or a pitchfork to the head. You know that means he must have been extremely drunk or exhausted or blindsided to have been taken out by her. ... So zonked at the time."

He groaned. "Okay, that's quite possible, but that still doesn't explain your laughter." She looked up at him and giggled again. He smiled. "What?"

"We now have yams."

"Yeah, what about yams?"

"And we have animal bites. That means animal sounds ..."

"Yes, so?"

"*Yipped in the Yams*," she cried out triumphantly.

"Oh, Lord, I'm so sorry I asked."

Instead of continuing that ridiculous conversation, he pulled her into his arms and kissed her.

Chapter 2

DOREEN WOKE EARLY the next morning. She stared around her bedroom in slight confusion for a moment. Then all the memories slammed into her. She bounced out of bed in excitement. Mack had promised to send her the cold case file that the captain suggested she take a look at. To even be offered the opportunity was a huge honor, and she wouldn't do anything to jeopardize the relationship she had with the captain, or the faith that Mack had in her. It would be a tough case though, and that in itself would be a challenge, but she was definitely up for it.

She called out to Thaddeus, who was perched on the roost in her bedroom. Thaddeus opened his eyes, glared at her while ruffling his feathers, then sank back into sleep again. "What's with you?" she chided, as she walked into the bathroom.

A long hot shower later, she came out, wrapped in a towel, bubbly and happy. There was just something about having found her place, her people, and her purpose in life. After everything that had happened in this last year, it felt very much as if that's exactly what she had accomplished. She quickly dressed, then leaned over and kissed Mugs, who was stretched out on her bed, not impressed with the early morning start. As usual, Doreen saw absolutely no sign of Goliath.

She walked down the stairs, whistling, then laughed. "Look at you," she said out loud. "Somebody gives you a cold case on a dead child, and here you are happy. What's wrong with you?"

Other than giving those loved ones some closure, Doreen had no good answer to that question. So she ignored it, went to the kitchen, and put on coffee. It was still freezing cold outside. Yet this had been an unseasonably warm winter, and she was okay with that. A nice way to experience her first full winter in Kelowna. With the coffee dripping, she wandered back into the living room.

Now that some of her money issues would soon be re-solved, she wondered just what she wanted to do with this place. All the auction money from Christie's hadn't hit her bank account just yet, and she needed to figure out what to do with it when it did, so she never had to worry about paying bills again. Her husband's estate would go to probate eventually, once the lawyers got through with it all. Plus, there was Robin's estate. So more paperwork.

Doreen shook her head at that. One windfall would have been enough, but all three of them ensured that she would never again find herself in such a desperate situation as she had been in last spring. From her husband's refusing to share any assets with her at all—while separated or during the divorce proceedings—to losing everything, including his life, was just so sad.

Many people might see it as karmic justice, but she re-fused to look at life that way. Everything in her world was just way too good these days. She had Mack, and she had to smile as she held her ring finger out for the morning sun to twinkle on the diamond. She had Nan's house, and she still had Nan—all of which, for Doreen, was an absolute blessing. Plus, now she had a purpose in her life too, something else she couldn't have imagined prior to separating from her husband. Back then she didn't have a life. She had been his showpiece, and that was it. Now she looked nothing like arm candy and couldn't be happier. She was so much more comfortable in her own skin that it was hard to envision her old life.

When the coffee finally finished, she turned on her laptop and sat down to see if she had an email or anything from Mack yet on her new cold case. Frowning, she didn't see one. She quickly sent him a text, asking when to expect it. She got a text back from him, saying as soon as he got to work. He was still having breakfast. She checked the clock and realized it had just turned seven in the morning.

She groaned at that and sat back with her coffee. Only so much she could do until he sent her the file, and it wouldn't be anywhere near fast enough for her. It was too cold to walk down the river, so she headed back over to her living room, wondering what she should do with this space. Of course that just brought up a discussion she needed to have with Mack.

After they married, she presumed they would live here in Nan's house, but Doreen hadn't talked to him about it. She couldn't imagine leaving this place. It was so perfect now that they had the deck and patio and everything outside set up. Not to mention that she absolutely loved living alongside the river. It just reminded her how they still had more to talk about, but she didn't think she would be very willing to budge on this house issue. Still, he seemed to like her house just fine, although it could use some renovations, and it certainly needed some furniture.

Blindly she started going through the possibilities of what she could do for furniture, only to realize that the bathrooms needed updating first, and the master bedroom could certainly use a facelift. Furniture really needed to wait until after that.

With a sigh, she surfed on the web for fifteen minutes but couldn't sit still for long. She got up, went to her bedroom, and stripped down the bedding, then started the laundry. She might as well do something useful while up at seven in the morning. She also didn't know if there would be any physical files to hand over. It sounded as if there wasn't much to go on because, if there had been, someone would have dealt with the matter by now. Mack didn't share much of anything about it, so she didn't know if he had even looked at the case file himself.

The fact that the box with the bones of the dead baby still sat in the morgue said a lot too. It appeared to be something that could never quite be forgotten, yet never solved. That just meant Doreen really needed to step up to see if she could put a name to those bones, maybe even create a face, something she didn't have any experience with. She'd certainly found lots of bodies around Kelowna, but, in this case, they were talking about a baby, found in, of all things, a patch of yams. *Yams.* Kind of weird, yet in a way it made sense because she always thought of yams as baby food. She didn't know why except that she'd seen a catchy ad for some years ago. It just stuck with her, even after all this time.

She remembered having some baked yams with her husband and had found them very sweet, but then they had been cooked with marshmallows and brown sugar and maple syrup. Her husband had been very disapproving of the dish, deemed an item to make her gain weight. That reminder just made her roll her eyes. She was trying hard to keep her memories of him decent and nice, instead of always worrying about how negative life with him had been. In order for her to move on to a happier life, she had to let him go, which was easier said than done.

She returned her attention to her computer and checked through her compiled list of Solomon's files to see if any of his research mentioned finding a child's body in a box. She did a keyword search of her notes on Solomon's files but didn't get a hit. Confused and frustrated, she got up and poured herself a second cup of coffee. Just as she sat down again, she got a text from Mack. She opened it quickly.

Hope you have a good morning. I'm off to work now.

She smiled and sent him a thumbs-up. She didn't want to say anything too pushy about the delay because he would just get his back up and would probably tell her to wait until he got his morning together or something—which was fair enough. Just because she was eager to have another case didn't mean that he would have the time, energy, or attitude to deal with this one, even if it involved her. While he was all about seeking justice and closure for a family who lost someone long ago, that didn't mean it wasn't a real impact on both his workday and his personal time, since they spent a good share of it together. It was all about give and take, and she would need to learn a little bit more about that, especially when she would soon be wed to Mack.

She frowned, realizing that she felt more than a little bit nervous about the whole upcoming marriage thing. Not a comforting thought. She'd barely even had a chance to get her head wrapped around her morning when Nan contacted her.

"Good morning," Nan greeted her in that bright, cheerful voice.

"Good morning, Nan." Doreen smiled. "You're up bright and early."

"I always am," she declared, with a laugh. "I wondered if you wanted to come down and have breakfast with me."

"Sounds good to me. I just poured a cup of coffee though."

"Ah, you and your coffee."

"Yes, me and my coffee." She laughed. "As you very well know, my coffee is a major joy for me."

"And there's no reason not to have things that bring you joy. Didn't some woman make a whole career about finding things to create joy in your life and getting rid of everything else?"

Doreen laughed. "Yes, and I agree with it in part, but, like everything that other people say, it has to be the right thing to do for you."

Nan chuckled. "And the right thing for you to do is put on a coat and come on down here and get some breakfast."

"Is there a special occasion?" Doreen asked, as she got up, sipping the coffee from the cup in her hand. "I am hoping to finish the cup of coffee I'm currently drinking."

"That will take you all of five minutes," she muttered. "Other than that, no, there's no particular reason to have you come, except that I would love to see you." Then she chuckled. "And I'm not saying that just because I'm feeling old and blue."

"That's good, because I would hate to think you are feeling old and blue."

"It happens, and unfortunately it happens a little too often sometimes," she muttered. "Otherwise everything is good. I think we're getting some new people in today too. Don't know if that's a good thing or not."

"You could look at it as new friends."

"I could," Nan muttered in a dark tone. "Or maybe they're here because they've heard about all our detective work."

At that, Doreen wanted to laugh, and she wanted to question that *our* detective work comment but realized it had become an important part of Nan's life. So no way Doreen would take that away from her grandmother.

"You could also look at it as a friend you haven't met yet," she reminded Nan. "Even if they aren't interested in solving cases or just how much goes on at Rosemoor, maybe that's a good thing. Maybe they need something to liven up their lives too."

Nan sniffed. "It depends."

"Here's another thought. They may like gambling," Doreen pointed out.

After a moment of silence, Nan replied in a slightly mollified tone, "That would help. ... These people around here have become a bunch of old fuddy-duddies about placing bets."

"Maybe because they're tired of losing."

"They should change their bets then, shouldn't they? Why would you continue to place losing bets?" she asked, as if it made no sense to her. "Change them to winning bets."

For Nan, placing losing bets made no sense, but a lot of people didn't necessarily know which side to bet on. Her grandmother seemed to have one of those innate abilities to place a bet and to know exactly what it should be at any given time. Not everybody had that same sense, and maybe that's how it should be. At times Nan had definitely been warned to behave herself, to stop the betting even, though she didn't take kindly to it. Now she had more notoriety than anything, and Doreen couldn't imagine anybody prohibiting Nan from her fun.

"Hurry up and finish your coffee," she ordered, with a chuckle. "I can hear the brain cells running through your head. We don't want to miss out on whatever is there, as it could be something important."

Doreen chuckled. "I'm getting the animals ready," she muttered. "I'll be down there in a few minutes."

She quickly disconnected and smiled as she looked around, considering the life she had created for herself. "You did good, Doreen. You did good."

Chapter 3

AS DOREEN DRESSED for her walk to Rosemoor, something about a new year always made her want to start fresh. Sure, they were well into January now, but the sense of newness was still there, having some special innate feeling that was different, that separated one year from another. It made her feel as if something extra came with the new year. Whether it was right or wrong, it always seemed as if, maybe, just maybe, something was out there just for her. Some years worked out better in that regard than others, but last year had been one for the books.

Not only had she managed to sell a lot of the antique furniture her grandmother had given her but Doreen had also involved her grandmother in several cold case investigations, making Nan's final years more interesting and giving her a sense of purpose too. That was important, and, if this was the only way Doreen could give back to her grandmother, then this was what Doreen would do. It was simply a matter of reining in Nan and the rest of her crew at Rosemoor into some semblance of control. Otherwise, wow—when they got out of control, they had the tendency to go off in every direction without a care to any limits. Nan and her merry band of Doreen's Deputies had become the talk of the town, and, no matter how wary Doreen felt about it sometimes, she loved that it made Nan so happy.

Doreen smiled as she called out to the animals, announcing that they were heading down to Nan's.

Thaddeus half flew and half stumbled down the stairs, with Goliath swatting at him as he did. Mugs was already at her feet when she turned around, his tail wagging so hard that his big square butt bounced more than it wiggled.

She smiled at him. "Buddy, you might just need to go on a diet."

He woofed at her several times, and she realized a diet wasn't all that likely to succeed. Nan would have treats down there at Rosemoor for them, just as Doreen assumed there would be some for her. And honestly, she was looking forward to eating them just as much as her animals were. She chuckled as she raced toward Nan's. It was cold outside, and there was a bite to the wind. Of all the things that she liked about Kelowna, this wintery stage wasn't as much fun as she might have hoped, even though it had been warmer than usual.

Not that she had any reason to complain. When she had lived in Vancouver with her husband, Mathew, it had always been wet, wet, wet. There was always such a chill down there just from the dampness, and she had struggled with it. And yet up here in Kelowna with her grandmother, Doreen had adapted to the cold as if life were completely okay. And it was; it was more than okay. She had her work. She had her pets—Thaddeus, Mugs, and Goliath—and she had Nan and Mack. Life was good.

The animals danced around as she headed down the creek. They looked to be completely content with anything and everything she wanted to do this morning. It was hard to argue with that. The animals were always so much fun, and she knew that Nan absolutely loved having them visit her. As Doreen neared the river, she hoped to keep the animals out of it, so she didn't have them soaking everything at Nan's apartment. Unfortunately that message seemed completely lost on Mugs. He walked right into the water, determined that it was the best place for him to be.

She groaned. "Mugs, get out of the water. Isn't it too cold? Plus, you'll be soaking wet at Nan's now."

He woofed at her several times and wandered around closer to the shore. She kept watching, hoping he would decide to come right back out, and he did—eventually. It just took him a little while. When he finally caught up with her, she hadn't gone too much farther, but his body language suggested, *Hey, you're taking off on me.*

She smiled down at him. "I'm not kidding, buddy. We've got to go."

He woofed and gave a big shake, splattering water everywhere, catching Goliath, who swiped at him. Mugs yelped a little bit, jumped back, and Doreen laughed.

"Now you know perfectly well that Goliath doesn't like water, but you did it anyway. And you did it right there beside him, so it's hard for me to feel too sorry for you."

He gave her a look and then raced after Thaddeus, who was still busy half flying and half hopping, strutting down the pathway all on his own.

She sighed. "Thaddeus, don't go too far."

Thaddeus just flapped his wings and ignored her.

"Why do I even bother?" she muttered.

She didn't pass anybody on the pathway. Mind you, most people preferred not to be out in these temperatures and certainly not first thing in the morning. She rarely saw anybody on the river at this hour. She thought maybe once it warmed up more people would appear, but it was hard to say. As she wandered a little farther down, she noted a few people gathering toward the turnoff but wasn't sure what they were doing. When she saw other dogs with them, she realized they were all just outside, giving everybody a few minutes of fresh air. Still, with Mugs dripping water, it was better to avoid any engagement.

She smiled as she passed them and continued on to Nan's. As soon as she got to Rosemoor, she headed for Nan's patio, even though she probably should be avoiding the grassy lawn and going in through the main door. It was always a little bit of a challenge, depending on who was doing the groundskeeping at any given time. Still, it was winter, and no one would be working on the lawns or gardens right now. Plus, Mugs was wet, and taking him in through the main door wasn't a great idea either.

Doreen danced over onto the patio, waiting for the animals to join her, and then opened up the patio door into the living room that Nan had left unlocked. Doreen smiled at Nan, as she called out, "Good morning."

Nan came over and gave her a hug and a kiss on her cheek. "Aren't you in a chipper mood this morning," she noted, as she patted Doreen's bright red cheeks. "Mack is obviously doing his job and keeping you happy."

She flushed at that. "Oh, I won't say that because it falls to me to make me happy too. Yet I'm definitely in a good mood. … Yes, I am."

"Yes, you are, and I can see that." Nan nodded, but her gaze was curious as she studied her. "The only thing that ever really puts you in a good mood is Mack and …"

Doreen repeated, "Mack and?"

Nan laughed. "Mack and a new case."

She nodded. "Mack and a new case, that is correct."

Nan was absolutely thrilled and clapped her hands glee-fully, like a child. "Oh, this is excellent news. We'll all be thrilled to have a new case."

"We just finished a case," Doreen pointed out, "so it's not as if we needed another case right away."

"No, but we love getting cases." Nan chuckled. "Wait until I call the gang over." And then she saw Mugs. Her face lit up, then twisted in mock horror as she realized he was wet. She grabbed a towel and tried to dry Mugs to his joy, thinking they were playing.

Maisie, one of Doreen's Deputies, arrived shortly there-after. Doreen smiled as she sat there with a cup of tea. There were no treats, which surprised her, but considering that she'd had more than enough in the last little while, she was totally okay with it.

When Richie showed up, basket in hand, his cane in the other, Doreen rolled her eyes and added, "You do know I'm perfectly okay if you don't come with treats one day."

"Good, because I can't always guarantee that they'll be there." He sniffed. "Can you imagine? These were barely coming out of the oven. You would have thought they would be all prepped and ready by this time of day."

"Why is that?" Doreen asked him, with a grin. "Just be-cause you're waiting for them?"

He nodded. "Absolutely because I'm waiting for them. The least they could do is be on time."

She laughed out loud at that. "I don't know that it works that way, but good on you for trying."

He grinned at her, held out the basket, and shared, "I

hear we have a new case." He pumped up his chest, took a seat, resting his cane nearby, and rubbed his hands together. "I can't wait to get started. It's pretty boring in this place without cases, you know?"

"What did you do before?" When his eyes twinkled, she held up her hand. "No, no, I'm good. No details, please."

"Didn't think you would want to hear more," he replied, with a smile. "However, anytime you want to talk, it's not a problem."

"Oh no, nope, no thank you." Doreen shook her head. "Absolutely not."

He burst out laughing. "That's okay. Mack will get you fixed up, no problem." She flushed at that and focused on completely ignoring him. He chuckled and let it go. "I shouldn't tease you, but it sure is fun."

"No, you shouldn't tease me," she agreed, glaring at him. "I really wouldn't want Mack to be upset by our talk."

"He wouldn't be upset," Richie stated, with a chuckle. "He would just laugh it off."

"Maybe so," she muttered, "but I'm not sure I will."

He grinned at her and shook his head. "Oh, you're always a good sport."

"Maybe," she muttered.

With everybody seated, Doreen went through the basket, placing items on a plate that Nan had brought out. "Are these croissants?" she asked in amazement.

"Seems to be," he confirmed, as he stared down at them in appreciation. "At least they gave us enough this time."

"How many people did you say you were feeding?" she asked, with a glance in his direction.

He shrugged. "Four, but then I also told them that you were coming. As soon as I tell them that, they're all over it, doubling up on the order."

She sighed.

Richie held up a hand. "I know you don't like that, but the last thing you want us to do is starve. If our brains are starved of food, we couldn't possibly work."

"Aha." She glared at him. "Does that excuse work for you?"

"I don't know," he admitted, with a cheeky grin in her direction. "Did it?"

She sighed. "You guys are quite something."

"We absolutely are," Nan agreed, with a bright smile in her direction. "Now, tell us about this new case."

"I'm still waiting to get the file," she began, "but … the captain has asked me to look into a cold case that's been sitting at the coroner's office for a very long time. And because they haven't had the chance and now don't really have the time to devote to it, he wondered if I wanted to take a quick look."

"You said yes, right?" Nan asked.

"Of course I did, but now I'm waiting for the file to come my way. I haven't gotten it yet, so I don't have too many details. I just know it's a box of bones. My understanding is that the bones are from a baby or toddler, found long ago, buried in a garden in a pillowcase, with some teeth marks on the bones."

"Good God." Nan stared at her. "They don't give us much to work with, do they?"

"If they had much," Doreen pointed out, "they probably would have done this one on their own."

"Right." Nan settled into her chair. "We certainly can't let a lack of information stop us on this one."

"No, and I'm not planning on it," Doreen stated,

"though obviously we will sometimes come up against cases where we can't do anything with them."

"But not this one," Maisie declared, munching away on a croissant in her corner seat.

"Exactly," Doreen agreed, "particularly if I've been asked by the captain to look into it. We want to put on a good showing."

"Oh, absolutely. This could lead to all kinds of cases."

Doreen chuckled. "And you would think, at some point in time, that this town would run out of cases."

"Oh, I highly suspect a lot of very old cases were never sorted," Richie noted in that heavy, serious tone of his. "When you think about it, so many things never seem to get resolved. Just knowing that makes you want to go back through every case and confirm we got them all."

"It'll be a while before we get there," Doreen pointed out. "Let's start with this one. But again, so far, all I really have to tell you is that I believe the bones have been sitting in the coroner's office for a very long time, so it's a very old case, and we may not have a whole lot of information to go on."

"Doesn't sound as if we have anything yet."

"No, we don't, at least not until I get the case file."

"But that fact that the captain is reaching out to you and giving you this one, now that's fascinating," Richie exclaimed, eyeing her in admiration. "You've certainly moved up in the world."

"I think in this case, … it's more about proving myself helpful in some ways," she suggested. "I'm sure that both the captain and Mack would put the emphasis on *some ways*, but there is the potential that the captain appreciates what we've done."

"Exactly." Nan beamed as she reached for another croissant. "I think it's absolutely wonderful."

"I do too," Doreen replied, with a smile. "Yet we don't have anything yet."

"Of course, so we'll reconvene." Nan brought out her pen and paper, while looking around at everybody. "How about tomorrow morning?"

"Sure," Richie said. "I'm guessing I can probably get more croissants tomorrow."

"Ooh, yeah, if you could do that," Maisie cried out, reaching for her third one, "it would be wonderful."

Doreen frowned and asked her, "Maisie, are you feeling okay? You seem really hungry."

"I fell asleep before dinner last night," she shared, with a wave of her hand. "So, I woke up starving. If I had known Richie was getting these, I would have been here earlier."

"I wasn't here earlier though," Richie noted amiably. "So, even if you'd been here, it wouldn't have helped."

Maisie just waved off that logic as not being her concern. "Maybe, but the truth is, this has been lovely and absolutely what I needed."

He chuckled. "In that case I'm happy to have made your day."

Doreen looked over at Richie. "I don't want you to get into trouble for this."

"No, I don't," he replied. "We all pay our rent around here, so we're perfectly entitled to eat. Thus, it shouldn't be an issue."

"Sure," Doreen muttered, "but I don't pay rent here and don't want you guys thinking you always have to feed me either."

"I know, dear," Nan replied, "and it's good of you to

always worry about such a thing, but we're also allowed to have guests. Honestly, I don't think anybody else is worried about it at all."

"Maybe not, but, as soon as you get new employees or a different manager, they might think that you're stealing or something," Doreen pointed out, "and we can't have that."

Just then came a knock on the door, and someone poked in their head. One of the staff entered, took one look, and nodded. "So, he was telling the truth."

Nan frowned at her. "Of course he was. Richie wouldn't lie."

"Of course he would," the woman countered, with a chuckle. She smiled at Doreen and introduced herself. "Hi, I'm Rachael."

"Hi, Rachael. I hope this is okay."

"It's fine, but we just never quite know for sure if Richie is, you know …"

"I do know," Doreen stated, as she rolled her eyes at Richie. "Half the time even I don't know if he's telling the truth, but today we are having a little meeting," she added.

Rachel laughed and nodded. "Okay then, good enough." And she quickly left.

Doreen looked over at Nan. "It doesn't seem *everybody* is a firm believer in this."

Nan stared at the door, a frown on her face.

Doreen reached over and patted her grandmother's hand. "It's fine."

"She was checking up on us," Nan declared in outrage, as she turned to Richie. "Did you see that?" Richie nodded, a frown furrowing his forehead. "Did you see that?" Nan repeated to Doreen.

"I did see that, and it's fine," Doreen added, still patting her grandmother's hand.

"What do you mean, it's fine?" Nan asked in outrage. "How dare they check up on us."

With a sigh, Doreen sat back. This would likely start something which was *exactly* what Doreen was trying to avoid. "They do have a significant overhead here, Nan. I'm sure they have to stick to a budget, and, if you're grabbing treats to this extent, they probably need to know that you're eating them."

"Of course we're eating them," Nan snapped in horror. "It's not as if any of us were raised in times when we had so much that we could afford to waste food."

"Maybe not," Doreen pointed out. "You also know that a lot of people do all kinds of things that they shouldn't do, and maybe it isn't appreciated on their part."

Nan blinked, then looked at her and asked, "Child, what exactly are you talking about?"

Doreen sighed. "I'm just letting you know that sometimes people do things that they shouldn't, and we want to confirm that the staff here isn't worried about whatever you guys are up to all the time."

Nan blinked, shook her head. "They really have no right to question us."

Doreen winced. "Maybe we shouldn't look at it that way. Maybe we should look at it more as …" She glanced around at the three of them, all looking at her expectantly. She took a deep breath and added, "Maybe they're just checking up on your welfare."

Nan sniffed at that. "Nice try, but that's hardly an improvement."

"Sorry, but this is an old folks' home, after all. I hate to rain on your parade, but sadly people occasionally die here."

At that, Nan's lips twitched. Then she went off in gales of laughter. "Oh my, I can't help but see this image of poor Richie here, dying with a basket of extra treats on his chest."

Richie grinned. "I'm not against that at all. I'll go out with a bang. If I can't die in bed, then I for sure plan to die with a full tummy."

That seemed to set off Nan again.

As her grandmother giggled and laughed, Doreen just shook her head, not exactly sure what she should be doing about this scenario. She may need to step in and talk to management to see if it was okay that she was here, eating their food. The last thing she wanted was to cause them any difficulties.

"It's fine," Nan told Doreen, as if reading her thoughts. She tapped her forehead. "I know you, child. You're already starting to fuss."

"Me?" Doreen asked, frowning at her. "Here I thought you were the one starting to fuss."

"Oh, never," Nan muttered, "but you should grab another croissant. I know how much you like them."

"Sure, but only if there's enough for everybody," Doreen noted, and still there were plenty. She reached for one and had a bite, smiling. "They really are good." She motioned at Richie.

He nodded as he snagged one. Not to be outdone, Maisie snagged yet one more, and Nan grabbed one too.

When only one was left, they all looked at Doreen, and Nan pointed. "That's yours, dear."

"Do I look as if I need more?" she asked humorously.

"Absolutely. I swear to God you're losing more weight." Nan stared at her intently, as she looked her up and down.

"I'm fine, Nan," Doreen muttered.

"You might be fine, but we can't have you so skinny at your wedding."

"Why not?" she asked, eyeing the croissant in her hand. "Isn't that what every girl dreams of?"

"Doesn't matter about every girl," Nan stated, "but, for you, it's always about trying to get weight back on you. As soon as you get on a case, you forget about eating, and all kinds of things happen."

She smiled at her, kissed her on the cheek, and said, "And I love you too."

Nan smiled, and tears came to her eyes. "You've been such a blessing, my dear."

Richie nodded. "Without you, Doreen, we would all have died of boredom by now," he added. "If I'd realized all this work was so much fun, I would have hassled my grandson a lot earlier."

She winced. "Not sure you should be hassling him now either," she pointed out. "You could be getting him in trouble."

Richie shook his head. "I called the captain the other day, asked him if I was bothering people, and the old chap was fine and understanding. He told me it was all good, and we were fine."

Doreen stared at him. "You did what?"

"I didn't want anybody to think I was some old dolt, causing trouble," he explained. "So I went to the source and asked him myself."

"That was well done," Nan declared, facing him. "And you didn't tell me?"

"I don't tell you everything anyway," he muttered, glaring at her. "Why would I? Besides, I just wanted to feel good about it myself."

Doreen smiled. "I love that. It's a great thing."

"It was. I think the captain appreciated it. I'm not sure that my grandson is all that happy about our work, but I ain't gonna stop, so he better get happy about it," he stated, with a smile.

"Did you check with him to see if you were becoming a bother?" Doreen asked him.

"Nope, I sure didn't," Richie declared. "Why would I ask anybody who will say yes?" And, on that note, he chomped down on his croissant, and everyone fell silent.

Chapter 4

DOREEN CARRIED THE last croissant back home, really appreciating that Richie had contacted the captain. She'd also laughed at the truth behind his comment about only asking people who would give him the answer he wanted. That was true of most people. And the fact that he recognized it, whether with a note of humor or not, she really appreciated that he at least was open enough to say it.

She checked her phone and still had no word from Mack. When she got home, now at least ten o'clock in the morning, she transferred the laundry and did a few things. Yet she was getting antsy because Mack still hadn't contacted her. She didn't want anybody having a change of heart about letting her work on a cold case. It really bothered her to think that bones were sitting in the coroner's office all this time, and nobody had gotten much further with it.

Surely every family needed closure. She'd heard horror stories about the number of unsolved cases in the US, and it was probably the same in Canada as well. Yet she'd never seen or heard the actual statistics. Still, it was shocking to hear just how many unsolved cases were out there, how many unidentified bodies were buried in unmarked graves, all because nobody knew who they were—complete families in some cases. It just broke her heart.

She put on tea out of habit, then realized she was already too full to drink more. By the time the laundry was done, she sat here, twiddling her thumbs. When her phone rang, she jumped. It was Mack. "Hey."

"Sorry, it's been pretty rough already this morning," he explained.

She heard the fatigue in his tone that she hadn't really expected. "Something happened?"

"Just the usual," he muttered. "Anyway, I'm about to send you the file. If nothing else, that should keep you busy for a little bit."

"So you have another case?"

"A trial," he snapped. "And, yes, I do have another case, but it's not one that you can help with."

"No, of course not. I'm only good enough for the cold cases."

Silence followed for a moment. "What?"

"Never mind. Never mind. You're tired, and you need to focus on what you need to focus on."

"That I do, but it sounds as if we need to talk."

"No, we don't." She laughed. "I shouldn't have said that."

"Interesting that you did say it though."

"Not really, just me sitting here, anxiously waiting for you to send the file. Sorry about that."

After a moment of silence, he said, "Fine, but we'll pick it up later."

She winced. "I think we're just fine without picking it up."

"Maybe, but you're the one who brought it up."

"I did bring it up, but then I apologized for bringing it up and told you to forget about it."

"Aha, and now you just sound guilty." When she gasped in outrage, he chuckled. "Now that sounds more like you."

She groaned. "Thank you for sending the file. It's been bothering me that this poor case has never really gotten anywhere."

"I don't have much to send you. We haven't had a chance to bring this one up out of the cold case files," he explained, "so I don't know if the digital file will be anything you can work with or not. Yet the captain is happy to let you have at it, so take that as a huge compliment."

"I will. You have a better morning." She quickly disconnected and was dancing with joy, now that she had the file.

And, with that, she opened up the document and started transferring notes to her notepad. There wasn't very much. In fact, there was a horribly small amount of information. So little that it made her heart ache. She read through what was here. The body had been found in a garden—a toddler, a female, approximately eighteen months old, with signs of abuse. As she sat back and looked at the short paragraphs of information and the few photos, she realized that this case might have more of an effect on her than she really expected.

Out of all the cases she had dealt with, anything involving children was always something that hurt her more than the others. Plus, to see a child who obviously had suffered prior to death was difficult. Then the unthinkable reality that nobody had any idea who she was made Doreen's heart ache. This was somebody's daughter. How could a child live for eighteen months and not be missed?

Doreen sat back, willing herself not to cry as she looked at the pitiful little bits of info they had. Had someone just buried this child in the garden? Or at least that's where the child's bones were found. The autopsy report noted some animal damage to the bones too. Surely none of that was okay. Were the bones so old that there really was no better option for burial? Maybe a lot of the damage occurred after death. Regardless it all bothered her.

That these bones had only been found when the garden bed had been turned over was worrisome too. The property had sold numerous times since the small bones had been discovered, so numerous residents had occupied the house over the years, while the bones remained undisturbed in the nearby garden. So, Doreen would need to start at the beginning.

She read a little bit more, finding that the police couldn't locate the owners of the house around the date and time when the body had been potentially laid to rest, per forensic testing. That left her with a lot more unknowns. She sat back, realizing just how much these cases depended on people remembering correctly events that happened decades earlier, potential witnesses who were quickly dying before she could get to some of these cold cases. Some people may have answers but may not even know it. These people would help if they knew that help was needed. Sadly, in most cases, Doreen couldn't get to these people fast enough, particularly the age of her potential witnesses in this case.

She sighed, her heart torn, as she looked at a photo of a small pile of bones. "It's all right, sweetheart," she muttered. "I know they call you Baby Jane, but we will find your legal name for you. And hopefully we can find out what happened to you."

The fact that this toddler had been in an unmarked grave and that there was damage to her body—aside from the teeth marks of animals—suggested murder. Yet Doreen also knew that everybody else wouldn't be quite so quick to judge. As she looked at the file, a note on the bottom stated *wrongful death*. Beside that, another note popped out. *The cause of death could not be determined.*

However, the report mentioned that excessive force had been used to leave the body in the state it was in. So, most likely, death was caused by physical trauma—beatings. She frowned as she thought about that. The child's age was determined to be eighteen months. With birth registries in town as a logical resource, this would still be a daunting task, without a name or an exact date of how long ago the child had been buried in the garden.

She couldn't exactly go through every registered birth and follow up to confirm each one lived past eighteen months, yet a part of her felt as if she may need to do just that. She also knew that would take her forever. It did cross her mind that maybe that was on the captain's mind when he told her that she was welcome to pursue this one. Anything to keep her out of their way while they finished catching up on all the current paperwork. And yet she was up for the challenge.

As she looked at the small photo of the bones again, she realized it wasn't so much that she was up for the challenge because of the captain or because of any time frames he might want to clamp down on. She was up for it because of the little girl. If nothing else, Doreen wanted to find out what her name was, what happened to her, and if justice could be served. She wanted to find out who was responsible for her death, before it was too late for them to pay the price. This child had already paid the ultimate price herself.

Chapter 5

AFTER FINISHING A few notes to herself, Doreen headed over to check Solomon's physical files. She was pretty sure she hadn't seen anything regarding this case that she'd summarized digitally, and it wasn't the type of thing he normally chased, but she wouldn't walk away and she'd talk to anybody about this case if she hadn't already checked everything at her disposal. She brought up the summary of his work that she had so painstakingly compiled and typed, then went through each of the physical files, wondering if anything was even close to her case, but she couldn't find one single thing that appeared to be connected.

Frowning at that, she realized this could end up being the one case she couldn't crack by pulling magic out of the air, when it seemed as if all hope was lost. She sat back, writing up her notes again, but this time in a little more organized and legible way. Then she called Nan.

"Hey," Nan answered, sounding a little off. "I had a talk with management." Nan sniffed. "Apparently Richie's antics haven't been looked on as well as he thought."

"I'm not surprised," Doreen replied frankly. "It is a lot to expect him to continuously come into the kitchen, taking things."

"In his defense, he is paying for it. We all are, to be honest, and we are allowed unlimited access."

"Yes," Doreen noted, "but I'm sure it tends to mess up their accounts and their planning for Richie to be feeding me."

"They did try to tell me something about that. Anyway, I didn't want to leave it this way and would never want you feeling as if you couldn't come down here at any point in time and visit, especially if it would be awkward if we had to be sticklers over a treat here or there."

Doreen chuckled, and Nan went on to say, "They did rush to tell me that you were more than welcome to come, and they weren't worried about that at all. They were more concerned about the amount of food taken away, making sure Richie was eating the food and not just stockpiling it. She brought up another resident's name, someone we did have issues with, and that's exactly what she had been doing. She kept extra food in her room until it went bad because she had this thing about not starving to death."

"Oh my," Doreen muttered, "that sounds terrible."

"I know, and, when Rachael mentioned that, I confirmed, *Oh, so as long as we're eating the food, it's all good,* and Rachael nodded," Nan explained, her tone turning cheerful. "Now, that's enough about us. Did you hear from Mack?"

"I did, and I have the case file."

"Ah, then you need to come back down here."

"First I need to head to the library and see if I can come up with anything," she shared casually. "No point in coming if I don't have any information."

"Was the file that empty?"

"Yes, the file was definitely that empty," she stated.

"Ooh, ouch, okay. So, we will really have to buckle down and work on this one."

"Yep, we sure will." Doreen chuckled. "Let me get out there and see what I can find."

"Afternoon tea then?" Nan asked. "We'll expect you here at two." And, with that, she disconnected without giving Doreen a chance to answer.

She shook her head as she stared down at her critters. "Wouldn't it be nice if I had a choice in some of this?" she muttered out loud. Yet her life with Nan had taken off and had become a world of its own.

Doreen wasn't even sure if she should start at the library. She was thinking about the cemetery too. She had already looked up random obituaries on the internet, plus she did know a couple people down at the cemetery—Dezy the groundskeeper and the woman in the office, whose name escaped Doreen just now.

So, with that in mind, she loaded up the animals in her car and headed to one of her favorite places to walk. Some people might call her macabre for walking the cemeteries, but honestly, it was so peaceful, and there was generally a sense of joy, without the feeling of loss that you might expect. She definitely sensed completeness and calm. Maybe that's what she was looking for.

As she wandered, she looked over and caught sight of somebody she recognized, doing maintenance. Dezy looked up at her and then waved. With the animals racing forward, she walked over to say hi to him. "Hey, Dezy," she greeted him, with a big smile.

"Haven't seen you around here in a bit." He eyed her intently. "Are you okay?" He reached down and said hello to Mugs and Goliath, who were both vying for attention. He chuckled. "These guys don't appear to have changed."

She shook her head. "No, they sure haven't, and they're still as competitive for attention as ever."

Dezy nodded. "I see that, but I won't complain because it's so nice to see them here."

She smiled. "I'm glad to hear you say that because I have to admit that this is one of my favorite places to walk."

"Of course," he agreed. "It's really peaceful here. I know people think I'm strange for wanting to work in a graveyard, but it's, by far, one of the nicest locations in my opinion."

"You certainly don't have to worry about anybody bugging you," she quipped, with a smile.

"No, I don't, and honestly, an awful lot can be said for that too." He looked down at Mugs. "This guy isn't getting any skinnier."

She winced. "I was noticing that a little earlier today. With the winter and the cold weather and all, we haven't been out on as many walks."

"Yeah, I can see that," he noted, as he studied Mugs's girth. "You need to watch that he doesn't get too big."

"I know," she grumbled, followed by a sigh. "He just won't enjoy life much if he loses his treats."

"No, but I think that goes for everybody in that situation," Dezy stated, smiling at her. "Now, are you here just for a walk, or are you here because you need something?"

"Both," she replied cheerfully.

He nodded. "I figured as much. So … what's going on? You got another case?"

"Kind of," she said, rolling her eyes. "It's a sad one though."

"Aren't they all?" he noted. "Any case that comes to you means that nobody else has been able to solve it. So you've got yourself a reputation. The problem with that is," he shared, waving his hands, "the pressure to maintain it."

She groaned. "And this case may be the downfall of my reputation," she agreed. "It's terrible."

"Okay, shoot," he said. "Fill me in on just what's going on and how I can help."

She frowned and began, "It's a strange one."

"Come on now. It seems as if you're stalling. What do you know so far?"

"I don't have very much information," she admitted, "and that's a problem and makes it even sadder."

"Okay, so just what do you have?"

She groaned. "I have the remains of an eighteen-month-old toddler. I don't have when she died, but they figure the bones are at least thirty-some years old, up to ten years older." When Dezy frowned at her, she nodded. "I know, so sad, … isn't it?"

"Tragic, but why do I find myself wondering if they are using this difficult case to keep you busy and out of people's hair?"

She winced. "I'm really hoping that wasn't the point, but I can see how maybe it serves both purposes. … If I can solve it, it's another one they don't have to worry about. However, I don't have much to go on. Not even a name. I don't have anything, except …" She paused. When Dezy gazed at her expectantly, she sighed and continued. "She was beaten pretty badly."

He winced, then shook his head. "Wow, that's not good."

"No, it isn't," she stated. "So, although this is possibly a no-win situation for me, I can't *not* have a look and will do my best."

"No, of course not," he agreed, shaking his head. "And back then, … we didn't have a ton of law enforcement around here, yet it wasn't that bad. Most of the people were good, strong, hardworking families."

She nodded. "And you've been here that long, haven't you?"

"I have," he replied, as he rubbed his chin, leaving a streak of dirt across it. "Yet I don't know anything about this one."

"No, but," she added, trying to collect her thoughts, "I guess the question I'll have to turn upside down is, does anybody know of a baby who went missing here locally? I could ask about a baby who people heard had passed away, and maybe nobody ever questioned how or why."

He shrugged. "That won't be an easy one for you."

"No, it won't," she acknowledged, trying not to get too dismayed about it. "Normally I have a little bit more to go on," she admitted. "But that's why the bones are sitting in a box in the coroner's office, so that people don't forget and that someday, … somehow, … we might have a light to shed on it."

"It sure doesn't do my heart any good to think of a little baby like that in a box on some shelf," he muttered in a doleful way. "Of course she'll end up in a box anyway," he pointed out, "but we want her properly buried, with a proper marker."

"Exactly," she said.

"I'm not sure I can help you though." He looked around at the graves and noted, "Everybody here's got a marker."

"I know. I guess I was just wondering if you knew of anybody who may have lost a child way back when."

"You're thinking that it would be somebody who lost a

child, but that nobody would necessarily know about it?"

She nodded. "Otherwise then I would think there would be a burial," she pointed out.

"Right, unless they were really poor, and they just wanted to bury the child on their property. Do you know where it was buried?"

"Yep, southeast Kelowna." Then she stopped and whispered, "The bones were found when they were digging up a patch to grow yams."

"Yams?" he repeated, looking at her.

She nodded. "Yeah, yams."

"Good God." He frowned. "They're not that hard to grow, so you could certainly grow them up here."

"I think they were turning over a bed or creating a new one, and … the bones came up with the soil."

"Wow," he muttered, shaking his head. "You sure do live an exciting life," he said, with almost admiration in his tone.

"Ha." She tried to hide her shivers from the cold weather. "Not sure *exciting* is quite the right word for this."

"There'll be the expectation that you need to solve it," he pointed out.

She nodded. "And that is precisely why I need help on this one."

"Right," he agreed, "but I don't know anybody who might have had a baby back then and lost it. I didn't ever see one. … If the child died that young, and the family lived out in the middle of nowhere, that doesn't mean that nobody ever even knew about her. It's just that her life was limited to her family maybe."

He wasn't telling Doreen anything she hadn't already figured out. She was just hoping that, somewhere along the line, somebody would know something. Doreen already knew she would have to go a little further afield on this one. Plus, this was just her first day, so she wouldn't let herself get upset about it.

Dezy shook his head. "All I can do is …"

"Is what?"

"I know it sounds foolish," he began, "but I do know a lot of people in town. I don't know the new people so much, but … I know an awful lot of the old-timers. The only thing I can think to do is maybe take a look through our records that we have of who is buried here and see if those names trigger anything. I can do that for sure, but no guarantees."

"No, no guarantees at all," she replied, "but, even that much, if it doesn't trigger anything, that is still information. Now, if it does trigger something, it could potentially lead me to the next thing."

"And that's what you do, isn't it?" Dezy asked, with a nod and a bright smile. "You get one little thing and then carry it on to the next."

"I do, and, if I'm lucky, somebody at the end of the long road of questions *knows* something, and even better is when we get to somebody at the end of the long road who *did* something."

He frowned and then nodded. "You're not likely to get any justice for her," he pointed out. "It's been too long. Thirty-five years is a long time."

"Sure," she agreed, "but thirty-five years, if you're hiding from a crime that you committed, isn't a long time. What if they were twenty or twenty-five back then?"

"Sure, they could be in their fifties or maybe sixties, … but they also could have been thirty or so at the time."

She nodded. "I know. It's a long shot, but the captain

did say I could look into it, and I feel obligated for this little girl's sake to find out what her name is and what happened to her. To call her … *Baby Jane* just hurts."

He winced at that. "I hear you there. That will never do. When I go in for my break, I'll pull out the records and start going through the names and see if anything comes to mind."

"That's all I can ask of you," she said, truly grateful. "Thank you for that. At the very least, it's something we can do, and all we can do is try." She handed him a card with her phone number on it.

And, with that, she gave him a bright smile and tugged at the animals. While she was here, she might as well get a walk in. If nothing else they would all get some exercise, and she could use this chance to clear her mind.

Chapter 6

DOREEN AND HER animals drove around, giving her time to think some. By the time 2:00 p.m. came, to meet the gang, she opted to drive to Rosemoor instead of going home and then walking back here. As she pulled up outside Rosemoor, a surprising amount of traffic came and went from the place. She frowned as she looked around because she never really came this way. She rarely saw the entrance to the place, not like this.

It was quite busy and really surprised her, giving her a new appreciation for the staff who worked there, trying to keep everybody safe and happy—a feat she had to admit could not be easy, at least not with her grandmother, who was a bit of an agitator in a way, but she wasn't malicious. Nan was just busy enjoying life.

Doreen frowned as she thought about that. Nan had been living on her own successfully for a very long time so probably didn't need someone curtailing anything now. As long as she was getting along and not causing any real trouble, it should all be good. Hopefully it would all be good.

With that thought in mind, Doreen headed to the front

door with the animals, then realized it made no difference at all, so she stepped around the garden beds and walked toward Nan's patio. As she approached, she heard a *harrumph* behind her. She turned to look, and a strange woman stood there, glaring at her. Doreen raised an eyebrow. "May I help you?"

"You could stop walking through the garden beds. You do realize how much everybody here puts into making this place nice," she stated crossly.

Doreen nodded. "I didn't step into the flower beds, but I did walk on the lawn."

"And that crushes the grass and makes it very hard for it to look perfect."

Doreen didn't say anything, just smiled and nodded and tried to walk away, but the other woman wasn't done chastising her.

"Unless you're one of those people who think the rules don't apply to you," she declared, with half a sneer.

Doreen winced at that and kept on walking.

The other woman called out, "Hope you're never in a position where you have to deal with people here," she said. "They won't look kindly on you over that."

Doreen held her tongue, even as she got to her grandmother's patio and stepped onto her grandmother's little private area. The angry woman had followed her here.

"Oh, so this is how you get into everybody's little special area," she pointed out, with a sneer. "Too good for the front door, are you? Or do you realize that animals aren't allowed, so this is how you sneak them in?"

Nan stepped out at that point, hearing something she didn't like.

Just as Nan opened her mouth to blast the rude woman,

Doreen held up her hand. "Thank you for the advice." And, with that, she put her arm around Nan, and they both stepped into Nan's little apartment and closed the door firmly in the other woman's face.

Nan gasped. "Who was that horrible woman?"

"I have no idea," Doreen said. "I think these days she's called a Karen."

"I don't know any Karens," Nan replied.

Doreen winced. "I didn't mean that's her actual name. I think she's one of those people who just likes to complain. She thinks that the world belongs to her and that she's righteous, no matter what she does."

Nan nodded and raised an eyebrow. "*Right.* So is she one of the new people you mentioned earlier would be new friends for me?"

"No, definitely not. Anyway, hopefully she'll leave us alone now. I parked out front with the animals because I'd been down at the cemetery, so I just thought I would drive here. This run-in just tells me to reconsider that."

"But driving here makes sense if you're already in the car. Yet, when you're at the house, walking here is the way to go."

"Which is precisely why I drove here just now," she said, with a shrug. "Anyway, it's all good. I certainly won't let her ruin my day."

"You are the most amiable and the *easiest to get along with* woman I have ever met." Nan stared at her. "You know it might do you some good to yell and scream at someone once in a while."

"Really?" Doreen asked. "I can't imagine what that would do besides freak out my poor animals."

At that, Nan crouched to give Mugs the greeting he'd

been waggling all around her for and hoping to get. As soon as he got a good greeting, he waddled over toward the food she always kept there for him. "Oh, dear," Nan muttered, "he is getting a little …" She cupped her hands over her mouth and looked at Doreen.

"I know." Doreen sighed. "He's getting a little chunky."

Nan giggled. "A little," she said, rolling her eyes.

"I'll put it down to the fact that we can't do very many long walks because of the weather."

"Oh, that's a good excuse," Nan replied.

Doreen groaned. "But it does sound like an excuse, doesn't it?"

"Of course it does, but that's okay. It's just that … Okay. We love Mugs just the way he is."

"Sure, but it's not healthy for him to be this way," she noted. "So loving him isn't enough if I'm not doing the right thing by him." Worriedly, she looked down at the very contented animal, who was once again checking out the kitchen, the food bowls, and the table. "He really does like his groceries though."

Nan giggled. "He's male."

Doreen rolled her eyes. "And yet we know all males aren't the same," she pointed out.

"Of course not, but, if you want to go by Richie and his propensity for bringing treats," she explained, "you know he and Mugs are a good match."

Just then the door opened and in stepped Richie. He held a paper bag in one hand and his cane in the other, as he precariously tried to turn and close the door.

"I've got it," Doreen offered, as she raced forward to close it for him.

He beamed at her. "You're such a sweet girl. Too bad

Darren didn't get there before Mack."

She stared at him and shook her head. "Darren is a decade younger than I am," she pointed out. "So, I really don't think he would be interested."

"Even if he was, the boy's not very fast on the uptake," Richie noted, with a sigh. "He'll be single forever at this rate."

"I wouldn't suggest that you do any matchmaking then. It'll just make people more upset, especially him."

"How can he be *more* upset? He doesn't seem to care about it now."

"I'm sure he cares, but he'll do it in his own time," she suggested.

He just grumped at her but shot her a cheeky grin. "Mack didn't waste any time, did he?"

She flushed. "Maybe not, though I do think he sometimes wonders if he made a decision too fast."

"*Nah,*" Richie argued, "he's smitten. We all can tell."

She shook her head and quickly changed the subject. "Okay, enough of that. Let's get down to business, since I do have the file now, such as it is."

"Wait, wait, wait." Maisie's frail voice came from the doorway. "I'm here. I'm here. Wait for me." She crowded inside, telling Richie to move his fat butt.

"I'm not fat," Richie cried out in horror.

"You should be," Maisie stated crossly. "With the amount of food you eat, you certainly should be fat."

Doreen, sensing a breakdown about to happen, stated, "I don't have much time, so let's get to the point."

Immediately everybody turned their attention to the case at hand. Richie grabbed the closest chair, pointing Maisie to the one farthest from him, on which she sat down with a huff. Nan took the only other spare seat. "Now, tell us what you know," Nan told Doreen.

"First off, it's not much," she began. "We have a dead eighteen-month-old little girl. She died approximately thirty-five years ago, give or take ten," she added.

"Ouch," Nan muttered. "So, what's the story? Who found her?"

"A family in Black Mountain, while preparing their garden to plant yams."

Immediately Richie jumped in and shared, "You know, if it was a good patch, a patch for potatoes would have been just fine for yams." He seemed to be warming up to the subject. "We had a lovely time growing those. Not only yams but sweet potatoes too. It all depends on what varieties and whether they want to put the money into getting some of the more exotic types," he added.

"Is a point in there?" Maisie asked.

"No, technically there's only sweet potatoes in North America, and the yams come from Africa," he stated.

"Oh, hush," Nan grumbled, looking at him crossly. "Nobody here cares about growing potatoes."

"You ought to." He glared at her. "Growing food should be everybody's concern."

"That's because you were a farmer along with being a cop," Nan pointed out. "I just pay for the food."

He frowned and then shrugged. "Good point. We needed people like you to pay for the food too."

"Exactly." Nan sighed. "Go ahead, dear, before anybody else jumps in on the wrong topic."

Richie glared at her but settled back, reached into the bag, and pulled out a scone.

Immediately Maisie gasped. "What's that?" she cried

out. "I didn't see any of those at lunch."

"Nope, I went into the kitchen and got them," he admitted, with a bright smile. "I figured I should get there before everybody else had a chance. Otherwise they would all be gone."

"They would all be gone because you keep taking them," Maisie cried out fretfully. "I feel as if I can't go anywhere now without first checking to see if you've gotten all the treats because then I'll lose out."

He stared at her in astonishment. "That's an awful lot of talking, when you could be eating," he pointed out, passing over a scone to her.

Immediately she shut up and munched on the scone.

Doreen wasn't sure what was going on around here with anybody today. They all seemed a bit on the cranky side.

Nan looked at her and whispered, "It's nap time, dear."

"Ah." She was embarrassed, feeling inconsiderate. "You should have warned me."

"You said this afternoon, so that's about the only time we have."

"Right, well, that's a good reminder. We'll do it differently next time."

"Yes, I highly suggest you do," Nan said.

"But now that we're all here"—Richie glared at them—"and yes, it is my nap time, and I am getting cranky," he admitted, his voice slowly raising an octave. "That doesn't change the fact that we have things to sort out here."

Doreen nodded. "You're right. I get that, but I still don't have a whole lot more for you anyway. The toddler was found in Black Mountain. The police have not brought up the records from the cold case storage area yet, but the house where the body was found has been sold and rented many times. So far the police have not located anybody who either had a baby or was pregnant in the relevant time period."

"It's not as if anybody would say they were pregnant," Maisie stated, frowning at her.

"Exactly," Doreen agreed with a nod and a quiet smile in her direction, making Maisie feel a little bit better, after all the outbursts.

"It still doesn't change the fact that we need to find somebody who knew the family," Richie said glumly. "We all know, when it comes to the death of a child, people don't like to talk."

"Yet we also know," Doreen pointed out, "as time catches up with people, sometimes they like to talk just fine."

He eyed her shrewdly. "That'll be your best bet in this case."

"It might be," she agreed. "Still, it'll be hard trying to find somebody who knows something but has kept it quiet all this time, or who maybe wondered about something but never brought it up." She nodded. "If it was me, and I had killed a child, I would have moved far, far away, very quickly."

"Sure, but, if you didn't think you would ever get caught, or if you knew you wouldn't get caught, or if you didn't want to draw attention to yourself, you might not."

She frowned at that part. "True. Maybe nobody moved at all. Plus, we can't automatically blame one parent, as either the father or the mother may have done it."

Richie frowned. "I really don't like this thought, but what if the mom moved away and left the baby with the father? She may have run off with a traveling salesman or something. It was done back then, and, if the husband was abusive, maybe she took off. And maybe she took off before the baby was killed."

"Or maybe he killed the baby and then she took off," Maisie suggested. "If so, who knows where they could be or whether the woman even knows that her baby is dead."

"Well, one thing I'll tackle is the genealogy sites," Doreen shared. "If I input the toddler's DNA, I might get a match." Then she frowned. "I didn't check to see if there was any DNA available of hers to input, but, if they have the bones, I might get the captain to pull some DNA."

"I would think that is done first thing with a dead body," Nan stated.

"It is and it isn't," Doreen noted. "Remember that this case has been cold for a very long time now and that DNA testing is a newer technique."

"But the captain gave this case to you," Nan added, "so he must think you have some ideas."

"I don't know about *some ideas*, but I would certainly like the chance to put a name to this little girl," Doreen stated. "It's so sad to think of her sitting in a box all this time, completely unclaimed because of this."

On that somber note, Richie agreed and looked at the others. "And we should start talking to everybody here."

Nan agreed. "I was going to suggest that," she declared, looking over at Richie, "but you wouldn't let me get a word in edgewise."

"No," he argued crossly. "It's my nap time, and I'm heading there right now. We've been given our orders, and we are to talk to everybody, to figure out who might know something, and to tell Doreen." And, with that, he lumbered to his feet and made his way unsteadily to the door. He turned to smile at Doreen and suggested, "Take the treats home with you. I've got another bag in my room." And, with a laugh, he headed out of Nan's apartment.

Maisie just stared at him. "He really isn't the best at

sharing, is he?" she noted fretfully.

Doreen reached into the bag, pulled out several of the treats, and handed them to her. "And he won't know if I gave these to you to take to your room."

Maisie looked at her in delight. "Thank you, thank you." And she literally ran out the door with them.

Doreen sat back and looked at Nan. "How about you? Do you need to take your nap too?"

Nan chuckled. "No, child. I'll have my nap when you leave, but watching you send everybody off is way too much fun."

"Goodness," Doreen muttered, "that's not what I'm trying to do, and you know that."

"I know," she admitted, "but you do it without even trying, and that is a skill I admire."

"Admire?" Doreen cried out. "How can you admire that? I'm trying to be good here, but I do feel like a referee."

"Ah, that's what all of us do here anyway," Nan declared, with a wave of her hand. "Going through a second childhood and all that, people get just as cranky and just as bad-tempered and just as jealous as they did before they were living here," she explained. "Even worse, it seems as if it gets compounded because they're here. Good behavior goes out the window. Manners go out the window, and then you add in the fact that everybody is tired, and, well, that's just all there is to it."

"In that case," Doreen muttered, "no more two o'clock meetings."

"I can see that," Nan said. "Honestly, I hadn't really expected it to go quite so badly. Certainly not so quickly."

"No, neither did I." Doreen laughed. "The good news is, … we got through it without anyone running me out."

Chapter 7

B Y THE TIME Doreen had gone to bed last night, she realized that she had gotten absolutely nowhere. She woke up this morning determined to make some progress one way or another, so she headed to the library. Luckily her favorite librarian was there.

The smiling woman looked up, then frowned. "*Uh-oh,* you appear to be working."

"I am, and it's a hard one," Doreen shared, looking around, not finding anybody else here at the moment. "It might be the case that kills me. Though I just got it, so I shouldn't be so depressed already," she muttered.

"Tell me more."

"Do you know anything about a toddler who died at about eighteen months old, some thirty-five years ago?"

She frowned, thought about it, and then shook her head. "No, … I can't say that I do, but that's just off the top of my head, without having had a chance to think about it."

"I think that'll be the issue on this one, jogging people's memories."

"How on earth did you find out about this case?" she exclaimed.

"You can blame the captain for that," Doreen stated, with a smile. "Apparently the bones have been held in the morgue, and, because the police just don't have any way to move on it, the captain suggested I take a stab at it and see if I could find any information."

"Oh, that's lovely," she cried out in delight. "You must be awfully happy."

"I am to a degree, but I would be happier if I had anything to go on. It's pretty slim pickings where the details are concerned."

"Of course," the librarian muttered. "If it was an easy one, they could have done it themselves years ago, but without the manpower to put into it …"

"Exactly," Doreen agreed. "All I have is that the bones were recovered from a garden in the Black Mountain area in southeast Kelowna, and the death appears to have been thirty-five years ago, plus or minus ten." Doreen sighed heavily. "Nobody really has anything more definitive than that. I will ask the captain if we have DNA. If we don't, could we get some? … That'll just be one of those conversations where, if you need me to do something here, I must get some information at least."

"The DNA would help a lot," the librarian agreed. "You could upload it to one of the genealogy sites. And, even if it doesn't get a direct hit, still, you may get half matches there," she pointed out.

Doreen agreed. "It would also still be there for anything in the future that might pop up."

"Exactly," she stated. "Just eighteen months old, poor baby. Wow. … Obviously we've had deaths at that age because, even when you think everything seems good at birth, it doesn't mean the child was born in good health."

"That's true, but—"

"So, an eighteen-month-old dying even thirty-five years ago isn't a surprise. I mean, look at sudden infant death. Have they figured that out yet?"

"But"—Doreen leaned in closer, lowered her voice, and looked around to confirm the two of them were alone—"the child seemed to have sustained beatings over time."

"Oh no." The librarian gasped, as she looked at Doreen in horror. "I always hate to hear about those cases."

"Yeah, you and me both." Doreen grimaced. "Something is just so wrong about a child ending up that way."

"Oh, absolutely." Shocked and still groaning at the idea, the librarian added, "So, we're potentially talking about a murder case then." She stared at Doreen, one raised eyebrow.

"Yes, we could be looking at a murder case," Doreen confirmed. "Yet we don't have anything more to go by at this point. So, for all we know, this was something else entirely."

"It could be an acute case of brittle bones or something. Back then I doubt there was even research about that medical phenomenon."

"Oh my," Doreen murmured. "I hadn't even considered that myself. I guess that's why we can't jump to any conclusions. I so hate to think about a little girl being lost and buried like that—or not even buried deep enough because of the animal activity noted on her bones."

"No, no, of course not," she agreed. "I really would love to help you. Just tell me what I can do."

"Exactly." Doreen nodded. "That's why, even as difficult as this case appears it'll be, I'll still have to do everything I can to solve it."

"I think you put your heart and soul into every one of

them," the librarian noted with a smile, "whether it's a child or not."

"I would like to think so," Doreen murmured. "Anyway, one of the things I wanted to ask you about was where I would find birth announcements from thirty-five years ago?"

The librarian raised her eyebrows. "Oh wow."

"Oh wow, what?"

"Do you have any idea how many you'll end up with?"

"I don't know," Doreen admitted. "I don't have a clue, but I don't know of any other way to get an idea of what we could be looking at."

"That's true," she said, "and, for this little girl, I would do all that too." She led the way to the microfiche at the back.

Not knowing the exact time frame they were looking at, Doreen had the librarian take her back fifty years, as she worked up to thirty years ago. Surely that would cover the estimated death of thirty-five years ago, plus or minus ten years. Then Doreen sat down with a hard sigh and muttered, "Okay, I'll see you in about fifteen years."

The librarian laughed out loud. "It won't take you quite that long, but see what you can come up with. Meanwhile I'll rack my brains on other ways to figure this out."

"Any and all help is appreciated," Doreen called out. "Don't worry about me. I'll just be back here, lost in the archives."

And, with that, she pulled out her notepad and set to work. It was pretty easy once she got the hang of it. She couldn't filter anything, so she manually reviewed each announcement. Much later, when a tap came on her shoulder, she jolted, then looked up to see the librarian again.

"Any luck?" the librarian asked.

"I've written down quite a few names," Doreen explained. "I wrote down all the births." She frowned, looking at her notepad. "I only wrote down the deaths if they involved infants or toddlers."

"Right, because not everybody would necessarily go through a formal funeral, but they might have sent out a notice," the librarian noted. "Smart thinking."

"Thirty-five years ago that area wasn't incorporated into Kelowna proper. So, as much as people seem to think it was fairly lawless back then or so rural that no one else was around, it really wasn't. It's not as if we are talking one hundred years ago," Doreen said. "There were still neighbors around, with professional medical help nearby. So, a notification in the papers would help people looking for answers."

"Oh my, yes. I agree totally. I'll leave you to get back to it." And then she took off.

When Doreen's back began to complain, she knew it was time to call it quits, at least for today. She straightened up and groaned as her back made a few snaps, crackles, and pops.

Another woman walking by winced for her. "Oh my, you really shouldn't be sitting there hunched over like you were for so long."

"I lost track of time," Doreen admitted. "That's a bit of a problem when I get caught up in my work."

"It is for all of us," the older woman stated, with a chuckle. "But take it from me that there is no amount of research that makes destroying your back worthwhile."

She moved on, leaving Doreen standing here, thinking about what she'd said. The woman was right to a certain extent, and Doreen would certainly have to be more careful. She didn't want to cause any long-term trouble for herself, but this little girl? … Just something about her had gotten a hold of Doreen, and she couldn't imagine not getting the answers she needed. It might take longer than she expected, and this might even be a case she had to shelve for a while, but she wouldn't ever let it go. She just couldn't imagine giving up on this one.

Not when Doreen knew a baby girl had been buried in a vegetable garden, discovered by scavenging animals, and then otherwise left for all eternity. Just the thought of it all hurt Doreen deeply. Maybe because there had been so much death in her life recently that Doreen just couldn't let this one go.

Chapter 8

DOREEN WOKE THE next morning to her phone ringing. It was Mack. She groaned as she answered it.

"Are you okay?" he asked, his tone sharp.

"Yeah," she mumbled. "While you were at trial and then working late last night, I did a bunch of research at the library. I guess I wasn't watching my posture."

"Oh, so that's what that groan was about," he noted. "Sorry, you do need to watch those chairs down there."

"I know. They're painful."

He chuckled. "I'm hoping to be done a little bit earlier with court today," he shared, "and I would suggest lunch."

"Oh, lunch would be lovely. Do you want to come here, and I can cook something, or do you want to go out?"

He thought about it for a moment. "It doesn't matter, but I was thinking about going out."

"Good, I'm up for that. You pick the place, and I can meet you there, or you can swing by and grab me."

"*Hmm*, maybe I'll just meet you there. That way I don't have to feel guilty about leaving the animals behind."

She burst out laughing. "Got to love how they've already got you wrapped around their little paws."

"It's always hard to leave them," he admitted. "So I've come to understand why you tend to take them everywhere."

"Yep," she agreed, "and it's not the easiest when I do have to leave them. But, for lunch out, I will."

"Ha, so it's just needing the right excuse. I don't know where you want to go. Maybe think about it, and I'll try to give you a call when I get a break."

"Sure, but if you've got any places that you want to go to, that's fine, though I wouldn't mind Asian—or more specifically Japanese or Thai?"

"Sure, a couple good places are downtown, if you're okay to come here," he suggested. "You can just park in one of the parking spots, and we can walk. Meet me at the courthouse, if you like."

"Sure," she said.

They set the timing tentatively for noon, and then he was gone.

She'd known he wasn't looking forward to court, but she couldn't imagine why anybody ever would. It was one of those things that you had to do as part of your job. At least *he* had to do it as part of his job. She couldn't imagine it being something anybody would want to sign up for. But then Mack was one of those guys to do it without complaint because it was his job. Doreen, on the other hand, was a different story, and she knew that about herself. Parts of the job stuff could get pretty rough and boring for her.

The thought of returning to the library was enough to make her cringe. She'd gotten through twenty years' worth of deaths, but she still needed to correlate any deaths against all those births. And that meant another day of slogging her way through microfiche.

When she went back down to the library, the librarian

looked at her and winced. "You look as if you had a rough night."

"No, I have a sore back," she muttered, "from those chairs."

The woman nodded sympathetically. "Sorry about that," she muttered. "You didn't get enough information?"

"I sorted the births and the obituaries yesterday," she noted, "but I didn't get a chance to cross-reference the births against the obituaries."

"Oh my, I hadn't considered that."

"I only wrote down any of the deaths at the time around when the child died, but I missed some stuff. Now I plan to run through the names that I didn't check, versus the names that I have here." She sighed. "It shouldn't take that long— at least not as long as yesterday took."

And, with that, she marched to the back, determined to make this as fast as possible. And it was; it was also very depressing because, in the end, she came up blank.

As she walked out to the front, the librarian looked at her, and Doreen shook her head. "Nope, no joy. I knew it was a long shot anyway."

"Of course," the librarian agreed sympathetically. "I can't say I've had any luck coming up with anybody who lost their baby at that age either. Not that I would know them personally anyway."

"No, of course not." Doreen sighed. "And again the whole thing is a long shot, but we'll do what we can do." And, with a smile, she walked outside. One of the other ladies who had been in the library walked out with her.

"What is it you're looking for?" she asked, with a nervous smile. "Sorry, I couldn't help overhearing what you were talking about with the librarian."

"I'm looking for information on a little girl who died around thirty-five years ago, give or take ten years," Doreen shared, with half a smile.

"Anybody who's been around that long," she noted, "will probably be in the old folks' home."

"That's true, and I'm heading down there soon enough myself." Doreen waved to the woman and headed to Nan's. It was only 11:00 a.m. Doreen figured that she could check in and could get an update from Nan's crew down there, and then she could have lunch with Mack, without worrying about this check-in. As she walked up to Rosemoor, she was determined to avoid any contact with the argumentative woman who had accosted Doreen earlier. As she got nearer to Nan's apartment and walked to Nan's patio, that awful woman appeared. Doreen quickly disappeared into Nan's apartment, hoping the woman hadn't caught sight of her.

Nan looked up and frowned at her. "I wasn't expecting you."

"I was hoping I could touch base with everybody and see if you guys had come up with anything."

"I don't think we've even had time, dear, but it's on everybody's agenda today. After the nap fiasco yesterday, you know …"

"Right." Doreen nodded.

"Naps are important at our age, you know?" she declared, with a bright smile.

"Of course they are. I was just checking in to see if you had anything to go on."

"Oh, dear. No luck so far, I assume?"

"No, nothing," Doreen admitted ruefully. "I did go back to the library and checked the obituaries against the births from that long ago."

"The question is whether it could have been a slightly different time frame. How many years did you cover?"

"I did a twenty-year sweep, starting fifty years ago up to thirty years ago, and checked the names of the obituaries against the names of the births, looking for something that would match our scenario, but I came up empty-handed."

"Which means what?" Nan asked, frowning at her.

"Which means—and I am not sure of this—but I highly suspect that it was murder and that whoever did this obviously didn't want anybody to know. So either they didn't record the birth, which I guess is quite possible in a home birth or something, or they didn't record the death. Or they could have moved, and nobody would have been the wiser."

"Right, all of which makes a whole lot of sense and un-fortunately is no surprise."

"Exactly," she muttered. "Yet I really want to get more information on this."

"You just don't want to disappoint the captain," Nan noted shrewdly.

Doreen winced. "Don't want to disappoint the captain, don't want to disappoint Mack," she admitted. "There, that's my weakness." She raised both hands in frustration. "I want them to see me in a good light."

Nan smiled at her, then walked over and gave her a big hug. "Oh, my dear, that's one thing you never need to worry about. They see you in a good light already."

"You think so?" she asked, frowning. "I'm not so sure."

"I'm sure. I'm absolutely sure. You don't need to worry on that account at all. Still, I understand what you're saying. You don't want to disappoint anybody, but nobody can get all the answers all the time. The fact that you've closed as many cases as you have is quite remarkable."

"I know. I know." Doreen frowned at her grandmother. "It still seems to be a cop-out."

"Not a cop-out at all," she murmured. "Just an acknowledgment that nobody—not even you, my dear—can solve every case."

She laughed. "True enough. But to change topics, I've got to run. I'm going to meet Mack for lunch today. Then go home and try to coordinate all the material I have into something slightly more cohesive than I currently have."

And with that she gave her Nan a hug and a peck on her cheek and left to join Mack for lunch and a bit of a break from the information rolling around in her head.

Chapter 9

THE NEXT MORNING Doreen was wide awake in bed, her mind running through the bits and pieces of information she'd gathered so far, and after returning home the previous afternoon, collated them into something that was a little easier to sort. Even listed possible scenarios, but absolutely nothing was pointing her in any direction. It was early yet in this case, so she shouldn't be so overwhelmed, but she *was* putting pressure on herself, and that was something she did need to watch.

She'd had so much success that now she felt a greater pressure to find answers, an expectation that she maintain her good record, but nobody could do that all the time. Besides, there was a reason these were cold cases. But even that pep talk didn't necessarily do its job.

She made her way out of bed, had a quick shower, then headed down to put on coffee. She couldn't imagine what life was like without coffee, though maybe tea would do the same if that's what you were raised with. That's certainly how it was in England, but it was coffee all the way for Doreen. As she waited for the coffee to brew, she checked her laptop for emails, wondering if anything of interest had come through.

When she found no new emails, she stared down at it and sighed. She needed to get in touch with Mack's brother to deal with more paperwork. She knew that he was waiting for something and would be sending her a bunch of things to decide on. She had him handling almost everything at the moment, just because it was easier to have one lawyer, even though some of this wasn't necessarily his field. She was sure it was a mess for him, yet having one person coordinate it all made her life a little bit easier.

Just as she was about to pour a cup of coffee, her email beeped, and she found something there from a lawyer regarding Robin's estate. As she read through the email, she shook her head. More paperwork was required, and everything was being sold. The dollar amounts were eye-popping. However, as long as Doreen had enough money for right now, she wasn't in any particular rush. Since Robin's estate was going through probate, there would apparently still be months of headaches to deal with. As with everything else, the legal process seemed to take a while.

The probate attorney had written that it would be eight to nine months before everything was settled. Doreen had just nodded and smiled. It's not as if she could do anything about that time frame. So she would not get involved more than she already was. She was content to sit back and to let it all play out. Thankfully the sale of Nan's antiques and a partial payment to Doreen gave her some relief.

She had confirmed with Mack's brother that it was an accurate time frame. Probate being something done to help maintain the fairness and the ethics of actual estate settlements, she could do nothing but sit back and sign the paperwork as it came through. As usual, she just forwarded all the paperwork to Nick, and, as he approved it, she signed and sent it onward.

There was always so much paperwork, so much legalese to read. Since she didn't want to get caught out in anything, it was just easier to funnel it all Nick's way. Not long after she had forwarded this latest email to him, he called her right back.

"Are you having fun with these emails?" he teased.

"Not really," she muttered, "and I know it's a big pain for you, but, with so many bits and pieces, I don't really trust anybody anymore."

"I'm honored that you trust me."

"There should be some advantage to … *family* connections," she quipped in a cheeky tone.

He burst out laughing. "I'm glad you're finally seeing some advantage to it."

"I'm not quite adjusted to the whole thing yet," she murmured, "but I am working on it."

"That's all we can ask of you," he noted. "While I have you on here, I would ask a favor." He took a moment and then came back strong. "Could you find time to visit my mother? She's quite lonely."

"Oh dear." Doreen paused. "I stopped by last week, but you're right. … I should be popping over a little more often."

"It's not that *should be* is involved in this," he replied, "and I don't mean to pressure you. It's just a matter of she's lonely, and we're all so terribly busy. I just know that a visit from you always cheers her up."

"Not a problem," she said, "and I should have thought of it myself. I think of that automatically with Nan, but I need to get into the same habit with Millicent."

He chuckled. "Stop putting so much pressure on yourself. You're doing a fine job."

"Am I?" she muttered. "I've just started a mess of a case—and from the captain no less," she added, "but I'm not getting very far."

"What's the case about?" he asked. "Wait, did you say the captain?"

"Yes."

"So, is it another personal case?"

"No, it's one they've had in a box at the coroner's office since forever," she explained. "A set of bones from a toddler was found quite a long time ago, thirty-five some years ago, and they haven't been able to figure out who she is or what happened to her."

"Not even what happened to her?" he asked, his tone sharp.

"She died of her injuries, and the bones showed what looks to be animal damage, but that's not what killed her. They are saying basically abuse killed her due to multiple factors, but there isn't a whole lot to go on."

"Of course not," he agreed. "It's been a long time, and for little bones especially."

"I don't know if they're more fragile and disintegrate faster," she noted, "but, in this case, there's not much information. I've been down at the library, trying to locate birth and death information, hoping to find a match."

He replied, "It wasn't really all that long ago. It's not as if we're talking the Dark Ages. You might want to talk with some of the older midwives in town."

"Oh my," she muttered, staring down at her phone. "I hadn't even considered that, but you're right."

"This is around the time when Mack and I were born,

and our mom may know of some midwives working back then."

"In that case I will definitely stop by and talk to her." He burst out laughing. "And no," she muttered, "I didn't need an excuse."

"I'm glad to hear that because I know how much she really appreciates any chance to visit with you."

"Yes," she murmured and then groaned, remembering her last visit. "She is lonely, and I get that, but what she really wants is a chance to ask me questions about when the wedding is."

"Given her age, I'm pretty sure that's something she would want settled while she's still doing as well as she is."

"She might want it settled, but I won't be pushed," Doreen stated adamantly.

"I get that, but, with your husband deceased, many people would think there's no reason to hold back."

"Maybe not," she conceded, "but it still doesn't seem to be settled yet *to me*."

"No, but we're getting there."

"Are we?" she asked, with a wry smile. "Even now I just forwarded you that email from the lawyer handling Robin's estate."

"And thankfully we're making progress on your husband's estate too," he added. "I'm staying on top of both, and it will come to an end at some point."

"You keep saying that." She chuckled. "Don't mind me if I don't quite believe it."

"Probate being what it is," he began, "definitely checks and balances have to be done. So far, everything is clear. Nobody's contesting Mathew's will, and his estate is all yours, particularly after the many years of your marriage.

Then we have all the other issues that came out," he noted, "and, if all goes as I see it, you will end up a very wealthy woman."

"Sure, sometime," she pointed out. "It's not as if it's now."

He asked, "Do you need money?"

"No, I'm fine."

"Are you sure?" he asked. "That's not something we want to happen."

"I still have all the antique money coming."

A sigh of relief from the other end came first, then his tone sharpened again. "But you said *coming*, not necessarily in your wallet right now."

"I've been paid for some of it already," she replied, "just not all of it. And that's because it takes like ninety days for the larger pieces."

"No, ninety days for all of it."

"Right," she muttered, "and the bigger stuff recently sold, so … ninety days from then."

"Okay," he replied, a bit unsure, "but, if you run into any trouble with that, you let me know."

"Will do, and, yes, I'll still stop by and talk to your mom."

With that, she ended the call and phoned Millicent, who cried out in delight.

"Do you have time to come for a visit?" she asked Doreen. "I was hoping to maybe talk to you a little bit more about Mack."

"I was thinking maybe early this afternoon, but I'm not sure if you'll have a nap later."

"I usually do," she admitted, with a chuckle, "but, if I know you're coming, I'll hold off."

"No, no, no, you don't need to do that. You'll just be more tired." Doreen looked down at her watch. "Of course you could probably just put on the coffeepot now."

"Done," she cried out in joy.

"Okay, I'll pack up the animals, and we'll be over in a few minutes." And, with that, she disconnected, looked down at the animals, and asked, "How do you feel about going over to see your other grandmother?"

Mugs just looked at her, rolled over onto his back, and yawned.

"Oh no you don't," she stated. "If nothing else we can go get some information."

She bundled up and grabbed her purse and the leashes. As she opened the back door, prepared to walk to Millicent's, she stopped as a cold blast of air hit her, then slammed the door shut. She looked down at the animals and announced, "Okay, we're driving."

Not a one of them argued with her as she headed to the car, helped them all up, hopped in, and turned it on. The engine took a minute to turn over. Even her vehicle reacted to just how cold it could be. Frowning at that, she waited for the engine to warm up and then drove slowly the few blocks over to Millicent's place. As soon as she pulled in and parked and exited the car, the animals raced up to the front door with her.

Millicent opened the door and let them right in. "If I'd realized it was so cold," Millicent noted apologetically, "I would never have asked you to come over."

Doreen stepped inside, barely holding back a shiver and smiled. "I may not be used to the cold, but I have to admit it caught me by surprise this morning."

"It'll do that to you every once in a while," Millicent

stated, with a beaming smile, "but I did put on coffee for you."

She laughed. "And, as you know, that will bring me over anytime."

Chuckling, the two women made their way into the kitchen, where Millicent poured Doreen a cup of coffee, and they sat down at the table. Knowing that Millicent would start talking about the wedding plans, Doreen jumped in with a little bit about her case.

"Don't know if Mack told you, but the captain wanted me to look in on a case that had confounded everybody so far. It's old and not something they have time to do anything about," she explained, "so I'm looking at it now."

Millicent nodded at her in delight. "That's lovely to hear. I'm glad that the captain trusts you with it."

"I don't know how much is trust as much as he's hoping that we can find some closure on a case that's bothered him all this time."

"I wouldn't be at all surprised," she agreed, with a nod. "So, tell me about it."

Doreen sighed. "It's a little troublesome, a little upsetting, because we—not we, but somebody in the past—found a child's body, a toddler really, in a garden. They were turning over the bed to plant yams and found the bones underneath the surface. I don't know how deep under the surface, but it was obviously time for it to come to light."

"Oh my." Millicent frowned. "I feel as if I've heard something about that."

"And you might have," Doreen noted, frowning at her. "It was around thirty or thirty-five years ago, so it would have been somewhere around the time that you had Mack and Nick."

"Right," she muttered, nodding. "I do remember a lot of discussions about it at the time." She shook her head. "I don't remember the details though."

"I'm not surprised. I'm not sure any of us have much in the way of details, and that's a bit of a concern too. We just have the bones, and I have asked the captain via email this morning if there was any chance of pulling DNA, so we can put it on the genealogy sites."

"Oh, I've heard about that," Millicent replied. "That's really clever."

"Even with that I will probably still need some help in order to sort out who could possibly be related to her," she shared, "but that might give us a start."

"Of course, of course." As Millicent stared off into the kitchen window, she frowned.

Doreen nudged her. "Are you remembering something?"

She shook her head, then stopped. "Kind of. I do remember something that bothered me. It's not as if we found things like that all the time."

"No, of course not," And then she stopped, confounded at her words. "What do you mean, *we* found things?"

"I'm pretty sure if you check the address where the bones were found, it's not that far from here. Kelowna has really grown in the last thirtysomething years. We used to be a collection of communities that all became one as the population grew. You can go from one end of the city to the other in under twenty minutes now. Of course the communities of Black Mountain, Joe Rich, Lake Country, and across the lake don't count as they aren't part of the actual city and might take a little longer to reach depending on traffic."

"Really?" Doreen mentally kicked herself for not having

checked out exactly where the bones were found. "That's interesting," she muttered. "Would you know your neighbors around here from back in the day?"

"Oh sure, but, even if the bones were *found* about thirty-five years ago, as you say, they could have been there for longer."

"That could well be true, but I'm not exactly sure. I would have to grab my notes and the case file and check it." That was something she had wondered herself. "I was down at the library, looking at all the births and deaths from that general time frame, but there's just so many."

"Oh my, yes." Millicent nodded. "When you're having babies, it seems as if everybody is having babies. You want to go to the doctor, and you can't because it's so full of other people's babies," she shared, with a laugh. "Maybe that's just the way it works, so that you tend to notice people who are in the same stage of life as you are. Still, it was pretty impressive to see just how many families were expanding thirtysomething years ago."

"And did anybody have any idea about what was going on back then?"

"Oh, you mean with the body? No, I don't remember anything specific ever said. You should talk to the midwife."

Doreen nodded. "Nick mentioned that too."

"He dated a midwife in town here at one point in time," she shared, with a chuckle. "At least she wanted to become a midwife. I don't know that she ever went through with it or not. For a while there everybody was using midwives, and then it seemed as if they went out of fashion, and nobody was."

"I think things probably come and go, depending on the surroundings and the people who you're involved with."

"That could be, and I do remember a mention of finding the body, obviously of a small child, but I honestly don't recall much more about it."

"No, that's fine," Doreen replied. She had to admit to being a little on the tired side. And a little disappointed. They talked for a little bit longer, as she finished her coffee, then she stood to say her goodbyes and to collect the animals to head back home again.

Millicent added, "You should probably talk to Lilybeth."

"And who's Lilybeth?" Doreen asked, frowning.

"She used to live around here. She was the midwife at the time."

"She lived close by?"

"Yes, for a while, she did. Though I'm not exactly sure what years she lived here."

"Any idea where she is now? Is she still in the area?"

"She's staying in a home but not Rosemoor."

"Right, several others are around town."

"There are, but I can't remember where she's at. Seems as if it might be the one down close to the river."

"If you remember the name of it," Doreen suggested, "I would be happy to check."

"I don't have any idea, so you need to check on that. If you talk to Lilybeth, she might have something to say. I remember her reaction to the body being found seemed a bit odd."

"In what way?" Doreen asked.

"I'm not sure. I just remember her reaction was … almost shocked, yet not. Something was off about it. I remember asking her about it, and she got offended. Yet the more she protested, the more I felt that she might know something."

"I will talk to her. That won't cost me anything."

Millicent laughed. "No, talk is cheap, but getting the truth? Now that's a whole different story."

Chapter 10

DOREEN PHONED THE Riverdale retirement home and asked if Lilybeth was there. The answer she got was positive, but she wasn't having visitors. "Oh." Doreen didn't expect that response. "If you would tell her that it's Doreen, the woman who works with all the cold cases in town, and that I had a few questions I wanted to ask about her years as a midwife. Maybe that would … change her mind."

The receptionist sounded doubtful.

Doreen asked, "Is there a reason why she doesn't have visitors?"

"Yes, she doesn't want any," the receptionist stated, with a snort. "We encourage our residents to be social, to interact with others, but, every once in a while, we get somebody who's more reclusive than we like, and that's Lilybeth to a tee."

"I understand. Please leave her my message, and we'll see." Doreen disconnected and frowned.

What was she supposed to do if somebody didn't want to talk to her? Why Lilybeth refused to talk was a whole question in itself, but there could be a lot of reasons for that. Realizing that worrying about it was pointless, Doreen turned her attention to going through the notes that she'd made at the library. Even knowing it was probably a complete waste of time, she still hoped it would trigger some other light-bulb moment as to how to go forward.

She had already sent a message to the captain, asking about DNA testing on the bones, so she could get it uploaded to the genealogy site. She didn't have any response yet. As she sat here, her phone rang, and it was the captain.

"The DNA has already been pulled," he began, sounding all gruff, "and we do have the results. As for what you're asking about, I'm okay with you uploading it."

"Good," she cried out in delight because that could be the only way to get some forward movement on this. Not that she would hold back either way, but it was nice having him onboard.

"No luck yet?" he asked.

"I'm hoping to talk to a midwife who was very busy during that era to see if she has any thoughts or information on that situation."

"Oh, that's interesting," he murmured.

"Why?"

"A lot of women back then used midwives," he noted. "I hadn't really considered that as an avenue."

"Maybe it's not a good one. I don't know yet," she said, with a chuckle. "I'm hoping to talk to her. She's over at Riverdale retirement home, but apparently she's fairly reclusive."

"Oh my, are you talking about Lilybeth?"

"Yes, I'm talking about Lilybeth," she confirmed. "I didn't realize you knew her."

"Yeah, I do know her. She was an old family friend for a while, but then something happened when I went into law enforcement. I know my mom was pretty heartbroken that she seemed to have lost Lilybeth's friendship at the same time, but Mom never really understood why."

"Do you think it was because you went into law enforcement?"

"I would hope not," he stated, with a grunt, "but people are funny, and just because I went into law enforcement doesn't mean everybody was happy about it."

"I'm sure your mother was."

"Yes, she was over the moon."

"Odd about Lilybeth, isn't it?"

"Yes, but, after her husband died, she was never quite the same again."

"What happened to her husband?" she asked.

"Oh, well, that was a sadness in itself. Her husband was murdered, a mugging while he had been in Vancouver. The authorities caught the guy, but that doesn't bring back Lilybeth's husband."

"Oh no," Doreen muttered, "no wonder she's reclusive."

"Exactly. She's a lovely lady. She really is, but she doesn't want to talk about what happened with her husband, and she certainly doesn't want to talk to strangers."

"Of course not. Who would want to dredge all that up again?"

"Right, anyway I will get the DNA results back for you, and you can set up an account and upload it."

"Perfect."

As soon as she got off the phone, she immediately set up an account on an ancestry site, ready for the DNA to be sent her way. Her mind was busy on the midwife, still reeling from the information that her husband had been murdered. All too often it seemed the people who spent their lifetime helping others got completely shafted in the deal. When bad things happened to them—with no rhyme or reason—it sucked on so many levels.

It wasn't long before she got the DNA report and had it uploaded onto the account she had opened. There was a small fee for it, but she didn't care. Once the request was submitted, she sat back, knowing it would take a bit before the results came in.

She smiled, having at least achieved something. That didn't mean it would bring any answers, but it did feel like progress. While she was sitting here, congratulating herself, her phone rang. Surprised, she looked down to see that it was Riverdale's number. She answered the phone in a light tone. "Hello, this is Doreen speaking."

"Hello, Doreen," the receptionist replied. "I did speak to Lilybeth, and she's reluctant to talk to you. She's not at all happy about it."

"Meaning that she's afraid I'll bring up something about her husband?"

"I think that's probably it, yes," she agreed.

"There's a cold case involving a baby from many years ago," Doreen explained, "and that's what I was hoping to talk to her about."

"Oh dear. I'll mention it again, but I don't know that she'll go for it." The woman was quite apologetic.

"I understand," Doreen replied. "I'm also trying to put a name to that baby who died so long ago."

"Right," the receptionist muttered. "I see Lilybeth's just coming out of the lunch room. I'll put you on hold and go talk to her real quick."

Surprised at that, Doreen waited, going through a few emails and cleaning out her inbox, until the receptionist came back on the phone. "That seems to have completely changed her attitude, so I'm happy to tell you that she has agreed to see you. Anything to do with babies, I guess, is okay."

"That makes perfect sense, since she spent a lifetime helping babies."

"She did, indeed." The receptionist laughed. "She can see you at two today."

"Oh my, that's perfect."

"I hope that time is okay?"

"It will be fine," Doreen declared, with a smile. "I can definitely make that work."

"Thank you," the receptionist said, with a relieved tone. "She is … fairly direct as to …"

"What she wants?"

"Yeah, that's a good word. Another would be … *militant*." And, with that, she disconnected.

Militant? Doreen frowned. That could be a challenge in itself.

Doreen didn't have too much time before her meeting with Lilybeth, so she quickly looked up directions as to where she needed to go, and, with that done, she cleaned up the kitchen. She also might need a few names from that era to jostle Lilybeth's memory and to help dial in the time frame. Grabbing her notes, Doreen jotted down the names of a few girls who had been born in that general period, wondering just how accurate Lilybeth's memory would be, especially after all this time.

Before long, it was time for her to get going. She looked at the animals, all waiting at the front door for her. Doreen then quickly called Riverdale and asked if she was allowed to bring the animals with her.

"Today is visitors day," the woman noted hesitantly. "It really depends on how well-behaved your animals are."

"They're very well-behaved," Doreen stated, "and I do find that most of the elderly people we encounter really do enjoy the animals."

"In that case," she replied, "we'll give it a try, but you may be asked to put them back in your vehicle if they prove to be too much."

"Fair enough," she said. "See you soon." As she packed up the animals, she warned them, "You guys need to be on your best behavior."

She almost heard Thaddeus snort in her hair, as he settled down for this adventure. Goliath just ignored her as usual, while clambering into the front seat, and Mugs took up the bulk of the back seat, his girth once again worrying her. He did seem to be already at an unhealthy weight. Yet she didn't really know enough about dogs, and, since Mugs seemed happy and could still run extremely well, she wasn't sure that she was doing him a disservice either.

Chapter 11

FOCUSING ON WHERE she was going, Doreen turned her attention to the road. Before long she was up and around the corner, and Riverdale was just a few blocks away. It was an eight-minute drive. As soon as she pulled in, she smiled to see lots of other visitors heading into the home. It was nice to think that people were coming to visit their families on such a cold and ornery day like this one. Yet it was a designated visiting day, and people were bracing the weather. So then they clearly cared about somebody they were coming to see. And that was lovely.

She walked into the front reception area, then stopped, turned, and headed to the front desk. She quickly introduced herself, and the woman immediately lit up.

"Now I know who you are," she exclaimed, as she leaned over the counter to look at the animals. "I thought you had more than just two."

At that, Thaddeus poked his head out from under the fall of Doreen's hair and cried out, "Thaddeus is here. Thaddeus is here."

Startled, she looked at him and burst out laughing. "Oh my. Aren't you adorable?"

Immediately Goliath pushed Mugs aside, his tail constantly wagging. Goliath preened in front of her, as if to suggest the entire world revolved around him. The receptionist came around the front desk and stroked his fur, talking to him, while simultaneously petting Mugs, who traveled around her feet. Doreen sighed, knowing there was absolutely no way to get out of this additional need for attention.

Suddenly, as if realizing that Doreen was here for a purpose, the receptionist gasped. "Sorry, let me show you where Lilybeth is." And, with that, they headed down the hallway. "She's in the sitting room in the back."

Obediently Doreen and her animals followed the receptionist. They headed to an out-of-the-way area, away from the general gathering of visitors in one of the main rooms up front. As they came to a sitting room, several people looked expectantly, as if waiting for someone special. Doreen sincerely hoped somebody showed up for them. There had to be nothing worse than sitting here, hoping someone would come and visit, only to realize they were too busy.

As they entered the room and headed toward the back wall, Doreen saw a tiny woman with an e-reader in hand, busily poring through the pages.

She looked up to see the receptionist come toward her and then frowned when she saw Doreen. Lilybeth stiffened and glared at her. "Where are the animals?" And then Mugs woofed, came around to her side, and sniffed her hand. "Ah," she murmured, a big smile on her face. "You did bring them."

"Of course," Doreen replied. "I did ask first whether I was allowed though."

"Oh my," Lilybeth muttered, with an eye roll. "If they

can stop us from having a decent time here, they will."

"Now that's not fair, Lilybeth," the receptionist countered in a cross tone. "You know we have rules to follow—all of us do."

"Sure, but we don't get to make the rules. You guys do."

"We make the rules to keep you safe," she explained and then looked back at Doreen. "If you want a cup of tea or something while you're here, let me know."

"She won't be here that long," Lilybeth snapped.

Doreen held her smile in place as she nodded at Lilybeth. "Hopefully we can get answers to the questions I have, and it will be painless for everybody."

"You're here," Lilybeth declared, still glaring at her, "so presumably not painless enough."

"Maybe not. I told the captain that I was coming to see you. He mentioned how he knew you quite well back then."

Lilybeth frowned at her and grumbled, "Right. You work with the police, don't you?"

"Sometimes," she agreed, with a nod. "It's part and parcel of the work I do."

"Of course it is," she snapped, "nothing but people poking their noses where they don't belong."

"And sometimes people need to poke their noses where they don't belong, or otherwise things happen, and people get away with things that they shouldn't. And, in this case, a child was buried in an unmarked grave in a vegetable garden and only discovered because someone wanted to grow yams."

"Yams," Lilybeth declared in astonishment. "That's not right."

"Exactly," Doreen agreed, with a smile. "Which is why I'm here. I'm hoping you can help me identify the child."

"Goodness, how on earth could I possibly identify a

dead baby?" she muttered. "Unless of course it's one of the ones I delivered, and then maybe …"

"And maybe that's a way to start," Doreen suggested. "May I sit?"

Lilybeth looked at her and at her animals, then grudgingly nodded.

Not sure how to take the woman's absolute lack of manners or joy in life, Doreen sat down and kept her animals close. A lot of other people wandered around, and she didn't want to upset anybody.

"At least you're keeping them well-behaved," Lilybeth noted, eyeing her critically.

"I wouldn't want to upset anyone by having them here," Doreen replied. "Some people don't like animals."

"Of course not, because those people don't have a heart."

Doreen didn't say anything to that, as it might open up a whole minefield of issues. "We don't even have a name for her."

"So, you don't even know who she is?" Lilybeth asked, with a headshake.

"No, at the moment, we don't. I don't know if you can help," Doreen began, "but did you know of any children who died about thirty-five years ago?"

Lilybeth sat back and let out a loud snort. "You expect me to remember that far back?"

"A lot of people have memories from that era," she noted, "but, depending on some people's mental health, maybe they don't."

At that, the old woman scrunched up her face. "I don't like the way you put that."

"It's a well-known fact that, as we age, some people remember things that happened long ago far better than something that may have happened last week," she shared. "And I have the case of an eighteen-month-old baby girl who was beaten to the point of death," she shared, almost choking up before pushing back the tears. "Then her remains were unceremoniously dumped in a garden plot, where animals chewed on her bones."

"Who would do that? Everyone deserves a Christian burial."

"That would be nice," Doreen replied, "and I'll be happy to confirm this little girl gets that, once I have her name."

Lilybeth's expression turned sorrowful, and she nodded slowly. "Child abuse happens so often. … Back then I don't think it happened any more than it does today, though it certainly did happen. I just think that we hear about it a lot more these days."

"Did you know of any families where the children were abused?"

Lilybeth looked at her for a long moment, then slowly nodded. "There were a couple." She sighed, then shook her head. "In one case, the family was killed in a house fire, and we found out afterward that the husband had murdered them all and then torched the house. Their last name was Smith, but they are all dead now." She frowned, paused for a long moment, then added, "The other family was the Winters, although I'm not sure it was around the same time frame, but it wasn't too far off."

"This little girl was found in Southeast Kelowna, the Black Mountain area." Then she told her the address.

Lilybeth's eyebrows shot up. "Back thirty-odd years ago that would not have been that far out of town," she noted, "yet just far enough that it's another world. Back then these were all small separate communities, unlike today where it seems they've all grown together. I still don't really know how I can help you."

"Did you help anybody in that corner?"

"Sure," she said, with a chuckle. "I helped a lot of people there, but most of the time I stayed closer to town. Sometimes the women came in to see me, and sometimes I went to visit them, but I can't really say that I would know who had an eighteen-month-old baby who disappeared."

At that, Doreen frowned at her. "And yet I didn't mention that she disappeared."

Lilybeth flushed. "If she was buried in the yard, she disappeared, didn't she?" she snapped, with a waspish tone. "And don't you get smart with me, young woman."

Doreen shook her head. "I didn't come here to argue with you. I would just like to give this child a proper burial and to mark her grave with her given name."

Lilybeth obviously was warring with something from the struggle evident by her facial expression, until finally she shrugged. "A couple families were in that corner. Winters was one of them, and I think the other was his brother-in-law." She frowned. "Another couple in that corner were fairly strict with the rod, after all that church-going preaching and whatnot. I don't remember the name though."

"Meaning that they beat the kids?"

"Meaning that, if the kids didn't behave, they were punished," she clarified. "And that was a lot more common back then than it is today."

Doreen could not imagine that, but back then it seemed as if you could do a whole lot and nobody cared. "And do you remember if a little girl went missing?"

"I have no idea," she stated. "I helped deliver a couple

girls in that corner, but I can't tell you which ones or to whom."

"No, of course not. So, Winters, and any other names?"

She looked at her and shrugged. "Just because they discipline their kids doesn't mean they would have killed them."

"Right," Doreen replied, "but it's also quite possible that they disciplined too hard. This little baby's bones, … they were broken, so she was likely abused."

Lilybeth winced and then nodded. "So, it's possible that it's them. But it could also be half a dozen others."

"Any other names than the Winters family? I've been looking through birth records and death records but haven't found anything that got my attention. So no sign of them or of a death certificate."

"If the birth were announced anywhere, or if there was a formal death certificate, I would imagine the child wouldn't have been buried in the garden."

"No, I wouldn't have thought so," Doreen agreed.

Lilybeth added, "It was illegal back then too. There were certainly some who wanted the afterbirth buried out in the garden, but that's a whole different case."

Doreen stared at her. "Did they do that?"

"Some of them did," Lilybeth said, "and that practice comes and goes on a regular basis. It's not as if it's new. Whenever you have women giving birth, you'll get all kinds of beliefs about what's proper and what's not."

"I'm not too bothered about the afterbirth, as long as they didn't bury children who died at their hands in the garden."

Lilybeth nodded. "I wouldn't either. I think that's all I can help you with."

Doreen pulled out a piece of paper from her notepad, wrote down her name and phone number, and handed it to Lilybeth. "If you think of any other names, give me a shout. I will be diligently tracking down any other birth and death certificates, seeing who's left."

"That'll take you a long time."

"It will, and it's one of the reasons I'm going the genealogy route, to see if I can speed things up a bit."

Chapter 12

ONCE SHE GOT back home again, Doreen followed up on her notes and then headed online to see if she could find anything about the Winters family. There were quite a few generations of them, if the news was anything to go by. There were some good and some bad stories about them, which was to be expected. The family was touted as supporting various organizations with their donations, including the local church.

She filtered her way through and came to a news article involving a Buck Winters and a domestic violence charge. She frowned, then checked out the number of years that had gone by. Sure enough, it fit right into what could be the time frame she was looking for. Of course it was a *could be*, not a definitive answer. Nothing was ever quite so easy in this world.

As she pondered the name, she kept searching, looking for anything that might also run along the same lines. She found several other articles, most of them more newsy than about crime. But she didn't trust any of that either. She wasn't sure when she came to distrust the news sources, but apparently it had already happened because here she was, looking at every article and wondering at the source, wondering if it could be trusted.

Finally she picked up the phone and called Nan.

When Nan heard her voice on the other end, she cried out, "Have you got something?"

"I'm not saying I've got something," Doreen clarified, trying hard to suppress a smile, "but do you know the Winters family?"

"Winters, Winters, Winters. Oh my," she grumbled. "If it's the Winters family I think you're talking about, they're bad news, with domestic violence, battery, petty theft, you know the type. ... Yet they were always in church, as if that wiped clean what they had been doing while out of church. ... I don't think they ever did anything criminal though."

Doreen winced. "News flash, Nan, domestic violence and battery is criminal."

"Oh, I know that," Nan replied, "and I'm not trying to minimize it. But, in my day, men could get away with certain things, without facing consequences."

"But this was only thirty-five years ago, not seventy-five," Doreen pointed out, "so there should have been consequences if they were involved at that level."

"Oh, I think they were involved," Nan noted. "I seem to recall some court cases. ... A rough bunch as far as I'm concerned."

"And are they still in that area?"

"Maybe, I don't know. I haven't really had anything to do with them."

"So, this is the question," Doreen began. "Is there anybody at Rosemoor with that name or with any connection to them? Or who would even know anything about them?"

"Wow, that's a really good question, but I have no idea. How did that get by me?"

Doreen chuckled. "I'll leave it in your capable hands to do a scout around to see if anybody at Rosemoor knows the Winters family because apparently domestic violence and possibly child abuse was something that they were known for."

"Yes, yes, yes," she agreed. "I don't doubt it. Do you really think she's a Winters' baby?"

"I have no idea," Doreen admitted, "and we can't say that either. We don't know anything for sure yet."

"No, but you're getting somewhere," Nan pointed out, her admiration coming through the phone, clear as a bell.

Doreen groaned. "No, no, not yet. I'm not saying anything along that line yet."

"Maybe not," Nan conceded, "but I, for one, am delighted that you're getting somewhere."

"I'm not sure I'm getting anywhere." Doreen groaned. "I'm running up against quite a number of issues."

"Of course, dear," Nan chastised her. "That is to be expected, but you will resolve them." And, with that, she disconnected.

Doreen groaned as she realized it was already four o'clock. When a hard knock came on her door, and the front door opened without ceremony, she realized two things. Mack was here, and she was probably supposed to cook some dinner. She frowned at Mack.

When he walked in, took one look at her face, he asked, "What's wrong?"

"Was I supposed to cook?" she cried out.

He walked closer and snagged her up into a hug. "It wouldn't matter if you were supposed to cook today. This isn't a military camp, and you aren't under orders. If you had something else to do and didn't cook, that's fine."

She stepped back out of his arms, searched his face, and then sighed in relief. "Are you sure? We could try a new restaurant," she suggested, "because honestly, I've just been so busy working on this case that cooking never even crossed my mind." She walked over to the fridge and opened it.

He stepped up behind her and nodded. "I see you forgot to buy groceries too."

She groaned. "I don't know about that. It doesn't look any different than the last time I was in here."

He chuckled. "News flash, to have groceries in your fridge, you have to buy them. You can go get them yourself or just order them, have them delivered. Some of the guys will even put them away for you. Regardless, you still have to do something to start the process." She glared at him, and he chuckled again. "So, either we go out to eat or we go grab some food to cook when we get back home."

"Honest to God, I'm tired." She looked at the fridge again and then rolled her eyes. "We could have an omelet."

"We could have an omelet," he agreed. He poked around in the fridge and noted, "Not a whole lot of protein in here though."

"You're tired and need protein," she noted.

"It's not just that I'm tired and need protein," he added, looking at her, "but you look equally tired. So, before you wear yourself down on this cold case, I would feel better if you ate properly." He chuckled and opened up the freezer. "We've got sausages here, and we've got eggs in the fridge," he stated. "Why don't I make a scramble—with potatoes, if you have any." He went to the pantry and pulled out two very sad-looking large potatoes. "I'll come up with dinner.

You go sit and tell me all about your day."

She looked at him in bemusement. "Isn't that my line?"

"What?"

"You go sit and tell me about your day?"

He laughed. "My day was all about court, and I can tell you that, at times, I absolutely detest lawyers." He chuckled. "Then I remember that my brother is one, so I don't really get to go off on that tangent either." He smiled as he washed and then chopped potatoes and tossed them into a pan.

She watched in fascination as, before her eyes, a very solid and hefty-looking meal was created out of what she would have considered nothing.

Twenty minutes later he nudged her toward the table. "Grab some forks."

And she realized he was done. "How do you do that?" she asked, feeling vexed. "You took nothing and turned it into a meal for two of us."

"It's hardly nothing," he pointed out. "You had sausage, potatoes, and eggs, plus some leftover vegetables and even cheese. So I just made a bit of a scramble. It should be enough to keep us both going."

"I would think so," she muttered, as she stared down at it in amazement. She sniffed the aroma coming off her plate and groaned. "I didn't even realize I was hungry." She took several bites, nodding and smiling as she did. "This is so good."

"And that is something else we'll have to watch with you," he noted. "You tend to get so involved in work that you forget to eat."

"I don't think I even know what hunger is half the time," she admitted. "It's as if I shut off everything because I don't have time for it."

"Yeah, and that makes sense too, but it's also not good for you." She just shrugged and didn't say anything. With a groan, he asked, "Okay, back to this case, how far did you get?"

"I got the DNA uploaded to the genealogy site." He raised his eyebrows. "The captain gave me the DNA report, and I told him what I was doing with it, and he approved," she explained.

"Interesting. Okay, that's good. Probably the first time ever that you did something that was preapproved."

She snorted. "I went to see Lilybeth in Riverdale, the old folks' home down by the river."

"Did she have anything to offer?"

"It took a bit, but she confirmed two families known for domestic violence issues. She didn't really come out and say that she didn't want to deal with them, but I got the impression that she would just as soon *not*." When he raised one eyebrow, she added, "One family is all dead, per Lilybeth, so the only family name she came up with for me was Winters."

"Winters?" he asked, frowning at her. "That's one of our local politicians, or he's trying to be."

"Oh no. Really?"

He nodded.

She snorted. "He's a politician, so, in my book, that makes him slimy."

"That would go right along with you saying lawyers are slimy," he pointed out, looking at her in concern, "and we both know we can't say that."

"No, but ..."

"No," he stated in a firm tone.

"Fine," she muttered. "Besides, the chances of it being

the Winters politician are pretty slim. After all, we are talking about a toddler found about thirty-five years ago." He pondered that, as he scratched his chin. "I think that Winters may be in his fifties, maybe mid-fifties?"

"Right, so hard to say then. Anyway, I need to go through what I have and get a series of births and deaths for the Winters family."

"I can run that through the database, if you want."

"Yes, please." Then she sighed. "Although I don't know if you have access to data from that long ago."

"I do, but it may not necessarily be in the online files. Thirty-five years isn't all that long ago," he pointed out.

"I know, but it's scary to think of abuse and killing a child as something done at all back then."

"It is, and there's only so much that time can hinder," he said. "Sounds as if you've gotten some things going."

"I've done a lot of running around. I've got Nan checking to see if anybody at Rosemoor knows the Winters family, and I'm doing some groundwork, but I'm not really getting anywhere."

He nodded. "But you do have a family name as a lead, which is something," he pointed out.

"I have a name of someone known for domestic violence. Honestly, Lilybeth didn't really want to talk about it."

"If you had seen some things that bothered you, would you want to talk about it?"

"I would not only *not* want to talk about it, I would not want to be associated with it, particularly if I did nothing about it." She frowned and sat back, staring at him.

"Think about what Lilybeth's job was. Think about what she was doing and about the pressure to keep her mouth shut, say about a political family or an unwed mother or something," Mack explained. "You can't judge her for it."

"No, of course not," She picked up the fork and had another couple bites, before putting down her fork again.

Mack eyed the amount of food still on her plate and motioned to it. "At least eat a couple more."

"Couple more what?" she asked, turning to him.

"Eat a couple more bites."

She stared at him, looked at her plate, and shrugged. "I don't think I'm hungry anymore." He frowned at that. She added, "I'm not … *not* eating for any particular reason. I just think I'm full."

"Maybe," he conceded, "but you also haven't eaten very much."

"I think I've eaten enough though." He let it go, but she could see he wasn't happy. She chuckled. "See? You eat way more than I do. I'm just not that big."

"You'll never get any bigger if you keep eating such minuscule portions of food either," he grumbled, "and no going after my dessert when it's dessert time."

She picked up her fork, then stopped. "Did you just do that?"

"Do what?" he asked, a grin on his face.

"Did you just try to bribe me with dessert?"

"No, of course not," he quipped. "I wouldn't do that."

"Yes, you would." But still, she shoveled several more bites of food down her throat and then stopped. "I don't even know if you brought dessert."

"Nope, you don't," he agreed, "but apparently you were still hungry because you just ate again."

She frowned. "I don't know if I'm hungry or not," she muttered. "I talked to your brother."

"How's he doing?" he asked in a noncommittal tone, as if he already knew.

"He's fine. I also had a visit with your mother."

Now he put down his fork and asked, "Was that okay?"

"It was because I didn't let her talk about the wedding."

He laughed. "That's one way to do it."

"I kept her busy with my cold case, asking her if she knew of anybody, of any child who might have gone missing or anything. She didn't seem to have any idea either, only to then mention Lilybeth's name."

"I think that's fairly common. Her age for one thing, and maybe just because of the nature of the case. A lot of people don't know how common domestic violence is, how common child abuse is. And, no, it's not just fathers. A lot of the time it's also the mothers."

"And that's just wrong," Doreen declared, staring at him.

He nodded. "It is, but just because it's wrong doesn't mean that we'll stop it."

"We should though," she stated, glaring at him.

He smiled, then tapped her nose. "Maybe so, but it'll take a whole lot more than just us being outraged over it."

"I know," she muttered. She took another bite and then one more. With a sigh, she put down her fork and announced, "Okay, now I'm really done."

"Oh, good. Now all the dessert's for me." She glared at him, and he burst out laughing. "You didn't even see me bring a bag in."

"What bag?" She got up and raced around the kitchen, like a two-year-old, looking for the bag. When she spied it, she admitted, "I didn't even see you bring it in."

"That's what I just said," he noted, with a laugh.

She sighed. "I have to admit that I am really preoccupied with this case."

"It won't be an easy one to solve," he noted, "so don't let a lack of progress get to you."

She shrugged. "I think it's already getting to me."

"It can't," he declared. "You've only had it a few days. That is not a lack of progress."

"Isn't it?" she asked. "It always feels as if I'm supposed to do something immediately to get there fast."

"Oh no," he argued, "none of that."

"None of what?" she muttered.

"You heard me. None of that. We're not expecting you to solve this stuff."

She frowned at him. "You're *not* expecting me to?"

"Obviously we're hoping you will," he clarified, holding up a hand, "but there's no expectation, no pressure. Nobody has been able to solve it yet. Sure, if we had a free moment, if we weren't dealing with all these old cases that somehow ended up solved and on our plates to finalize, we would be looking at some of these cold cases ourselves."

"But you never quite get a chance because you're already swamped without them," she added, with a nod. "And I understand that, but something's so disturbing about knowing that little girl went undetected for all that time and then was only dug up and discovered because somebody wanted to grow yams."

"And it's a good thing he did. Otherwise she could have been there for decades more."

"I know," she whispered. "It's just so heartbreaking. How could one toddler be forgotten? And, even as it is, she's been at the morgue all this time. And she was in the garden bed for how long? She was supposedly found thirty-five years ago, but how long was she actually there?"

"Exactly," Mack agreed.

"Let me check my notes." She got up and brought over her notes and reread them. "Okay, so she was found in the garden bed thirty-five years ago, but no telling how long she was there."

"Yes, that is how I remember it too," he replied. "I've looked at those bones a couple times, but I can't determine anything from them. Short of having a hit off the genealogy database, we don't really have much to go on to find answers."

"Isn't that sad?" she asked.

"Yeah, but hopefully you'll get something started."

"I'm hoping so," she muttered, as she put down her notes. "Found thirty-five years ago."

"Exactly." He nodded. "Was that confusing?"

"No, but I'm looking at a longer time spread. The coroner said up to ten years, so buried for forty-five years ago is also possible."

"But even having a range is okay for a starting point," Mack noted. "Part of the journey is trying to figure out just what you have for options."

"Maybe," she muttered.

"Just carry on knowing that she was *found* thirty-five years ago, and we still need to find whoever killed her back then."

"So, was she born approximately thirty-seven years ago?"

"If the coroner was correct on lower estimation on how long she had been in the garden bed."

"Oh, good God, I'm getting confused on the time frame."

"Well, she was in the garden bed, found thirty-five years ago, and laid in the box in the coroner's office all that time period since, but we don't know when she first went into the ground."

"That could have been a lot less time. Plus, what about the animal marks?"

"That's something else we don't know. It was a consideration at the time that potentially she had been buried, but not deep enough, and was dug up by animals, then over time the bones were covered over."

"Oh, good Lord," she muttered, staring at him in horror.

"It happens."

"Yes, I imagine it does," she muttered. "It apparently did." She shook her head. "Still sucks though."

"It absolutely still sucks," he stated. He got up and put on a pot of coffee. "Are you ready for a treat?"

"I'm absolutely ready for a treat," she replied, jumping to her feet.

"Let's get the dishes done first, and then we can sit in the living room," he suggested.

By the time they settled into the only two chairs in the whole living room, he looked around and smiled. "Have you thought about getting furniture?"

"Yeah, every time you suggest we go sit in the living room," she teased, with a laugh. He grinned at her. "One thing I did want to mention ..." She stopped to consider how she should ask this, but she did need the question answered. "How in love with your house are you?"

His eyebrows shot up. "It's just a house to me. Why?" She nodded but didn't say anything. "What's going on in that brain of yours now?" he asked.

"After we're married," she began.

"Yes." He leaned forward. "After we're married, what?"

"I want to live here."

He looked at her, then slowly nodded. "I'd already assumed that's what you would want to do, so it never occurred to me that there would be another avenue."

"That's good because I really do want to stay here."

"Understood," he said, "and I don't have a problem with that. Besides, you're on the river, and that's pretty darn nice." He stared out the window and frowned. "You do have weird neighbors though."

She burst out laughing, and he grinned at her. "I'm sorry about Richard," she said, rolling her eyes. "He is definitely different."

"Richard and who else lives there in his house?" he asked, staring at her.

"I don't know. I don't know if it's just Richard. Nobody ever mentions a wife, but I do hear voices."

"I've heard a couple different voices," Mack shared, "but I'm not sure exactly what I've heard. Sometimes it seems to me it's just him talking to himself or maybe it's a radio or something."

"I know. I've had the same thoughts." She laughed. "I don't know whether he'll be happier or will feel worse about your moving in." Mack stared at her, and she shrugged. "I think he considers me a nuisance, and maybe having a cop as a neighbor would make him feel as if I won't be a bigger nuisance."

There wasn't much he could say to that, so he just shook his head and smiled. "Anyway, I'm happy to move here," he replied. "This house is closer to your grandmother too. And my mother's place."

"It absolutely is," she murmured. "And I know Nan put so much time and effort into this place."

"She put a lot of time and effort into *filling* this house," he pointed out. "I don't know that she put any time or effort into fixing it up."

"You're probably right there," she muttered, as she looked around. "And I guess we could do some things to fix it up."

"Maybe one of the first things would be to buy some furniture."

She burst out laughing and nodded. "I guess when it comes to people your size, it's a little hard to sit in this furniture."

He looked at her with a mock-injured expression. "My size?"

She shook her head. "You won't pull me into that argument," she muttered. "All I'm saying is that you're big enough that you probably want a full-size couch."

He nodded, then he hopped up to take a look at one of the walls closest to the dining room.

She walked beside him. "What are you thinking?"

"We could take out this wall," he noted. "It's not structural. That would open this all up."

"Do we need the dining room?"

"I don't know, do you?" he asked, turning to look at her. "It's one of those things that was in older houses but is much less common in newer homes."

"Right," she muttered. "I guess I never really thought about it."

"And we can leave it if you want, but this room isn't used very much."

"No, but I get the feeling that maybe it should be my office."

"Or we can turn it into an office for two, since I might need a home office myself," he suggested.

"Oh, right. *Hmm*, so much to think about."

The next hour was spent discussing options on how to set up any new furniture in the house. By the time he left, after explaining he needed to turn in early because he had a very early morning tomorrow, she was left wondering how much these renovations might upset Nan.

Chapter 13

WHEN DOREEN WOKE up the next morning, she was not rested, feeling she would betray Nan by doing anything to the house. So, wanting to nip that in the bud as fast as she could, she hopped up, made her coffee, grabbed her phone, and called her grandmother.

"Aren't you up early," Nan noted, with a yawn.

"Sorry, did I wake you?"

"No worries, though I do need my beauty sleep these days unfortunately," she shared in a quiet tone, "but I'm fine. What's bothering you, child?"

"Now why would you think something is bothering me?"

Her grandmother burst into laughter. "It will be a while yet before you can hide the signs from me, dear. Something's got you all aflutter."

"I was talking to Mack last night about which house to move into after we're married, and he was happy to move into this one."

"Oh good. That should make you feel better."

"Yes, but then we were talking about what we might need to do because he'll need an office, and I'll need an office, *blah, blah, blah,*" she explained. "Then I got worried, wondering if you would be upset if we made renovations to your house."

After a long moment on the other end, Nan burst into laughter. "Oh my, absolutely not. It's your house, child. I would be very happy for you to burn the thing down and build yourself something new."

"Oh my, I couldn't do that," she stated in shock.

"It's not a bad idea. That thing is old and won't take too many more renovations without coming apart at the seams. You do whatever you two want to do. I'm just glad you like it enough to want to stay there."

"Oh yes," she agreed, "and I absolutely love being right on the river. Plus, we've done so much work in the back-yard."

"That's true. You have," Nan agreed, the smile in her tone evident. Then she yawned again.

Doreen was sorry she'd woken her. "You need to go back to sleep," she declared abruptly. "I'm so sorry for calling this early."

"No, no, no," she muttered. "For all you know, the next time you call, it will be my last morning, so don't ever apologize for that."

"Oh, ouch. That's a maudlin way to talk."

"It feels that way to me, child. We lost another member of the home last night," she shared, sorrow in her voice. "Remember the old guy we moved here who lived not far from you on the river there?"

"The one who kidnapped you at gunpoint because you didn't pay enough attention to him? Yeah."

"He passed away in his sleep last night. It was a good way to go, don't get me wrong. It was an absolutely good way to go, but it just reminds us all that our time here could be shorter than we think."

By the time she disconnected, Doreen herself felt sad. Not exactly the way she wanted to start her day, but the thought of losing Nan after finally having her in Doreen's life again made her incredibly sad. Recalling all their adventures together since Doreen had moved here, she was devastated to think that event was something she would have to face.

Yet it was unavoidable, considering Nan was eighty-something. Doreen wasn't even sure how accurate that eightysomething mark was. Nan was a pro at hiding things that she didn't want people to know, and her age would definitely qualify in that category as something she didn't want everybody else discussing. She wasn't vain, but a little bit of flattery went a long way in her case.

With a sigh, Doreen got up and wandered around the house, considering Mack's suggestions last night about renovations and furniture needed. They had been good suggestions, brilliant really. It would be a matter of trial and error to see what would work, or so she figured. It was still a pretty big house for just the two of them, yet it wasn't even close to what she'd shared with her husband. Still, having her grandmother's two-story house also meant cleaning all that space. So that wasn't something she was very good at either. Yet it was something to consider.

Just then her phone buzzed. She picked it up and saw it was Lilybeth. "Hello, Lilybeth. Is that you?"

"Yes," she whispered. "Look. I need to talk to you, and it needs to happen fast, before I decide I can't do this."

"I can come right now, if you like," Doreen offered.

Lilybeth seemed startled. "Seriously?"

"Yes, of course," Doreen replied. "I know it's early, but, if you're up, and I'm up, there's no reason not to. Unless Riverdale has visiting hours, and I can't come until a certain time."

"I have no idea. I've never even considered that."

"You call it," Doreen suggested. "And either I will come down now or will come down in a little bit."

"Let's not raise any eyebrows or cause any gossip," she decided, "so in a little bit is fine."

"I'll meet you at say, … ten o'clock?"

"Ten o'clock it is."

"Do you want to tell me what it's about?"

"No, I don't," she snapped. "And, if you're unlucky, I'll change my mind before you get here."

"Maybe you should tell me now," Doreen urged, "just in case."

"I did write you a letter, and it is here," she stated, "but I do think I should probably tell you first in person."

"Has it got to do with this little baby girl?"

"I think so, but I can't be sure, and I don't want to make any accusations if I'm not certain. I did speak to a couple people I used to work with, the ones still in the industry, the ones who …" She paused and then started fretting. "You told me to think about it, but how do you think about that and not react?" she muttered.

"I'm sure it's hard for you, for anyone really."

"Anyway, I did write you a letter, and I'm leaving it at the front desk. If anything happens to me," she shared, "at least you would have that." And, with that, she disconnected.

Doreen repeated out loud, "If anything happens to you? Good God, what is going on now?" She had a sense of something really wrong with this picture, so she quickly dressed. Although it wasn't even nine o'clock, she raced to the retirement home to see if Lilybeth would see her sooner.

As she walked in, quite a cacophony was going on. She looked over at the receptionist and asked, "Is there a problem?"

The woman nodded. "Yes, unfortunately one of our residents has just passed away."

Doreen froze, closed her eyes, and muttered, "Lilybeth, by any chance?"

The receptionist eyed her in shock and then slowly nodded. "Yes, how did you know?"

"Did she leave a letter with you for me?"

"She did. Is that what you're here for?"

"I was hoping to talk to her while I was here, but she did mention how she had left a letter for me."

The receptionist reached behind the front desk and handed it to her. "Here is the letter. She brought it down to me earlier."

"I was hoping to talk to her about it, but …"

"I'm sorry," the other woman said sincerely. "That time has gone."

Doreen watched and waited, feeling a strange sense of déjà vu as the EMTs loaded up the woman's body in the ambulance and took it away. Doreen looked over at the receptionist. "Do you have any idea what happened?"

"It looks as if she just had a heart attack. She was a loner here, and frankly I was really surprised that she even agreed to speak with you."

Doreen nodded. With that, she walked outside, got into her vehicle, and drove straight to the police station. As she walked in, a couple cops looked up and smiled at her. One waved, and she smiled back and asked, "Hey, is Mack here?"

"No, Mack's at court," one of them replied.

"Oh, shoot, I knew that." She groaned. "How about the captain?"

At that came a booming reply from the far side, "Doreen."

She turned and smiled. The captain stood there, rubbing his hands together. "Have you got something for me?"

"I've got something, all right," she replied. "May we talk?"

His eyebrows lifted, and he nodded. "Absolutely. Come on in." He led the way to his office.

She sat down and began, "Obviously I haven't got all that far on the case yet, but something happened this morning that I'm afraid may be connected."

It took a minute to get it all out, but, when she finally did, he sat and stared at her. "Seriously?"

She nodded. "I have the letter right here, and I haven't even opened it yet," she shared. Then she unsealed it and quickly scanned the contents. "Good God," she muttered, staring at it. She laid it down on the desk in front of him, and the two of them read it together.

He sat back, stared at her, and whistled. "Holy moly."

"I know, and the trouble is, she's the one who was just taken out in an ambulance as I arrived at Riverdale. I asked what happened, and the receptionist told me that it looked to be a heart attack. I had just spoken to Lilybeth a few minutes earlier, and she had already dropped off this letter at the front desk. I was to meet her at ten, and something about this just caught me as wrong, and I raced down there," she shared, with tears in her eyes. "I honestly don't know what happened, but I swear to God that I think she was murdered. I think she was murdered before she could tell anyone else what she told me. I'm just hoping that the front desk doesn't tell anybody that Lilybeth had left the letter for me there."

"Because now you're worried about your safety," he noted, turning to her.

"No," she stated, frowning. "I'm worried about that receptionist's safety. She's a nice lady. What if somebody thinks she read that letter?"

He stared down at the incriminating letter in front of him, and he shook his head. "This isn't something to just march out into the world with," he stated, with a nod.

"I know. That's why I'm here," she replied. "And unfortunately Mack's in court."

"He is, and he'll be there all day. You, my dear," he noted, shaking his head, "have this penchant for trouble like nobody else I know."

She smiled at him. "I do seem to burst things right open, don't I?"

He nodded. "I've got to admit that you're pretty darn good at it too."

She chuckled. "The bottom line is that we have a chance to solve this cold case, but we have to do it in such a way that nobody else gets killed. And I'm afraid that it's already too late."

Chapter 14

WHEN DOREEN GOT home, her mind was racing in circles. She opened up the rear kitchen door to let the animals out in the backyard for a few minutes, but it had turned blustery and cold, so not exactly welcoming weather. They quickly did their business, then came inside almost immediately. She smiled at them. "I hear you. It's not quite the weather we're used to, is it?"

Yet she and her animals were safe, warm, and had a beautiful cozy house, so everything in her world should be perfectly fine. Yet it wasn't, and now the captain was on it. Still, she knew that it would be a challenge, given the information in the letter. She had left the letter with him, but he had made a copy of it for her. She took it to her kitchen table and sat down again to reread the information that Lilybeth had revealed.

She had definitely pointed the finger at the Winters family, the one with the political influence. Doreen wanted to roll her eyes and say, *Of course it was*, but didn't have any reason to believe that this particular politician had anything to do with that unnamed toddler's disappearance. She certainly had to be even more mindful than usual as to who and what she proclaimed about them, since one of the Winters family members was in the public eye. It was tempting to just blame the entire family, but that wasn't fair either. Yet Doreen's focus right now had nothing to do with saving the Winters family name and everything to do with this little girl who'd been treated so terribly in her very short life.

Once she had a warm cup of tea, Doreen sat down and researched a bunch of history on the Winters family. She went through it all, finding article after article. They were fairly well known and appeared to be highly sought after in business deals. They were movers and shakers in the world and dominated the field where they had made millions, and everybody else was left to play their penny-ante games.

She didn't want to think that the Winters family had something to do with this, but somebody knew something. Plus, that little girl's bones had been held in the coroner's office all these years, and nobody had spoken up about it, which bothered Doreen more than she could say.

She continued researching the Winters family, getting to know the ins and outs. They were prolific in business, but less so in children. There appeared to be two brothers still living, with one sister passing away about ten years ago, and another sister passed about twenty years ago. Doreen got an urge to check her email and found a response from her genealogy request. As the file opened, and she began to have a look, she realized it contained exactly the name she was looking for.

She whistled as she sat back, reaching for her phone and calling the captain.

"What, already?" he asked.

"The genealogy just came in from the DNA upload of

the toddler's bones," she noted. "It came back as a partial match to some cousin, second cousin, whatever. It's within the same family, the Winters."

Dead silence came on the other end. "Good God," he muttered, taking his time. "We'll have to get into the thick of it now."

"Except, from what I've just found, and I'm sure you have better records than I do, two brothers are still living, but the two sisters passed away ten and twenty years ago, respectively. Clarence is the would-be politician from the news articles, and Carl appears to be running the big business side of the Winters family around the whole world."

"Yes," the captain confirmed. "We've had all kinds of dealings with them. They've skirted the law but never really technically crossed it. Of course we already knew that, but, as to their two sisters who have passed away, we don't know if someone in the family was involved in that."

"Right," she replied, "but no way somebody in that prominent family had a baby for eighteen months before it disappeared, not with nobody knowing anything about it."

"No, this is the mother of all cover-ups," he acknowledged, "but trying to figure out how to proceed will be a challenge."

She frowned at that. "Not really."

"How do you figure that?"

"Well, first it's a matter of figuring out which direct family member could be connected."

"And you've got an answer for that?"

"We'll have to get DNA from the siblings," she stated, "and we'll just have to start matching."

"We can't just ask them for it because they have every right to refuse," he pointed out.

"Sure, but Clarence Winters, the politician, he smokes, so if we get to a political rally or someplace where we can pick up a cigarette butt—"

He laughed. "I think you've been watching too many movies."

"And you're right. I probably have," she admitted. "But does that work or not?"

"Yes, if you can get something that has his saliva, we can run the DNA on it," he confirmed, "but that'll take a little bit longer."

"That would at least give us an idea of who we're dealing with because we don't have an exact match in the system, only that we have the familial link. I'm forwarding you the results," she said, rummaging around in her phone. "It targets the family, but all kinds of half sisters or half relatives are here, hence the different names. I'm not seeing anything that's a full match. We should check birth and death records though."

"No, of course there's no match," he muttered. "That would make it way too easy."

She laughed. "We at least have something, and we know we're on target as to what family it is, which is a whole lot more than we had."

"You've got that right," he agreed, his tone gaining in assurance. "Now that we've got this far, there's a very good chance we can close it." He seemed surprised.

She laughed. "It sounds to me as if you didn't really expect that."

"I should have," he noted. "Of course, having the DNA makes a huge difference."

"It absolutely does," she replied, "but it won't be the closing evidence, and unfortunately we now have a current murder on top of it."

"I'll talk to Mack about that when I can," the caption shared, "but he's tied up in court and will be for a while."

The captain didn't tell her that he would follow up or would get back to her, but she understood. She was the minion in this case, and he was the boss. When she disconnected, she looked down at the notes she had taken and phoned Nan.

"What'd you find out?" Nan asked by way of a greeting.

"Wow," Doreen muttered. "I don't even get a hello?"

"No, I called you earlier."

"Did you?" she asked, as she looked at her phone's call history and winced. "I didn't even see the missed call. I'm sorry."

"No, I figured you were off hunting, and we know better than to disturb you because that's when all kinds of stuff happen."

"Yeah, it happens all right," she muttered. "You know anything more about the Winters family individually?"

Nan asked, "You mean the politician?"

Such a wealth of disgust filled Nan's tone that Doreen had to laugh. "I think he's trying to run for office or something."

"Yes, that would be him," Nan confirmed. "There are a couple brothers, and there were two sisters, but both have passed on."

"So the brothers are here?" Doreen asked.

"I'm not sure about the brothers. Maybe there are secondary cousins or other family members nearby. We still probably wouldn't find them here at Rosemoor. This is one of the less hoity-toity places. We're getting a heck of a name now though," she muttered. "Still, for a lot of people, this isn't exactly a place that anybody with money would come."

That was the first Doreen had ever heard of that. "So why did you go there?"

"I wanted to be close to you," she declared.

"Oh, do you want a change to another one?"

"Good God, no," she exclaimed. "Can you imagine? A new place would just be crying to kick us out."

Doreen winced at that, and then she laughed. "You could be right."

"You know I'm right, and it would be an absolute nightmare. They would be begging us to leave in no time."

"You could behave, instead of terrorizing people."

"I could," she teased, "but where's the fun in that?"

"I'm not sure *fun* is exactly the way we're supposed to be looking at this either," Doreen stated in a dry tone. "Anyway, it would help a lot if we could find out any information there is to be had about the Winters family."

"Sure enough," Nan confirmed. "I'll talk to the gang." Then she asked, "Did you ever talk to Lilybeth?"

"Yeah, I did," she said, with a snort. "That's the other half of the problem I'm dealing with right now."

"Oh, I heard she wasn't a very friendly person."

"It doesn't matter how unfriendly she was," Doreen noted. "She died this morning."

After a long silence on the other end, Nan, her tone thoughtful, even contemplative, replied, "I guess that's one of the problems when you're dealing with our age group as witnesses. You only have so much time with any of us."

"That's true, and I won't argue that point. However, I also think Lilybeth was murdered."

And then she disconnected.

Chapter 15

DOREEN WAS STILL giggling when Nan called her right back.

"Now that was dirty pool, child," she said crossly. "You shouldn't hang up on me after dropping a bombshell."

"Aha, and yet—"

"I know. I know. I've done it to you too," she admitted, with a sigh. "Now, what do you mean she was murdered?"

"I was supposed to see her today. She called and told me that she left me a letter, and, if I was lucky, she wouldn't change her mind before I got there. So, I dressed and raced down to Riverdale. When I got there, the receptionist told me that they'd had a resident pass that morning. And I just knew who it was."

"Lilybeth," Nan cried out.

"Yes, she supposedly had a heart attack."

"Oh dear, that timing is definitely suspicious," Nan noted, with determination in her tone. "And that completely changes things. We need a meeting. You need to come down here. I would normally put it off for another little bit," she muttered, "but we can't do that, not now that people are dying."

"Not only that people are dying but that I'm not sure it's over just yet."

"Meaning?"

"She left me a letter, and it's a doozy."

"What's in it?"

"She points a finger at the Winters family."

"Oh, good Lord."

"But, of course, she didn't say which Winters."

"Why would she do that? Why put out an accusation and not make it clear as to who was responsible?" Nan asked, clearly vexed. "That's just wrong."

"Maybe, but she was torn about putting into writing something she could only guess at and didn't know for sure."

"*Hmm*, then I have to wonder what she was up to that she even mentioned anything."

"I think because she knew I would want to talk to her again, and maybe she just wanted to clear her conscience. You know, to share something she knew that maybe had something to do with something."

"Something to do with something to do with something, good God," Nan stated crossly. "We don't have time for this. We need answers. And none of us are getting any younger. … As Lilybeth just pointed out, all of us are in danger of a heart attack from one minute to the next."

Doreen winced at that. "Thanks for the reminder."

"You know as well as I do," Nan stated in a cross tone, "that we just can't afford to sit around and wait for people to think about it. We are old."

"On the other hand, an awful lot of people are clearing their consciences and going to the great beyond in a whole lot better shape because of it."

"But what good did it do her?" Nan snapped. "Particularly if she didn't die of a heart attack, and we have to take that into account as well."

"We absolutely do," Doreen agreed. "I've just come from the police station, and I know how much they're all on it as well."

"You already told Mack?" she asked.

"Mack's in court all day, so he doesn't know yet," Doreen shared, a shiver running down her spine. "I went directly to the captain."

"Oh my," Nan said, with admiration in her tone. "You're really moving up these days."

"I'm hardly moving anywhere," she claimed, "and I just shivered at the thought of his booming voice. I went to him because he's the one who asked me to look into this in the first place. So, when I find a case, a potential murder case, that looks to be connected, of course I have to say something."

"Of course, of course," Nan agreed. "You absolutely have to. Lilybeth may not have led a blameless life, but nobody deserves to have the last days of her existence on Earth taken from her like that."

"How would anybody give her a heart attack though?" Doreen asked.

"It could have been something as simple as a threat, since you and I both know that some days aren't so good, so it doesn't take much to scare any of us. This cold case of yours was relatively new to Lilybeth though. So, if she had a guilty conscience or in any way felt as if she hadn't done her full duty, then I could imagine it wouldn't have taken much to tip her over. You'll never prove murder then."

"Maybe not," Doreen murmured. "At least she left me the letter that stated she thought it was connected to the

Winters family."

"And yet you won't read the letter to me and tell me a little more?" Nan asked in a coaxing tone.

"I'll bring the letter down, but again it has to be top secret. You're not allowed to spread this to anybody."

"I would never," she stated in horror.

"No, but you will with the crew, with Doreen's Deputies, who you think are involved and helping us."

"If they're helping, they need to know of the evidence, child. We all need to be helping, and that can only happen if we know the truth."

"Yes," Doreen conceded, "but I also can't have any sign of this information getting out."

"Right, it is an active murder case now, isn't it?"

"Lilybeth's death absolutely is an active case. I don't know what that'll look like though. As you said, it's pretty darn hard to charge a heart attack as a murder of somebody who was what? Eighty-seven? She could have had a heart attack worrying about the meeting she had coming up with me."

"Oh, so does that make you a killer, dear?" Nan asked.

"No, it doesn't make me a killer," Doreen replied in exasperation. "It does make me a concerned citizen though."

"And how would anybody know you were looking at any of this and that Lilybeth could be a danger?"

"She had spoken to a couple colleagues, after she and I first spoke. I don't know if she told somebody about the letter she was writing. Maybe somebody knew I was looking into this case and had somehow stumbled onto Lilybeth and realized she had information they might be worried about. Maybe Lilybeth possibly mentioned something to someone," she pointed out to Nan. "Even innocently, some people could have taken it the wrong way."

"They absolutely would," Nan agreed. "Let me talk to the gang, and let us know when you're coming down."

Doreen glanced at the time. "I could come down now. I didn't get a whole lot of sleep last night, and I was hoping to take a nap."

"A nap." Nan giggled. "We'll all have to start booking our naps now. If you're so tired that you need them, you can only imagine how it is for us."

"It's not that I'm so tired," she clarified, "but my mind does a whole lot better when I'm rested, when I am free and clear to think about all the things that can go wrong."

"Of course you are," she replied. "I'm just teasing you, my dear."

"And you might be," Doreen noted, "but I do take this extremely seriously."

"I know you do," she murmured, "and, just so you know, we do too."

"You better. Particularly now that there's a chance that somebody murdered Lilybeth. That's not something we'll be happy about."

"Of course not," Nan agreed.

"Anyway, I'll come down in a couple hours, after you've all had your rest."

"And your rest too," Nan added, with a chuckle.

"And me too." And she disconnected.

Chapter 16

DOREEN DID STOP for a nap and did sleep. She rolled over and sighed at that revelation, since she had stretched out on her bed just to think for a few minutes. Something was so nice about being able to lie down on a bed, knowing that you don't have to do anything and that you'll still make it one way or another. As she stretched out her arms and legs, she realized that all her pets were holding her down.

She groaned as she cuddled up to Mugs and asked, "Do you think we should be getting up now?"

He gave a gentle *woof,* and she smiled, hugging him close.

"You really are a special love bug," she murmured, up against his chest. "Not sure how I ever got so lucky."

And she really didn't know, since Mathew hated the dog yet had allowed her to have him. Something was so very special about having Mugs in her life that made everything so much easier. As she softly stroked his nose and his ears, Goliath rolled over and gently placed his claws on her arm and tucked in to remind her that he was here too.

"You guys are right. I do feel guilty," she muttered. "And

yet I don't know what else I could have done."

She did feel as if she had messed up with Lilybeth somehow, and it didn't make her feel good at all. Somehow that poor woman had died, and Doreen was certain it was a consequence of something that happened at Riverdale. Maybe Lilybeth had asked for the paper to write the letter on, or maybe somebody had heard her handing off the letter to the receptionist.

Pondering that, she picked up the phone and called to speak to the same receptionist who had given her the letter.

As soon as she identified herself, the woman replied, "Oh, it's you again." An odd note filled her tone.

"It is me," Doreen confirmed cautiously. "Is there a problem?"

"Not a problem per se, but management is not very happy about the letter."

"Why?" she asked.

"They just don't want to be involved in something like that."

"Something like what?" she asked. "It's not as if Lilybeth was involved in anything, unless you read the letter."

"No, no, no, I didn't read the letter," she stated.

Yet Doreen thought the receptionist denied reading Lilybeth's letter way too fast for Doreen to believe her. Still, Doreen listened as the receptionist continued her tirade.

"It's not as if I've had five minutes of time anyway."

"So, what do you mean by *involved in anything like that*?" Doreen asked, trying hard to corral the suspicion in her tone, but recognizing that she was failing.

"Lilybeth told me."

"What did she tell you?"

"I don't think I should tell you."

"Considering that I've already taken the letter to the police, and I can just as easily ask them to come down and talk to you," Doreen stated with a little more force than intended, "it would be appreciated if you would just tell me what she told you."

"Police?" she repeated in a faint voice.

"Yes, the police."

"Oh dear."

"Yes, … *oh dear* is right."

"It's just that she mentioned a wrong had to be righted, and she'd been waiting all her life to figure out how to do it and thought that maybe this time she could get it done."

"Did she explain what it was?"

"No, she didn't," she snapped. "And that's all I have to say on the matter."

"That's fine," Doreen stated. "That's enough."

"It is?" the receptionist asked cautiously.

"Yeah, it makes perfect sense."

"I'm glad you think so," she muttered. "She didn't sound all that clear when I talked to her."

"Lilybeth was dealing with the pressure of age, not so much guilt but the idea that her time was running out."

"Oh, we do get that here because the residents have so many regrets. I keep telling them that it's well past the time to fix it."

Doreen laughed. "That hardly seems like something to tell an elderly person facing death in the foreseeable future."

"Well, if they really wanted to fix things, they should have done it when they were in better shape to do so."

"I think people tend to put off the hard things, hoping they won't have to deal with it. Then, as they get older and older, they realize it'll still be there, and it'll still bother them."

"That's precisely my point. They shouldn't have done whatever it was in the first place."

It must be nice to be so righteous, Doreen thought. But, for her, it was never quite so black-and-white and never quite so easy to consider.

"I have to get back to work," the receptionist added. "I hope that's all. I don't want to deal with this anymore."

"It will be all unless the police need something," Doreen said cheerfully.

"There's no reason for the police to come here at all," the receptionist stated in a shrill tone. "I've told you everything."

"Good, and, in that case, I thank you for your assistance. Have a good morning."

It was obvious that the receptionist wasn't impressed, but Doreen had gotten used to not making people's days. Honestly, plenty of times people were just pissed off by the time she left. She shrugged and headed back to the kitchen, looking at the coffeepot, then realized she should probably just head straight down to Nan's. With any luck, they could put some of these issues to rest as well.

And, with that, she loaded up the animals, still feeling a little on the tired side. It was not so much tired as maybe … *Hmm*, she pondered what it was, as she walked down the creek. The needed word skipped her mind as to what she was feeling. As she approached Nan's patio, the door opened, and she walked inside.

Nan asked her if she was okay.

"Melancholy," she shared, as she looked at Nan. "That's the word I'm looking for."

Nan raised her eyebrows. "Who's melancholy?"

"Me," she claimed. "It's not so much that I'm tired. I

guess I'm more in a melancholy mood."

"If you say so," Nan murmured, as she hurried her inside. "Not sure why you should be though."

"Yeah, but you see? That's the thing. There isn't necessarily a need behind this feeling. It just is. A woman died, and I don't know whether that was supposed to happen or if it was just an accident." She shook her head, collecting her thoughts, but she was all over the place. "It does feel very much as if people got involved and hurt Lilybeth, when there was absolutely no need."

"If there was no need, then why would they do it?" Nan asked, frowning at her.

"Because the one thing that I do know is," she replied, warming up to the subject, "people are lazy and only would have done that to shut down Lilybeth, especially if she absolutely knew something. But then again, maybe they didn't know about the letter," she pointed out.

Nan had crouched to the floor, busily greeting the animals. She looked over at Doreen and added, "Times like this are when I worry and think you shouldn't be doing this kind of work."

Doreen waved her hand, dismissing the concern. "And I get that," she said. "It's also one of the reasons why sometimes it's a little harder to sort everything out. It's not so much that I've done anything wrong. It's just, when you think about what people do to each other," she explained, "it hurts."

"People will do things that can hurt each other, some on purpose and some not," Nan shared. "The trick is to not let them hurt you."

That was the logic according to Nan, and then the rest of the crew arrived.

Their whole meeting seemed off. Nan, Maisie, and Richie all seemed older today. By the time Doreen stepped outside and headed back up the creek again, the same melancholy sense prevailed. The clouds had gone gray, and an eeriness filled the sky around her. She looked up and around, then muttered to the animals, "Seems a storm is coming. Let's see about getting home a little faster."

And, with that, she picked up the pace, the animals almost running at her side. She had Thaddeus tucked up into her neck, and by the time she made it to her property and crossed into her backyard, she really felt a chill, as the wind picked up. She shuddered and raced to the kitchen door, then opened it and bolted inside, slamming it behind her. The animals milled around, as they shook off the dampness from outside.

"I don't know what that was," she noted, as she took off her jacket and stared outside. "It's definitely a weird weather pattern right now."

Weird was one thing, but a *weird weather pattern* was completely different. She frowned as she moved from the kitchen area through to the living room and checked out the front window. Everything was normal out there.

With a sigh, she put on the teakettle, even though that was the last thing she wanted, after all the tea during her visit with Nan. This had been the first time Doreen had wondered at just how fast everybody appeared to be aging, and that was another depressing thought.

As soon as she settled in one of her two living room chairs, she remembered her discussion with Mack about furniture. He was such a big man, and she really did need to do something about getting furniture so that he could sit comfortably here too. Or maybe he has some he wanted to move over. She'd have to remember to ask him about that.

It was such a strange feeling to think of having him here all the time. He'd barely been here all week because of the court case, and she understood that. Yet it was strange to think that she needed to do something like that for him, as he would probably not feel comfortable enough to do it on his own. And why would he?

Just because she expected him to go make a furniture purchase for her house because that's what her ex would have done didn't mean that's what Mack should do. He just wouldn't. It was her house, after all, and he would never cross that line.

She sighed and almost immediately her phone rang.

"Good," Nan declared, "now we're alone."

"What are you talking about?" Doreen asked.

"Richie shared something with me that he didn't want anybody else to know about. So, I had to wait until everybody left, but I couldn't get rid of Maisie."

"I was wondering what was going on down there," Doreen noted. "It was definitely an odd visit."

"It was an odd visit, and I apologize for that," Nan said briskly. "Yet at least you know that we're taking all our work seriously."

"Okay." Doreen frowned at that.

"So Richie was involved with somebody way back when."

Doreen rolled her eyes. "Of course he was."

"Don't be disrespectful," Nan said in a chiding tone. "We've all lived very long lives, you know?"

"Of course you have." Doreen sighed. "I didn't mean to be disrespectful to either of you. I just appear to have trouble doing anything in this town without coming up against one of your former relationships."

"It's to be expected," Nan declared. "Wait until you're our age, and you're dealing with the same thing."

"I hope not. At least not now that I'm engaged to Mack."

"There is that," Nan agreed in delight.

Doreen frowned, as if Nan suddenly remembered how a real relationship was supposed to work. Doreen just shook her head and sighed. "Okay, so who did Richie have an affair with that he didn't want anybody to know?"

"Richie specifically doesn't want his family to know about it."

"You mean, he doesn't want Darren to know about it?"

"I would think so, yes," she declared, with a snort.

"And here I thought everything was more of a conquest for him."

"He's had a bit of a change of heart about that. He wants his family to think well of him when he's gone."

"You don't think they will?" she asked.

"I think they will, but you know. … When we get older, we change how we view life."

"If you say so," Doreen replied calmly.

"I know so. We all do things in our youth. Then later in life, when we look back, we see that maybe it wasn't the best thing we ever did."

Doreen waited, but Nan didn't have anything else to offer. "Okay. So who did Richie have an affair with?"

"I got the impression that he might have had an affair with the mother of the Winters clan, and her name was Iris."

"Iris?"

"Yes, the old man was Buck, and Iris was his wife."

"And you think that Richie may have had an affair with Iris?"

"Yes, I think so."

Doreen considered that for a long moment, and then she asked, "Do you have any idea if there happened to be a child out of that relationship?"

"I don't know," Nan replied.

This confirmed Doreen's thought in her own mind. "Yet it's possible?"

"But we don't know for sure."

"Good God, Nan, let's get to the real question. Is there any chance this unidentified child in the morgue could have been Richie's daughter?"

Nan took a deep breath and muttered, "I don't know, but it's possible."

Chapter 17

DOREEN HAD A lot to think about. When Mack finally called her just before dinnertime, she smiled when she saw his name on the screen. "Hey," she greeted him cheerfully. "How was your day?"

"Don't ask," he declared in a dry tone. "And it's not over yet. I still have to meet a couple of the lawyers and go over some of the testimony for tomorrow."

"I'm so sorry," she replied. "You must be exhausted."

"I knew it would be a tough week. I just wasn't expecting this level," he muttered.

"No, of course not," she murmured.

"And you, … are you okay?"

"Of course. I'm fine," she stated.

He laughed. "And, even if you weren't, you would say you were."

"If there was a problem, I would tell you."

"Would you though?" he asked in a wry voice.

"I would," she declared.

"I hope so. Somebody mentioned how you came into the shop today."

"I forgot you were in court."

"Right, yeah, I'm definitely tied up this week. I'm just hoping that, if I'm lucky, I'll be off the hook next week."

"I hope so, for your sake."

"Our testimony should be done here pretty soon," he shared. "Once that's over, things will get back to normal."

They talked a little bit longer, and then she asked, "We talked about the Winters family in town, right?"

"A politician, a big-business guy, and, other than that, not a whole lot to say. Don't think they've crossed the law, at least not very much to my knowledge," he conceded. "I have heard a few rumors about less-than-kindly dealings in terms of business, but I don't know of any court cases up against them."

"Right," she noted. "That makes a difference, doesn't it?"

"It does because, if nobody is charging them with anything, it's a little hard for us to go after them, not without solid probable cause of any wrongdoing. Why? Are you coming up with them connected to this case?"

"Kinda," she said. "I'm still digging. … I'm really just happy to hear your voice."

The surprise was evidence in his tone, when he replied, "And that is exactly something I needed to hear at the end of this long day. I thought about coming by," he added, with a sigh, "but honestly, I'm just tuckered and need to get some sleep."

"Then you do that," she agreed. "It's all good in my corner." When he hesitated, she added, "Honest."

"You would tell me if it wasn't, right?"

She chuckled. "Absolutely I would."

When she disconnected, Thaddeus glared at her phone from his position atop the kitchen table.

"I would," she stated defensively. He cocked his head to one side and glared. She shrugged. "It's not as if there's anything he can do about this mess right now. And, besides, for the moment, we have to honor Richie's secret," she muttered. "I don't know how much we can do with that anyway, though one of the options is to take his DNA and to run it through the system. That'll take a while."

She frowned at that and then sent the captain an email, asking what the procedure was for getting DNA from possible suspects. She didn't hear anything that night, but the next morning, bright and early, the captain got a hold of her.

"It's not so much that it's a very expensive process," he explained, "but it's a time issue."

"Right," she noted. "I would need more evidence before we get there. What if the DNA was collected by somebody else, and we ran it through?"

"If it's a match," he said, "that's a job well done for you. At least it may give us, … say, a direct familial match. Then we could go for more than that."

"Right," she muttered. "Okay, I'll keep working."

And, with that, she disconnected, then sat down and tried to do a time line, but it didn't exactly line up. As she reviewed it, she realized she needed to talk with Richie, but with Richie only. Not the rest of the gang. She picked up the phone and called him. When he answered, his tone was heavy and sad.

"I know what you're calling about," he muttered.

"Either I can come down, and we can talk a little bit together," she offered, "or we can just do it now on the phone."

"It would probably be better if we do it face-to-face. I'm

not a coward."

She chuckled. "You've lived a good life," she stated. "I don't consider that cowardice in any way."

"This was one of those times when I was a coward."

"Let me gather the animals, and I'll come down to you."

With that, she looked longingly at the coffeepot, realizing she should have had a cup of coffee before calling him, but it was already too late now that he was expecting her.

It seemed as if these seniors got up so early nowadays that there was just no time for anything or anybody else. Richie would probably say it was more about everybody needing naps in the afternoon, and they really liked their naps. Which Doreen understood, having had one or two herself. But she was eager to get at this and to get something resolved. She was eager to get at something tangible, at something that would be a step forward, or even a lead they could follow, some real progress. Even ruling things out would be welcomed at this point.

She wasn't trying to finish this before Mack was back on duty—although that had crossed her mind—but it would be nice if she could find more information. That way, when he did get back, he could hopefully just step in to nab the bad guys. At least that's how she wanted it to be. She chuckled at that because, although bad guys were everywhere, it seemed as if she found more than her fair share of them.

She packed up the animals, and, bundling up against the cold, although it was bright and sunny out, she walked down the river toward Rosemoor. As soon as she got there, she confused the animals completely and bypassed Nan's apartment to head down to see Richie.

When she knocked, he opened the door and stared at her with a sad puppy-dog look that made her smile. She asked, "May we come in?"

He nodded and stepped back out of the way. "You might as well," he grumbled, all too surly. "Lord knows everybody will know soon enough."

"Not necessarily," she replied. "There's no need for anybody to know if it isn't needed."

He looked at her, a smile brightening his face. "You think so?"

"I would hope so," she declared, with a nod. "Now, tell me what went on back then."

He shrugged. "I was in a dark place. I'd been with a long-term partner, and she broke up with me. I didn't handle it very well and went looking for solace in the arms of another woman, and, well, that's just what happened."

"Okay, that much I get but which woman?" she asked.

"Iris, of course."

"Hang on a minute. Was she not married at that time?"

He winced and then nodded. "She was married. She was, but she was also, in a way, separated."

"In a way, separated? What does that mean? Did the husband see them as separated, or were you stepping on toes?"

"I thought she was separated and didn't think I was stepping on toes," he declared with a huff. "But according to Claudia, her daughter, Iris wasn't separated at all."

"Did you believe Claudia?"

"I wasn't sure who to believe, and I didn't have much choice in believing any of it because, somewhere around that same time, Buck found out about us," he muttered. "And that's when Iris told me that they were taking a separation."

"What was the reason behind the separation?"

"She told me how Buck had beaten her up, and she

wasn't willing to be a punching bag anymore."

"So why was it a temporary separation?" she asked.

"That's what I asked her," he stated, nodding in agreement. "Iris said it was temporary because he was supposed to behave himself."

"Wow, I'm not sure that's really an option either."

"No, I didn't think it was, and I don't think she understood what she was asking for. Yet it didn't matter because that's what she thought. And Buck, … once he found out, … well, I've got to tell you that he gave me a pretty-good licking himself. I was big and strong, but I wasn't mean," he explained, speaking in a low tone. "That Buck, he was mean."

She winced at that. "I am so sorry."

He gave half a shrug. "It was part of a whole lesson about not really understanding marriage and the give and take in all that, plus whether that was really what people were talking about in life. She was new to me in the sense that I hadn't really ever met anybody who swept me off my feet," he admitted, looking everywhere but at Doreen. "We were together for about ten months, and, when that broke up—and because of the way it broke up—I was in really bad shape after that." He hung his head and took a deep and shaky breath.

"Of course," she replied, with a nod. "How were you *not* supposed to be upset when you're thinking that you're having a relationship with somebody special, but she's just spending time with you while she figures out the rest of her life?"

He looked at her, and his shoulders sagged. "It was too soon. I was vulnerable and should have realized that."

"You can turn yourself inside out and up and down forever, or you can realize that it was a mistake that you learned from, and life moves on."

"I didn't really get a chance to make a mistake, to learn from it, and to have life move on because I was too busy getting kicked to the ground," he stated in a harsh tone. "And then everybody found out about it, so that just made it all even worse."

"I'm so sorry. Being the town joke isn't fun."

He looked at her, his gaze lighting up as he realized she understood. "You know from experience, don't you?"

"I sure do," she said, with a smile. "But, back to you, it wasn't good and didn't do anything for your self-confidence, which would have taken quite a hit as well."

"I didn't even know what was happening. I didn't know what I did. I loved her as if there was no tomorrow," he muttered, "and, yet for her, apparently it was just for today."

"And maybe she needed to know that somebody out there could love her, that someone wouldn't beat her up. Maybe that's what she needed."

"So why did she go back to him?"

"I don't know, but now I'll ask you a really tough question."

"You think I don't know what that question is?" he muttered, glaring at her. "You think I haven't thought about it since you brought it up?"

"And yet did you have any idea who we were talking about?"

"No, except that I know Iris had a baby. And it was a while past us."

"When you say *a while*?"

"That I don't know exactly," he admitted. "I was kept out of the loop. She wouldn't see me anymore. I just heard through the grapevine that she'd had a baby, and it pissed me off because it meant that she'd gone back to him right away, and that what we had together didn't mean anything."

"Or … she felt she had no choice. She was married, so she went back to her husband, as a good wife of that day, and did what she thought was the right thing to do at the time, trying to make up with her husband."

"Maybe," he muttered, staring at the wall behind her. "But now you've got me wondering if I had a child back then and didn't even know it."

"Did you ever ask her?"

"No, I tried to talk to her once, and she told me to get lost, and that it would be really bad for me if I didn't."

"She threatened you?"

"I saw it as more of a warning," he clarified. "I think she was telling me that, if Buck found out again, … if I was found out talking to her, then it would go badly, more than the last time."

"Of course. It's not as if he would forgive, would he?"

"No, he would not," Richie declared, with a headshake.

"As a man who finally married and had a family of your own, you know what he was feeling."

Richie stared at her and slowly nodded. "I do understand that part," he conceded, "but still, I left a part of my heart there with her."

"Hopefully your wife didn't know."

"No, and she's been dead and gone these many years," he shared sadly. "Only after you lose everybody do you start looking back over your life and wonder how many more losses you can take and still not break."

"I don't know," she replied. "I don't have any experience with that level of loss. Although my life has been a mess lately, I think it's got more to do with the level of love you felt."

He stared at her, his gaze lighting first, and then his whole face. "That's a good way to look at it. I did love her," he admitted, "so whatever came from it would have been okay by me."

"I guess the question then is, have you ever had your DNA checked?" she asked.

His eyebrows shot up, and he shook his head. "I don't think so."

"Are you serious? None of your family ever put their DNA into one of those genealogy sites and checked it out?"

He shrugged. "I have no idea. You can talk to Darren about that." Then he winced and shook his head. "No, wait. Oh, please don't."

"Right." She then asked, "Will you let me get your DNA tested? I'll just pay for it privately," she added, wincing to herself.

"I can pay," Richie said. "I would like to know if that's my baby or not."

"Of course you would," she agreed. "Okay, let me get a kit, and we'll you tested. I don't know what it costs."

"It's expensive," he noted. "I heard somebody talking about it not all that long ago."

"Okay then, and you're okay to pay for it?" she asked, looking at him questioningly.

He nodded. "I will."

"Okay, good." And so she grabbed the animals, then turned to him and added, "I'll get it as soon as possible."

"Of course." He gave her a bright smile, but the smile soon fell away. "Don't say anything."

"No, I won't," she said. "I won't say a thing. Then, once

we get the DNA results, if you want to say anything to anybody, you can do it yourself."

"Will do," he agreed, with a nod. "I highly suspect it will be something I take to my grave."

"And that's okay. That's a decision you get to make, as long as—"

"Right," he muttered, "depending on what the DNA test says in regard to this baby. I hear you," he muttered. "Good enough."

And, with that, she packed up the animals and headed out.

Chapter 18

BY THE TIME Doreen finally got home, she felt a little bit ragged. She also had absolutely no updates, and the captain hadn't volunteered any update on the poor midwife's death either.

Could it really have been just a simple heart attack? Or was something much more nefarious going on? Her instincts had been to run right to Mack, but, with his being tied up in court, she hadn't had much choice but to go to the captain. So, if he saw this as anything more nefarious, she didn't know.

She had to admit that it had been really helpful to have Mack around most of the time to talk to about all the things that she needed to discuss in relation to her cold cases. He was really good about that. And he was good for so much else too. So it was a hardship not having him around, and maybe that was a good lesson for her to learn.

She put on the teakettle and looked down at the DNA kit that she had up on her laptop screen. She tried to buy one in town but hadn't had any success. So, she ordered it without letting herself think twice, knowing it would be a few days yet before it was delivered. She quickly phoned

Richie, but he didn't answer. Frowning, she thought about that and realized it could just as easily be their card game night or something. As she glanced around her kitchen, she sighed, wondering at what point in time she would become a person with no concept of a nightlife.

It was odd to see Mack, as he walked in the door a little bit later. He looked at her, then seeing her face, asked, "Are you okay?"

"I'm fine," she replied, walking over and giving him a hug.

His arms closed around her frame, and he just wrapped her up. There was something so comforting and safe about that large expanse of a capable man just holding her. When she pulled back, she looked up at him. "It's a very strange cold case."

He nodded. "Let me grab a coffee, and you can tell me all about it."

"Are you sure? You're so busy with the trial that I know you don't have the time to get involved with this."

"No, I may not get involved, but that doesn't mean I can't be here on the outside, getting an update," he shared. "I've already talked to the captain about it a little bit."

"Right, and a little bit is a help," she muttered, "but I'll say this just once, and you'll never hear it from me again."

His eyebrows shot up. "Okay, what will I never hear again?"

She collapsed down beside him and said, "I really miss you on this case."

He looked at her in surprise, put down his coffee, then leaned in and pulled her into another hug. "Sometimes on these cases, we just need somebody to talk things over with. It's not that they're hard or complicated. It just helps to get another viewpoint."

She nodded and settled back. "And I know this is one the captain doesn't want to move on with, not unless we have better proof," she muttered, preparing her air quotes, "because the whole family is, shall we say, *posh*."

He laughed. "From somebody who's come from posh as you have, I doubt they are posh in the same sense."

"Maybe not," she admitted, with a smile. "But I don't really consider myself posh anymore."

"I don't know that you ever did," he pointed out, with a gentle smile. "And that's a good thing because now you are you, and we much prefer you as you really are, than as someone trying to be what they think they are supposed to be, even if it's *posh*."

"Let me tell you about the change in this case now." Then she filled him in on Richie. Mack stared at her and then whistled. "Exactly," she agreed. "Now I've ordered a DNA kit for him, and we'll go through the process and upload it on the ancestry site because he's not sure whether Baby Jane could have been his child or not."

"Interesting," Mack muttered in a far-off tone of voice.

"What are you thinking?" she asked him.

"I'm just wondering if Buck may have found out the child wasn't his, then abused the poor child. It's not as if it's the child's fault—"

"You and I both know that children pay for all kinds things they couldn't possibly deserve, despite what their parents think."

"Unfortunately that is very true. It will be interesting to see the results from the DNA. That old devil Richie," Mack noted with a chuckle, shaking his head.

"He's pretty upset about the idea that it could be his

daughter. He has sons, but he never did have a daughter," she noted.

"Ah, so it's the one that never was."

"Also, just because Buck abused his wife doesn't mean he was into abusing children."

"Also … just because Iris told Richie that Buck hit her and spun a story, we don't know for sure that it was true."

"Right," she acknowledged, "and I don't have you on the other end to run some data in terms of arrests and criminal records."

"Did the captain not do that?"

"I don't know," she said. "I don't know if he would do it personally or would give it to somebody else to run. Even so, I don't know that he would share the findings with me. I'm not usually in the loop of things."

"I can do that in the morning," he muttered, and then he stopped and swore. "No, I can't. I'm sorry. I have to start my day at the courthouse."

She winced and reached out a hand. "I'm sorry you have to spend so much time in court. That must be miserable."

"It's part of the job. Once in a while you get a case where you wish they would just let you go back and do the job you're supposed to be doing. Instead they keep dragging you in to find other experts on all this stuff," he muttered. "And it's fine, and we're winning the case. Still, it would just be nice if it didn't have to be this way. This part of my job is no fun."

"Of course," she agreed, "especially when you go through all that hard work to capture somebody …"

He nodded and then raised an eyebrow, as he focused on her. "That's why I'm always on your case about making sure the evidence is clean, so we know for sure the case is locked down and tied up."

She winced at that and then laughed. "Right, and I'm hearing the admonishment in your tone."

"Every once in a while," he noted, his lips twitching, "you do get a little bit overenthusiastic, and, without the proof, we're really stuck trying to prove something in court."

"You mean, *without* the evidence," she pointed out. "However, I have done pretty well in getting you the evidence you need."

"What you've done in most cases," he clarified, looking right in her eyes, "is gotten confessions. And thankfully, so far, nobody has really been trying to back out of those confessions."

"What happens in that case?"

"It depends on the circumstances," he replied. "Sometimes the juries think it's just the lawyer's recommendation that the defendant should recant their confession, thinking they'll have a better chance at trial. And sometimes it might work that way. I don't know." Mack shrugged. "I just try to do my job and to bring in the cases and to put the best evidence we can come up with into the prosecutors' hands, and then leave the rest to them."

"Until they take you to court."

He groaned. "Until they take me to court, and I have to back up everything," he muttered, with a chuckle. "It's not as if this one will be bad. It's just … there's an awful lot of problems."

"I didn't even ask what court case it was."

He looked at her and nodded. "I was surprised you didn't because it's your neighbor Steve."

She looked at him and blinked. "Oh my."

"Yeah, *oh my* is right. We moved the court case ahead,

and we have a second filing happening. Of course Steve's been heavily involved in other crimes—fraud, tax evasion, and the list goes on and on. And we need him. They offered him a deal to get the rest of the people he's involved with."

"What does he have?"

"He's got some connections to the gangs," he muttered. "So, we need him to roll on some of them, but, in order to do that, we have to convict him for these murders first."

"I thought you were supposed to make a deal before conviction."

He laughed. "That's very true, and normally that's exactly what would happen. In this case, however, he's being quite cagey, thinking he'll be let off without a problem."

"He'll get let off with all those bodies buried on his property?" she asked in horror. "Actual bodies were found there."

"We haven't quite gotten through all that yet in this trial. Yes, all those bodies were found on his property, and his DNA was all over the bodies. It's a pretty iron-clad case from that perspective, but we need more than just getting him convicted on all these crimes."

"Right," she muttered, shaking her head. "I can't even begin to understand all that. I don't know why you don't just lock him away and throw away the key."

He laughed. "At times I agree 100 percent, but we still have to do our due diligence."

She smiled and nodded. "You didn't eat, did you?"

"Did you cook?" he asked, staring at her.

"Uh, … no. I didn't really have a whole lot of free time, since I was busy working on the case."

His lips twitched, and he nodded. "And if working on the case versus cooking was your choice …"

"Then working on the case would win." She chuckled. "Yet, when I went looking to buy a DNA kit, I did pick up some pork chops." She hesitated, then frowned at him. "I just don't really know how to cook them."

He burst out laughing. "If you don't mind, I won't barbecue pork chops today, not given the weather out there."

"I know," she agreed. "It's miserable out there. I was thinking the bad weather would be over soon."

"Oh, we'll definitely have a very early spring, but, right now, Old Man Winter is being cranky, so we'll leave him to it for tonight. Let's just see what we can do about cooking those suckers inside," he suggested, walking to the refrigerator. "How many did you buy?"

"Four," she replied, looking at him. "I was thinking three for you and one for me."

"Normally I would be totally okay with that," he stated, "but I want to confirm that you're eating more." Frowning at her, he added, "So, it's okay to share two and two, you know?"

"Sure, it might be okay to share two and two," she conceded, with a smile, "but I also bought asparagus."

"Ah, so that's what you're looking forward to."

"I really am," she admitted, still smiling.

Together they sorted out exactly what they would do, as they prepared their meal. Then, with her watching the asparagus she was steaming, he did something to the pork chops that she didn't quite understand. Yet they came out crispy on the outside and moist and tender on the inside.

"I just wrapped them in parmesan," he shared, by way of explanation.

"I don't even think I saw that," she muttered.

"No, I think you were too busy worrying about the asparagus."

"It is important," she muttered, as she gave him a smirk.

"It absolutely is important," he agreed, grinning, "but, while you were doing that, I was doing this."

"Oh, fine," she muttered. And very quickly they were sitting down to a delicious meal.

While they happily dug into the food, she asked, "Will we have to bring Richie into this?"

"I don't know," he stated. "I don't see why we would, unless it happens Baby Jane's DNA is a match to his DNA. If Richie is the father of the unidentified toddler, and the DNA testing shows that conclusively, then it's a whole different story. At that point, it's likely we would have to go back through his life."

"He says he didn't know anything about a baby. So, if it does turn out to be his and—"

"Do you believe him?" Mack asked, cutting her off.

She pondered that, thinking about the old man and how emotional he'd gotten. "I do. I think, in this case, if that had been his child, and he'd known about her from the beginning, he would have done anything he could to look after her."

"Is he *that guy*, but no one knows until it is right in front of you because of the gruff exterior he puts on at times?"

"Yes, but I do believe him. He also wanted very much to look after Iris. But Buck, being her legal husband, was apparently pretty angry about Richie's involvement with his wife, so that wasn't to be."

"That's understandable too," Mack replied. "Nobody would be too happy about some other guy being with their wife. Plus, we have to remember how things were back then."

"Do we though?" she asked, sounding angrier than she

should. "Buck still abused his wife."

"If we can believe Iris," Mack reminded her. "I would have to check if any domestic violence calls were made to the cops back then. Even if we have those 9-1-1 calls, and even if she went to the hospital with unexplained injuries, why would she ever go back to Buck?"

Doreen snorted, turning to look at Mack. "I know perfectly well why she went back to Buck."

Mack winced, then snagged her into his arms and pulled her close. "Sorry, I didn't mean to bring up that ex of yours—even if by association."

"And you didn't," she declared. "It's just one of those things that I am constantly reminded of. People bring up Mathew so casually and so often. Thus, when it comes to Iris, I understand what she felt." He nodded. "Sometimes I felt as if a mineshaft waited for me, with every step I took."

Mack didn't stop her as she vented.

"And no marriage should be that way, so full of fear and anger. … I know that I should have left him the very first time he hit me. I knew better than anyone else how bad things were in our marriage," she muttered. "Yet I didn't have the self-confidence or the monetary wherewithal to get out there and into the world. The worst part was that I let Mathew take away my own sense of self."

"But now you have both," Mack pointed out.

"Sure, but at what cost?" she asked. "Since I went through that experience, I'll never judge a woman who stays. It's way too easy to judge, standing on the outside looking in."

"When you get some of your settlement money in, you can always do something to help the local women's shelter, if you wanted to."

"Oh, I hadn't considered that," she exclaimed, looking at him.

"Once you figure out your finances," he suggested, "there are all kinds of places that would be more than happy to get some money from you. In the case of the Kelowna shelter, it would help support other women who are trying to change their lives and to get out of bad situations."

"It doesn't seem to matter where you live, that horrid scenario is probably happening worldwide. Maybe not everywhere, but I imagine it's pretty global as issues go. It's way worse in a lot of other countries," she added, "and not even considered a crime in many."

"So true, but that's not where we live, and you're doing just fine now."

She smiled as she looked up at him. "I am doing fine. Do you want some tea or something?"

"No, I think I'll head home. I need some sleep." He smiled at her. "And you need to put all this to rest, at least for tonight."

She winced, not sure what to say to him. When she didn't reply, he went on.

"The DNA for Richie will take quite a while, so don't worry about that. Nothing you can do until the kit gets here and you take the swab and send it off," he explained. "Then you'll still have to wait for the results."

"I know," she grumbled. "It's just frustrating, and it seems as if I'm always waiting, which is definitely not my strong suit."

"It is frustrating to wait, and I understand that it isn't your strong suit, but that's one of the things I love about you," he declared, giving her a big smile. "It's good for you to see how much trouble some of this evidence-gathering stuff can be."

"Good for me? Why? I find it quite depressing."

"Exactly," he agreed, "but it's also very depressing to have a case get thrown out of court because evidence wasn't collected properly or was tampered with or was otherwise suspect in some way."

She winced. "Yeah, got it. I hear you."

He laughed, then bent down to cuddle Mugs, who seemed to be looking for attention ever since Mack had arrived. "Don't you just love this guy?" he said, as he squatted to give him even more of a cuddle.

"He seems to be feeling particularly unloved at the moment," she muttered. "Not sure what's going on, and they're all a bit out of sorts. Could be the weather, I guess, and our lack of walks."

"Could be our heavy conversations. Animals are sensitive to our emotions," he noted. "Maybe they don't understand that we're irritated at the process, at the players in the case, instead thinking we are arguing, just wondering if everything is okay here at home."

"Maybe because you're not here all the time?" she asked, looking at him.

"Because I'm not here, because you're off doing something else, and"—he smiled at her—"I rather imagine they're picking up on your impatient energy just as easily."

"That's probably quite true," she agreed, with a nod. "They're also not sleeping as well as they could be."

"Have you had any nighttime visitors?" he asked, his tone sharp.

"I don't think so. Nobody knows me."

"Says you, but it seems as if everybody knows about you, and not everybody has a positive opinion."

"I do get that. Sometimes I make enemies without even trying."

He smiled. "The enemies don't matter. You're making the right friends, and that's what matters more."

Chapter 19

WHEN DOREEN WOKE the next morning, she remained in bed, watching what appeared to be snow falling outside the big bedroom window. She was pinned in by two animals, and—for her, right now—that seemed perfect. She tucked up closer to Mugs, who was stretched out along one side of her. Goliath had found his position atop her legs. Thaddeus was asleep on his perch hanging from her bedroom ceiling. She smiled at them all, as she reached down awkwardly to pet the ones in bed with her. "You guys could find positions that were a little easier to reach, you know?" she muttered.

Neither of them moved. Thaddeus woke from his roost in the bedroom, then squawked and made an awkward attempt to land on the bed, ending up half on Mugs and half on Goliath. Neither appreciated the new arrival. Mugs grunted and rolled over, while Goliath hissed and swatted at the bird. Thaddeus didn't particularly care. He ignored both of them and walked up Doreen's chest to flounce down on top of her, looking for his own cuddles.

She smiled as she reached for him as well. "I have no idea what today will bring," she muttered to all of them, "but it looks to be a good day to stay in bed, if you ask me."

Mugs yawned and stretched out one paw. She took that to mean yes. Goliath had just closed his eyes and didn't show any sign of wanting to open them again. "I'll take that as a yes too," she muttered.

Thaddeus squawked, "Thaddeus is here. Thaddeus is here."

"I know, big guy. How are you doing?"

"Big Guy, Big Guy, Big Guy, Big Guy." Thaddeus went off on a tangent about his fellow bird buddy.

"No," she said, hoping to shut him down as fast as she could. "We're not going to see Big Guy."

He glared at her and cried out again, "Big Guy, Big Guy." Goliath swatted at him again. Immediately Thaddeus hopped higher up so that he was just out of Goliath's reach, glaring at the cat the whole time. Then he went back at it. "Big Guy, Big Guy, Big Guy."

She groaned. "If there was ever anything guaranteed to force me out of bed fast, it's you when you won't stop caterwauling."

"Big Guy, Big Guy, Big Guy."

She sighed, then tried to roll over and realized she couldn't move at all because of the animals. She sighed. "Okay, fine. We'll stay here for a few minutes."

But even just lying here, her mind started working on the issues. Mack had stayed quite late and then had raced home, knowing he had to be prepped and ready for court this morning. She felt so sorry for him. It was obvious that this stage of his job was causing him all kinds of pain. She hoped she hadn't contributed to it, but it was quite likely that she had. Not that she would change any of her actions, not when it had brought all these people to justice. Yet somehow some of them always seemed to get off. She didn't really understand that, but, hey, she would still continue doing what she could do.

With a sigh, she disturbed all the animals and eventually got out of bed. As she headed to the dresser, looking for something warm, she found some heavy loungewear that looked cozy. She tossed her pajamas in the hamper and quickly dressed, then flumped downstairs in her big fuzzy slippers to put on coffee. As soon as she checked on her emails, she saw something there from Mack.

Checked this out at the office first thing this morning for you. Have fun.

She opened it up, and he had sent a couple announcements on criminal activities and convictions. Sure enough, one Winters male had been convicted of domestic violence. Buck, of course. She whistled and nodded.

Now she had something. Domestic violence didn't necessarily mean much, but it did show a violent side.

Then she sent back an email, asking Mack for the cause of death on both daughters—at his convenience. She gave him the two names. She didn't know whether anybody would be interested in their deaths, but she wouldn't let that stone go unturned either. Now she needed to find any newspaper clippings or any other information on the daughters' deaths.

Why hadn't she thought of that before? She groaned as she shook her head.

She also hoped that the DNA kit came in soon. Then she could deliver that to Rosemoor. However, if it didn't come in today, her trip to see Richie would have to be pushed back. Frowning, she walked her way through a simple breakfast and then hopped into her vehicle, leaving the pets behind, as she headed to the library, where she could hopefully get some information on Buck's two daughters.

If nothing else the librarian herself might know something. As Doreen settled in at the microfiche machine, the other librarian on duty came back to see her.

"Hey, you're here again. Must be working on a case."

Doreen smiled at her and nodded. "I am. Did you ever hear anything about the Winters family?"

She frowned at her. "They're a pretty famous family in town."

"I know. I know," she confirmed, with a wave of her hand. "There were two daughters, both long dead and gone."

"Oh, Claudia and Meredith."

"Yes," Doreen confirmed, trying to keep her face neutral and her tone calm. "Any idea how they died?"

"I have no idea," she replied, with a headshake. "I don't imagine a whole lot of medical assistance was available in Kelowna back then. We probably only had like 150,000 residents at the time, and the Winters family was out on a big piece of property out of town—at least back then it was considered outside the city limits."

Doreen frowned at the librarian. "We're still only talking ten to twenty years ago," she pointed out. "Not the Stone Ages."

The librarian laughed. "I don't know." She shrugged. "It seems as if it's the Stone Ages when we talk about them though, doesn't it?"

Doreen sighed. "Anyway, I was looking to see if there was anything about their deaths here."

"You probably could get it from the archives."

"Yeah, that's what I'm trying to do," she pointed out.

It wasn't her regular librarian, which added to her disappointment, because that favorite librarian was always a really good source for information. But this one seemed to be more interested in asking Doreen questions, and that was not helpful.

By the time she'd gotten through the microfiche, the little bit that she had found didn't resemble anything that she had hoped for. She wandered the library for a little bit, looking for a couple books to take home just to read. Then she saw a man standing in front of the librarian's desk, talking to her. He was sketchy. Something was off about him. She listened to him and realized from the pictures she had seen on the internet that this was the wannabe politician of the Winters family, Clarence Winters.

She tried to study him without being observed, but it wasn't that easy. He looked over at her once or twice and frowned. When he caught her gaze, she just smiled in a noncommittal way and refocused on the bookshelves in front of her. But her mind couldn't focus and she had trouble finding anything that interested her—particularly as she was constantly checking to see what he was up to. Not a whole lot else she could do, and if she wasn't going to spend some time finding something to read for fun, she really needed to just walk out, and that's what she did.

As she walked past them, she heard him talking about increasing the library's budget. She rolled her eyes at that. Anybody who listened to that BS was somebody just wanting to be buttered up because honestly, politicians were always quick to spew a whole truckload of promises. Yet, once they got into power, the real game started. They didn't even understand how things worked until they got into power, and then they realized that the budgets were already 100 percent spent, twelve times over. So, all their little promises were never kept.

She stood outside in the early morning air, considering how her absence so much lately could likely contribute to whatever was bothering Mugs—perhaps all her animals. Maybe it wasn't even that. Maybe Mugs was just tired these days. She could relate.

She got back into her car, and, as she turned on the engine, she realized that Clarence Winters was walking toward her. He had *that* smile on his face. Still, she wasn't exactly sure if he was trying to garner votes or what. She didn't really know if there was an election coming up. She was always so busy with everything else and hadn't necessarily gotten involved with that stuff in town. Politics didn't interest her in any way. Still, she also knew that, if change was to happen, it had to happen at the grassroots level of the people. As he stopped to talk to her, she slowly rolled down her window.

"Hi, I'm Clarence Winters," he announced, with a big smile. "I saw you in there."

She nodded. "Yeah, sorry, I wasn't trying to eavesdrop on your conversation. I needed a bit of help from the librarian, but it looked as if you guys would be a while, so I just left."

"Oh dear, oh no," he said, waving his hands in a big expansive movement. "That's not it at all. You can certainly go in and talk to her now if you want."

"No, that's fine. I'll catch her later," she replied. "It wasn't important." Then she looked at him and frowned. "Do I know you?"

He almost preened. "I don't know. I'm running to be the next mayor in town."

"Oh." She nodded. "Maybe that's where I've seen you

then, on the posters."

"That could be. It would be nice to think that the posters were working." He gave a self-deprecating laugh.

"I'm relatively new here," she shared, "so I don't know anybody in town. At least the ones I do know aren't in politics."

"Right." He nodded.

It's almost as if he realized she was fresh blood, so he launched into his soap box about how he wanted to increase the library budget and increase the playgrounds and parks for the kids, making it much more of a family area.

She just listened with half a mind, but, when she got an opportunity, she turned it around. "So, that means you've got family here yourself then. I presume you're one of the old-time families in town."

He laughed and nodded. "Absolutely," he stated enthusiastically. "There were four of us kids, but now there's just the two of us."

She detected a mock sorrow to his words. "You've already lost two siblings?"

He nodded, and this time managed a little more sorrow in his tone. "Yes, my brother and I are the only ones left. We lost my two sisters quite a few years back."

She nodded. "I'm sure your parents are happy to know that still the two of you are here to carry on the family name."

"Oh my, yes. My mother has passed, but my dad is still alive," he shared, with a big merry laugh. "Buck Winters is going strong, a bit of a cantankerous old coot, but he's still a force," he admitted. "Yeah, we were terrified of him growing up," he shared, with a headshake. "Those were the days, and now it's all about compassion and empathy and completely different parenting. I think they call it gentle parenting."

There was almost a snideness to his tone. "No clue," Doreen muttered.

"You don't have any children?" He eyed her intently.

She shrugged. "Nope, not yet."

"Are you single?" he asked, his gaze assessing.

"Engaged," she said, holding up her ring.

"Ah, of course you would be. It's hard to find any beautiful women around who aren't hooked up already."

"Not sure about the hooked-up terminology," she said, instinctively disliking this man more and more, "but we're definitely happy to be together."

"And that's the way it should be."

"And with the four of you kids, there must be quite a load of grandkids and great-grandkids for your father," she added, with a happy sigh. "I do enjoy hearing about big families."

"Not so much for us." Clarence waved his hands about carelessly. "We weren't terribly prolific," he muttered, as he glanced back at the library. "It's all in the archives. The family is old-time, and we've got all kinds of history."

"Oh, that sounds interesting. Maybe I'll look into it a bit."

"If you're interested and if you'll vote," he began, "all you need to know is that I'm right here and that I'm the guy to take care of your interests."

"I like to do a little research on my candidates. I know I'm a bit of a dinosaur, but I want ethics and morals and some honor system going on with my politicians."

"Of course, of course," he conceded, with a bright smile. "If you've got any questions, feel free to ask."

"I might at that," she replied. "Thank you."

He turned and walked away, but his steps were rapid, as if he had places to go, people to see.

She wasn't even sure what it was about him, but just the fact that he was a politician seemed to be enough to get her back up. She drove home, her mind full of all kinds of things, and realized that what she really needed was access to the police records and the obituaries.

On that note, she sent the captain a text message. **Can I ask for assistance from someone on this cold case, so I don't have to bother you all the time?**

He called her a few minutes later. "Hey, Doreen. What do you need?"

"I need to know what the two Winters' sisters died of," she replied. "I'm not sure how or where you would get that information, but I presume you have something in the database."

"*Hmm.*" She heard the sound of a keyboard clacking in the background. "Both died of heart attacks," he shared, a few minutes later.

"Heart attacks? Both of them?"

"Yeah, both of them. Why?"

"Lilybeth also died of a heart attack," she pointed out, and a dead silence came on the other end.

"Oh wow. You really don't pull your punches, do you?"

"I don't find that being quiet gets me answers," she muttered. She wrote down her notes on this. "I guess there's nothing else in the database, is there?"

"No."

"*Hmm,* so no family doctor listed by any chance?"

"Ah, no, I don't see that, but you could talk to the coroner."

"Ooh, I like that idea. And is it the same coroner you

currently have, the one I'm working on the box of bones for?"

"Yes, and I think she would be quite interested in talking to you."

"Lovely. Send me her name and contact details, if you don't mind, and I'll give her a quick call and see if I can set up a coffee with her."

"You do that, but be prepared to have the coffee down in the morgue. She's married to her work."

"Got it," Doreen noted, "and honestly, a tour of the morgue would be right up my alley."

He groaned. "Oh, Lord, I should probably not even be putting the two of you together," he said, with a snort. "In a way, you're two peas in a pod."

"That's not a bad thing," she pointed out. "Besides, I haven't really been able to make many friends in town. Especially women."

"She's the same as you in many ways. Although she's highly academic and scientific, while you're driven by some uncanny instincts," he noted, "be prepared, as she's always focused and very driven."

"Right, so academically speaking, we're definitely not on the same page," she restated, with a laugh. "And she's single, which I'm not really anymore," she pointed out.

"That's right. You aren't." The captain chuckled. "Have you guys picked a date yet?"

"Nope, we sure haven't," she replied. "I've hardly even shaken off the dust from my last marriage. It's hard to believe that I only arrived in Kelowna last spring."

"Yeah, that Mack of ours, he's a fast worker," he quipped, with a jovial tone.

She smiled. "Which is also why he knows better than to

pressure me to set a date."

"Ah, and I hear a hint of warning in your tone. Got it." This time his laughter was big and full.

She smiled. "I'm glad everybody is happy for us. If Nan has her way, it'll be quite the event."

"Have it at your place, so you can keep the venue cost down if you want," he suggested, "but still prepare for a good one hundred people to be coming through there on that day."

She looked out the kitchen window into Nan's backyard and noted, "This place might handle that, but it will be touch-and-go."

"It sure would, but, if it was a lovely day outside, it would be a great place to have a wedding."

She smiled. "I'm not against that. I just hadn't really considered it. Yet you're right. The venues are so expensive."

"And, if they're not for you," the captain added, "you don't have to do it. The wedding should be for you two and should represent what the commitment you're making to each other means to you. It's not about all the pomp and the ceremony, with the right dress and all that. It's all about the simple things."

She was surprised to hear that from the captain, of all people.

"It's about knowing that your life is connecting to Mack's in all the ways that matter, at a level that nobody else can really appreciate, beyond their own marriages," he shared.

She smiled at such wholesome advice. "Thank you, Captain. I really appreciate hearing that. The Rosemoor lot is ganging up on me."

"Of course they are." He chuckled again. "You're pretty

well obliged to invite everybody from there."

"I don't see how I could possibly get away from it," she agreed. "There's been talk about having a reception down there too."

"You could do that as well," he noted. "If they have the room, that might not be a bad idea. Or you could have an alternate reception for them," he pointed out. "And, if you're planning on a honeymoon getaway, don't forget to remind Mack. I hate to even bring it up, but he'll need to put in for holiday time."

"Right," she noted, "definitely something else to add to my list of considerations."

"I'm sure we can give him whatever time off he needs, but the sooner, the better in terms of planning everybody's holidays."

"I understand," she said, amused. "It's one of the nuts and bolts of all this planning, isn't it?"

"It really is," he agreed. "Weddings all sound fine and whatnot, but there are some really big nuts and bolts, particularly if you'll rent a venue. Personally I absolutely love the idea of a fall wedding at your place. With the river and the sunlight, it would be gorgeous. Even the families could bring the kids, and everybody could play in the river."

"You know, that's not a bad idea," she noted. "It would be much more like me, wouldn't it?"

"I don't know about the kids and the families," he pointed out, chuckling, "but the relaxed and casual good-friend vibes, definitely." Somebody called out to him. "Now, as much as I am enjoying this, I've got to go." And, with that, he ended the call abruptly.

She smiled as she phoned the coroner. Elizabeth Harley was the name she had written down. When somebody answered the phone, Doreen stated, "I'm looking for Dr. Elizabeth Harley."

"If you called this number," the woman said in exasperation, "I would presume you understood it's my number."

"I did dial this number," Doreen replied, with a note of humor, "but just because you answered this phone doesn't mean you were the coroner herself. After all, you might have an admin or an assistant or someone who took all your appointments and handled your calls."

"Who am I talking to?" the coroner asked in crisp tones.

She laughed. "Sorry, I'm Doreen."

There was dead silence for a moment. "As in Mugs, Goliath, and Thaddeus? Their Doreen?" the coroner asked cautiously.

At that, Doreen burst out into bright, clear laughter. "Absolutely. I am *their Doreen*," she confirmed. "And, if I'm lucky, they're also mine."

"Ha, animals will take every ounce you've got to give," she muttered, "but they'll still retain their own personalities."

"They will, indeed," Doreen agreed, still laughing. "And I'm okay with that."

"Sure, your animals are absolutely nuts," she muttered, "but they appear to be loyal to you. I have heard so many stories that I feel as if I know them."

Doreen gave a long-drawn-out sigh. "And sadly those stories were probably all true."

At that the coroner's tone warmed considerably as she laughed and laughed. "So, what can I do for you?"

"The captain suggested we meet, since he's asked me to look into the case involving a child's body, with those bones resting in a box on your shelf," she explained. "I've already made some progress, though I'm not sure I've gotten as far as

I can yet. I did have a few questions about the deaths of two women who could be related—meaning related to the dead toddler's possible family."

"Good God," Elizabeth said, fascinated. "You've already ID'd the family?"

"Yes, the Winters family." Then she quickly explained about the child's DNA that she uploaded and the genealogy results.

"So, the child's distant relative was related to this Winters family. Can you send me the child's DNA results?"

"Absolutely," Doreen said, and she quickly forwarded the email.

The coroner brought it up while they were on the phone. "Oh, that's interesting, very interesting. Okay, so we have a partial match on the child's DNA, so definitely in the Winters family, but why did we have the Winters DNA in our database to begin with?" It took a few minutes, and then she muttered, "Ooh."

"Yes," Doreen replied, with a smile. "Buck Winters was charged with domestic violence and convicted of it sometime in the past. So, as part of the local investigation, the authorities got his DNA and put it into their criminal database."

"Right, and I did pull the DNA off this child. Let me see. Wow, it was about eight years ago."

"And, until I had a DNA match, we didn't really have a family name or anything to go on," Doreen shared. "It's fascinating how the genealogy searches are growing. And to think this all begins when a second cousin was found per the DNA."

"That's happening all over the place now, right?"

"The younger generations want to know more about their history, and it's getting all the older people caught up in their past wrongdoings."

"Exactly," Elizabeth noted. "Oh, I found the DNA of Iris Winters in the police database. … Oh my. Now we have a direct match between the unnamed child and Iris Winters, but not to Buck Winters himself, the one with the domestic violence record."

"I wondered about that. So it's not his child but seems to be the child of Iris Winters, who is deceased. So, as far as we can tell, that's where we're at. I don't know how we got Iris's DNA into the database, but I'm sure glad we did."

"So you're interested in the two daughters of Buck and Iris Winters. Why?" the coroner asked.

"I was hoping for more information on their deaths."

"My online death records show they both had heart attacks," she shared, as she went through files on her computer. "Nothing suspicious."

"Did you attend those deaths?"

"They weren't unusual deaths, but the mother had also died unexpectedly of a heart attack."

"Right," Doreen noted. "And that doesn't pull any triggers for you?"

"Women in particular die of silent killers, such as high blood pressure and heart attacks all the time," she explained. "Sometimes it's a stroke first, and sometimes they go right into a heart attack, and they die very quickly. That's one of the reasons why women should be looking after their blood pressure." After a moment she asked, "How's yours?"

"I have no idea," Doreen stated flatly. "The fact that I haven't been taken out by a dozen assailants already remains a credit to my animals but certainly not to my health."

"You need to look after that," she declared, warming up to her subject.

"By the way, there's was a recent death, a woman's body, Lilybeth. … Lilybeth, Lilybeth. I'm trying to think of her last name. Chirkoff."

Elizabeth confirmed, "Oh yes, her body came through here, and I believe the funeral home is picking her up today."

Doreen asked, "And, to you, that was a normal heart attack?"

Dead silence came on the other end, and then Elizabeth replied stiffly, "Is there something you're trying to say here, something about my qualifications?"

"No," Doreen stated, "not at all. While Lilybeth is not any blood kin to the Winters family, she did point the finger at them in connection with Baby Jane in your morgue. So what I am wondering is whether we have someone who's been getting away with murder for quite a while." And then she explained her telephone call with Lilybeth right before her death.

"Good God," Elizabeth replied. "Nobody told me anything about that."

"I did remind the captain this morning."

"I do have a couple emails from him in here," she noted, "but I didn't really get that as a message."

"That's one of the reasons I wanted to know about the Winters sisters. So, we now have three women, all in the Winters family, all dying of heart attacks, so all *could be* genetic."

"That's absolutely how genetics work," Elizabeth stated. "Yet, with Lilybeth having also passed so suspiciously and quickly from a heart attack, that worries me a little. Since she's not related to the Winters family, it would not be a death based on the Winters's genetics."

"True. I understand there are drugs on the market these

days," Doreen began, "drugs that can bring on heart attacks. So, I guess I'm asking if you could possibly take a sample of Lilybeth's blood, tissue, or whatever you need, and test for any of the drugs that might have done that."

"Her representative didn't want anything disruptive done to her body."

"Right," Doreen muttered. "I don't know what her family might be like, but wouldn't they be worried if some suspicions surrounded her death?"

"*Great*," Elizabeth replied. "I think the funeral home is due to be here anytime, so I've got to go." And, with that, she disconnected.

Doreen stared down at her phone. If Mack had been available, she would have called him and filled him in on that conversation. While she felt the captain would be very interested, he was also very disconnected. But, then again, he was running the entire department, whereas Mack, being Mack, was just trying to keep her out of trouble. She smiled at that, and almost instinctively, as if he understood, Mack phoned. She answered it in a bright, cheerful voice.

His tone, however, was much less cheerful. "What are you up to?"

Chapter 20

D OREEN FROWNED AT her phone. "Why would you
even ask me that?" she cried out. "You're supposed to
be in court, looking after things."

"Yeah, and then I just got this feeling."

"I was just thinking that, if you were around, I would
talk to you about this. However, you're busy with the court,
so I can't get you sidetracked with all this other stuff."

"Fill me in," he snapped, and his tone brooked absolutely no alternative.

She groaned. "I just got off the phone with Elizabeth
Harley."

"The coroner?" he asked.

"Yes, the captain gave me her name and number."

"Oh no, the two of you together? That could be bad
news."

"Why? The captain mentioned something about our
being very similar, but, at least on the surface, I don't see it
at all."

"On the surface, no, but, if we go one layer deeper, you
definitely are."

"In what way?" she snapped.

"You are both terriers. The minute you find anything even slightly suspicious, anything at all, you both jump on it."

"She's gone back to Lilybeth's body to pull some tissue and blood samples," she shared.

"Who's Lilybeth?"

And she realized that he had no idea. She quickly filled him in.

"Good God," he muttered. "Right, that's the woman who died of a heart attack in the retirement home. And yet that thing is expected."

"No," she stopped him. "Certainly at that age you can die at any moment. However, she died of a heart attack with absolutely no signs of being in danger of having a heart attack."

"That you know of," he pointed out.

"That's true. But, since Elizabeth was under the impression that nothing was suspicious about Lilybeth's death, Elizabeth didn't do an autopsy because the family representative didn't want it, given her age."

"Exactly, and, given her age, that's a very common thing," he pointed out. "We only do autopsies on suspicious deaths." Doreen went very silent. Then he sighed. "Right, so as far as you're concerned, this was a suspicious death."

"Exactly," she pointed out. "And I do believe Elizabeth may agree because she disconnected abruptly, since the body was due to be picked up by the funeral home at any moment. She wanted to deal with something and just ended the call with me."

"Yep, that would be Elizabeth. Absolutely that would be her. We'll see if she comes up with anything," he noted. "That in itself will push everything else to the side because that would mean … you do understand that, if it's not a heart attack, then it's murder, which means it's not a cold case anymore?"

She groaned. "I get that, but it wouldn't be a murder in your eyes if I hadn't poked into it."

It was his turn to groan. "You're always poking into it."

"The captain asked me to look into this, and honestly, Elizabeth seemed quite thrilled about it. I did tell her about uploading the toddler's DNA and finding a connection to a second cousin related to the Winters family, and that led us to old Buck Winters, who had his DNA taken at one point in time, which must have led to getting Iris's DNA too."

"Right," he muttered, "the Winters family, yes."

"And Iris Winters is a direct match to the dead baby's DNA—but not Buck Winters."

"Wow. That's a whole different story."

Chapter 21

AFTER TALKING TO Mack, Doreen realized that things were getting a little bit convoluted, but he was right. Just because the baby was related to a member of that Winters family tree, it did not mean they had anything to do with the child's death.

However, the family would certainly need to provide some explanation as to where the child had been and who had been looking after her because a toddler should not be left alone on their own. Whatever caregiver had been involved with that child was somebody Doreen wanted to talk to. Although they were still far from finding out that information just yet, Doreen felt that they were suddenly a whole lot closer.

She also recognized that Mack was trying hard to warn her that, if Lilybeth's death ended up being a suspicious death, Doreen would be kept out of it, as deemed a current case then. Of course that wouldn't make her happy, yet it also gave her a lot of credibility when it came to pushing her way into Mack's world again. So that would always make her chuckle. He might not appreciate it, but she wasn't against it in the least.

She went back to her notes, knowing she would have to wait for test results from Elizabeth Harley. Doreen wasn't even sure that the coroner would pass them on to her. Why would Elizabeth? She would most likely go to the captain—or whoever was involved in any pending murder investigation. As far as Doreen was concerned, this was her case, given to her by the captain. Still, she also knew it could get torn from her hands as soon as there was anything for them to act on, like a current murder investigation.

She groaned at that, just in time to get a call from Nan.

"So," Nan began, "how are you doing?"

"I'm doing fine. Did you guys get anywhere?"

"We did and we didn't," she replied.

"Did anybody know the sisters, Claudia and Meredith Winters?"

"I don't know," she declared, with a snort, "but I do have a couple people for you to come talk to."

"Good. I'll just eat some lunch, and then I'll come straight down."

"Sounds good. I'll go have a nap."

"Are you okay?" Doreen asked, her tone sharper than she meant it to be.

"Of course I'm okay," Nan stated. "Why wouldn't I be?"

Doreen winced. "No reason, it was just the way you said that."

"I'm just tired," she admitted. "We've been playing table tennis, and I am not used to running."

"Table tennis, as in Ping-Pong?"

"Yes," she stated crossly, "and I got beat, as in resoundingly beat. I thought I was in better shape, but all that running? ... My goodness. Honestly, I thought it was on purpose. Some of these younger people in here, they just can't let us old geezers alone. They've got to remind us of everything we've lost and how much of that is our fitness."

"Oh goodness," Doreen muttered. "Well, you have your nap, and I'll talk to you as soon as you're awake again."

"Fine," she grumbled, "but come on down, say, maybe around 1:30 p.m."

"Okay, I can do that."

And, with that, Nan disconnected.

She might have a solid reason for being tired, but still, it was enough to trigger Doreen's anxiety over losing her grandmother, especially after having just found her again. So much goodness was in that woman and so much fun, so much loving spirit, that Doreen didn't want to lose her at all. Of course it would happen one day. Doreen just wasn't ready for that one day to be today.

And who was she kidding? It would never be the right day when Doreen could just say, *Oh, I'm okay to lose my grandmother today.* That's not how life happens. Unfortunately for Doreen, it seemed to be very much on her mind these days, but then she was dealing with a lot. If Lilybeth's death had triggered one thing, it was the fact that death happened when you least expected it.

Here Doreen had been, waiting to have a meeting with Lilybeth, even racing down there because she was a little concerned about Lilybeth changing her mind about the meeting. And, for the first time, Doreen wondered how panicked and how upset Lilybeth had been. Would she have done something to herself in order to avoid talking to Doreen about it? "Oh, gosh," she moaned.

Feeling Mugs nudge her, she sat down on the kitchen floor beside him and hugged him close. That would be a terrible thing to find out. It would be awful if Lilybeth had felt so pressured to talk to Doreen that Lilybeth had hurt herself to avoid it. That thought wouldn't ever let Doreen sleep again. She didn't want to think that she was adding to people's pain. She was trying to help, not to make things worse.

Of course Mack would say that sometimes, when you opened these kettles of fish, there was just no way to know who would get hurt and who would face trials and tribulations that they just couldn't handle. And now Doreen was worrying if that's what she had done with Lilybeth. Doreen hoped not; dear God, she hoped not. For Lilybeth to go at her time was one thing, but that didn't mean she had been ready for somebody else to help her along the way either.

Confused, tired, and depressed, Doreen got up and made a sandwich for lunch, meanwhile figuring out something for dinner. If just for her, she couldn't care less. And that was the problem. If for Mack, as in maybe he would come by later today, she could prepare something, even if just some pasta. She smiled at that because she absolutely adored pasta. She'd heard about a website where you could enter in selected elements of what you had in your fridge and pantry, and it would create a recipe for you, or it would find a recipe using those ingredients.

It didn't take her long to find the website, and then she checked out her fridge. She had black olives and feta cheese. On her countertop, she had tomatoes. In her pantry, she had pasta and not a whole lot else. Yet she had olive oil—which she knew Mack used a lot of all the time—and, before she knew it, she had a recipe that looked incredibly appetizing in front of her. Wondering if she could tackle it on her own, she decided to give it a try and, with that, set up for dinner. Then she sent Mack a text. **Pasta for dinner, if you can**

make it.

She got a thumbs-up in return and smiled because, of course, he would be happy with it. He would be happy because he wouldn't have to cook. She really should do a whole lot more in the way of cooking, and having Mack busy like this was a good thing for her. It pushed her to try more things.

"It's not that I'm incapable. I'm just, well, … maybe incapable," she muttered to herself. Mugs nudged her again, and she smiled, bent down, and gave him a great big hug, only to find Goliath right there, waiting for his turn. Everybody was just so needy today. Maybe it was literally because she was too.

As soon as the wedding talk came up, all kinds of shivers would go down her back, reminding her that she really was doing this. She loved Mack and absolutely wanted to be with him, but the thought of marriage and everything she'd gone through before wasn't something she wanted to face again. Yet Mack was nothing like Mathew. So her marriage to Mack would not be a repeat of her marriage with Mathew.

Groaning, she wondered if it was even fair to marry Mack, when she wasn't completely healed from all that prior trauma. Did anybody ever completely heal from all that? She wasn't so sure.

Chapter 22

DECIDING THAT IT had warmed up enough outside, Doreen packed up the animals, all quite happy to take a walk. She headed out the backyard toward the river. The animals were all delighted to follow along in her wake at first, then very quickly overtook her as they raced to the river ahead of her. She didn't have Mugs on a leash since this was his home territory, his backyard, so to speak. And generally he was really good with anybody here. Of course there was always a chance along the river that they would meet somebody who didn't like dogs, but, so far, it hadn't been an issue. Doreen was grateful for that. The animals were such an added light in her life that she couldn't imagine how lonely other people must be without something similar in their lives.

As she wandered alone down the pathway heading toward Nan, Doreen remembered so many of the cases she had dealt with, and it brought her a lot of joy to think that she had helped out at least some of the people and had got justice for some victims.

Obviously she couldn't help everybody, and some didn't want to be helped. She couldn't do much about that, but, as long as she continued to do as much as she could, maybe the authorities would finally get through this backlog of cases. She didn't know what she would do then, aside from moving to the next town and starting all over again. She burst out laughing at that because she didn't want to move anywhere. Somehow, in the midst of all this turmoil, she had managed to make Kelowna her home, cementing into her heart and soul where she belonged. She was absolutely ecstatic that Mack had no plans to take her away from Nan's house either.

Kelowna was his home as well, and, if he was happy to move into Nan's house with her after they married, then that was a perfect solution. At least she hoped so. And, with Mack's great building skills, she could tag along and help with his renovations just as much as she could, knowing that would be enough for him. To do things together was a joy.

Her thoughts still meandered as she considered changes they could make to the old house, as she arrived at Nan's place. She walked through the front door, smiled at the receptionist, then took the first hallway down toward Nan. As soon as she got there, the door opened just in front of her, and Nan went to step out, looked at her in surprise, then stepped back in again.

"Isn't that quite the timing," she said in delight.

"Does that mean you've had your nap?"

"Of course I've had my nap," she declared, with a wave of her hand. "Come on in, child. You look frozen."

"We walked this time," she stated, with a smile at her grandmother, "and it's definitely a bit chilly."

"It's more than a bit chilly, but that's okay. It put some beautiful color in your cheeks."

"I don't know that I needed any color in my cheeks," she

pointed out. "But, if it made you happy, it's all good."

Nan burst into laughter. She bent down and spent a few minutes cuddling Mugs, who seemed to be absolutely over the moon to see her. "Oh my, the animals are quite something today."

"I know. So much so that I wasn't sure what was going on."

"If something is going on, you can bet it'll involve you," Nan stated, her gaze astute as she glanced over at her granddaughter. "These animals are barometers for our emotions. Are you upset about something?"

"No, not really. Maybe a bit melancholy, that's all."

"Oh dear," Nan muttered. "You're not having second thoughts about marrying Mack, are you?"

A moment of silence fell all around her, and she realized that Nan still had the door open, and people were making their way into Nan's apartment to join her. Doreen groaned. "No, Nan, I'm definitely not having second thoughts about marrying Mack." As soon as she said it, a collective sigh wafted through the room.

"I'm glad to hear that," Nan stated. "We know you are still working through things from that disastrous first marriage of yours, but it's good to hear you say it."

Immediately the grins all around shone bright again.

Doreen shook her head at them. "Mack and I are fine," she declared, looking from one person to the next, "absolutely fine."

"That's good," Maisie replied. "We would hate for you to muck up things now."

Doreen glared at her. "Why would my changing my mind be a muck up?"

"Because every woman needs to be married."

Her jaw dropped at that. Doreen wanted to blast into her, but her grandmother was right here.

Nan interjected, "Enough of that talk. My granddaughter will make a decision on her own and in her own time."

"The decision is already made," Doreen declared firmly. "Mack and I are getting married."

"But when?" cried out Maisie. "I so want to be alive to see it."

Doreen groaned as she stared at everybody in the room.

"I'm just glad that hottie detective wasn't here long. She was after your man, and you wouldn't be wasting time getting married if she were still here."

Doreen snorted. "Who is she talking about?" She looked at everybody, then frowned at Maisie. "I have no idea who you are talking about."

Nan sighed. "Insley."

"Oh," Doreen muttered.

"Yes," exclaimed Maisie. "Insley was a harlot and was after your man."

Doreen turned to Nan, frowning.

"No matter, child. She was transferred to Vernon, so don't you worry about a thing."

"But," Doreen replied, "*was* she after Mack?"

Nan patted her granddaughter's cheek. "Now don't you worry, child. Mack is crazy about you. Any woman would want what you have," Then Nan turned to glare at Maisie. "And Maisie knows that." Nan tipped her head to silence Maisie.

Doreen shook her head. "Regardless of whatever all that was, I get that you're all in a rush, but I am not. I still have fallout from my divorce to deal with. I still have to take care of Mathew's estate, which is very complicated. I still have all kinds of issues to work through, and frankly I haven't been legally single for very long."

"Yes, but it's been a few months, and that's long enough," said another woman testily, who'd walked inside to join them. "In our day, if you were single past five minutes, something was wrong with you."

"It's a good thing that it's not your day anymore then," Nan quipped. "Come on now, everybody. Give Doreen some space. We talked about this, and she doesn't need any of us butting into her private life."

"Of course not," Maisie agreed, "but we don't want her to change her mind either."

"For heaven's sake, I won't change my mind," Doreen exclaimed in exasperation. "What brought that on?"

They just shrugged, and Maisie stated, "But you're not necessarily setting a date right now, are you?"

"How many of you have had family recently get married?" Several of the women nodded with bright beams of joy across their faces. "Right, and did it happen immediately, or did they need time to make arrangements, to book venues, and things like that?"

"Oh my, yes," one of the women agreed, one who Doreen didn't think she'd ever seen before. "My granddaughter took well over a year before finally walking down the aisle."

"Exactly. So why is it that I can't have the same time frame?" Doreen asked.

They all stopped and considered it, and the woman grudgingly admitted, "I didn't like waiting then either, but my granddaughter wouldn't let me change her mind."

"Of course not," Nan stated. "She wants to have the wedding of her dreams, not your dreams."

The other woman looked at her, blinked several times, and her shoulders slumped. "You know, if somebody had given me that reminder before the wedding, I would probably still be closer to my granddaughter." When Doreen frowned at her, she shrugged. "I guess I was a little pushy, and she didn't appreciate it."

"Of course not," Doreen noted. "I think a lot of mothers-in-law tend to have that problem too."

"Not to mention mothers," the woman added. "My daughter-in-law got herself more or less kicked off the wedding planning too."

Doreen smiled. "And that probably didn't bother you in the least, did it?"

"Nope, it sure didn't," she admitted, with a chuckle. "Even though both of us had been banned from the preparations, we both did attend the wedding, and everybody made up. However, it did leave a bit of a pall over the celebration."

"Of course," Doreen agreed. "It's another reason why I don't want to get pushed into a date. I'll do me. And, when *me* is ready, and not one day before, will I share the date with anyone."

Richie had just walked in, heard that, and agreed. "You do that, sister," he crowed. "You tell these ladies how to handle that. They're all up into everybody's business every day, and it's about time someone told these two to back off." Richie pointed to the two ladies whom Doreen had not yet met.

"And you love it," Nan said mockingly to him.

Doreen wasn't sure what was going on with the inmates today, but everybody was feisty and cranky. She walked over to Nan and asked, "So, what exactly do we have going on here?"

"Right, down to business, that's my granddaughter," Nan declared, with a beaming smile.

"We have things to do, remember?" Doreen asked pointedly.

"We do, indeed, and I have a couple people here to introduce," Nan began, looking around to the feisty elderly woman. "So this is Lynda."

That woman even now looked as if she wanted to say something about her granddaughter's wedding.

"And Lynda knew Iris."

"Did you now?" Doreen asked, turning to face Lynda.

Lynda nodded. "We were friends for quite a while, but she was a tormented soul."

"Tormented?"

"Tormented," she repeated. "She lost a child and never really recovered."

"A little girl by any chance?" Doreen asked her.

The woman frowned at her and then nodded. "How did you know?"

"I didn't know," she muttered. "It's just something I was expecting."

"I don't know how you could possibly be expecting that answer, but, yes, that's right. Iris lost a little girl, and it really broke her up."

"Of course it would," Doreen muttered. "Nobody wants to lose a child."

"She already had four children, but this little girl was the light of her eyes."

Doreen asked, "What happened? Do you know the details?"

"I don't know. I didn't know her back then, at least not closely. Yet I knew that she had lost a child, so it was just one of those things we didn't talk about. Honestly, several of us lost children and pregnancies back then. Most of us went back fifty-plus years—sixty to seventy years for some. I will say that the medical care the younger people have access to today seems to be a whole lot better."

"And yet, still there are problem pregnancies and deliveries in some cases," Doreen noted. "There are no guarantees, even now."

"No, of course not," Lynda admitted.

"Did Iris ever get over it?"

"Oh, sure, in the sense that she functioned on a daily basis, but there was always this melancholy look to her."

"Of course. I get it. And did she ever say what happened or why her child died?"

"No, she didn't." Lynda stared at Doreen and shook her head. "I'm not sure what purpose it serves to bring that up now anyway."

"Who was her husband?" she asked, sidestepping the comment.

"Oh." Lynda frowned for a moment. "I think his name was Bob. No, but it started with a *B*, I think."

Doreen nodded. "I do have it written in my notes somewhere. ... Buck. It was Buck."

"Winters, it was Iris Winters," one of the women cried out. "I knew her too."

"Yes, but, Corrine, you didn't know her as much as I knew her," Lynda stated.

"She never mentioned losing a child to you?" Doreen asked Corrine, the other newcomer.

"No, she didn't. Every once in a while, at a certain time of the year, she would get very quiet. Sometimes she even wanted to go to church."

"And was she …" Doreen frowned, not knowing quite how to say it, but the question needed to be asked. "Was she a church-going woman? A *good woman*? I know that's a judgment call to even know what that means."

"I know what you mean, but, yes, she was a good woman. She certainly was faithful to her husband."

"Was she?" Doreen asked.

"Yes, Buck Winters was not somebody you could fool around on and then live to tell the tale," Corrine declared.

"Right. Did they ever separate, do you know?"

"I think so, at one point in time, and then she came to her senses. He provided for her in a big way," she declared.

"Was she happy?" Doreen asked.

She frowned and then looked over at Doreen. "Even with all that money, I would have to say I don't think she was, but I'm not sure anybody would have made her happy. She was just very … I guess I would call it *depressed* all the time."

"As if something had happened in her life and she hadn't quite adjusted?" Doreen asked.

Corrine nodded, grimacing now.

"Yeah," Lynda added carefully, "and I think a lot of that went back to Buck. He might have provided for her, but I don't know that he loved her as much as he wanted to possess her. As in what was his was his."

"I won't argue with that," Corrine replied. "You're probably right."

"What about the two daughters? Claudia and Meredith?" Doreen asked.

"Both of them were interesting women," Lynda noted. "They both married, both had what? One or two children each? Both had heart attacks about … a good ten years apart,

I guess. They were very close to their mother, and I'm not sure that they were necessarily close to Buck."

"Could anybody get close to old Buck?" Doreen asked. "That would be my next question because, if he was a difficult person, getting close to him may not have been something anybody could do—not even his own wife or his daughters."

"I think you're quite right. He was, he still is," Lynda corrected herself, while rolling her eyes, "quite a force. He's also cranky to boot."

"Understood. I've heard rumors about domestic violence. Is that true?" Doreen asked everyone.

"Yeah, old Buck," Richie chimed in, "he was convicted of it, but I think he only served house arrest."

Lynda nodded. "His wife was dead and gone by then."

"So did Buck have a girlfriend at that time?" Doreen asked everyone.

"I think so," Lynda replied, "but I am not sure. Believe me that Buck always had somebody to look after him—or always had a woman about for whatever reason."

"So, he had a roving eye, yet he kept a very faithful wife at home?" Doreen asked.

"Yes, but again I'm not sure how much of Iris's faithfulness was because of love versus duty versus fear," noted another newcomer, peeling her gaze away and avoiding eye contact with anyone.

Doreen looked over at her. "What is your name?"

"I'm Madelyn," she said. "And I may not have known Iris as well as a lot of people, but I worked in the hospital, and I do know that she came in a couple times with bruises and flimsy excuses for them."

Doreen winced and Madelyn nodded. "I told her that

she didn't have to stay, and she gave me the saddest look, just the absolute saddest look, and told me that, yes, she did have to stay. One time I told her that people could help her, and she panicked. She said that there was no forgiveness for some people."

"And how did you take that?"

"It sounded as if her guilty conscience was speaking in some way," she replied, "but she was such a gentle soul that I don't know what she could have possibly done that would make her feel guilty."

Doreen nodded and didn't say a whole lot. Everybody was curious but being respectful.

"I presume you're onto another case now," Lynda said.

"I am, indeed."

"And it involves that Winters family?"

She nodded. "It involves that Winters family."

"There's no easy way to say it," Lynda stated, "except that the Winters family is messed up."

"All of them?" Doreen asked, with an eyebrow raised.

"Yes," confirmed Madelyn, "all of them."

"And have you seen that violence in all of them before?"

"No, but we saw a couple women come through the hospital back then. Now I haven't been active in nursing for quite a while now, but my daughter is a nurse, and I've heard her talk about some of the local families, and that's one name that she brings up regularly. It bothers her that the women will never press charges."

"They're a political family," Madelyn pointed out, then snorted.

"The one son is, Clarence, but he's no longer married," Lynda shared. And you won't see any charges show up against him, as he would just buy them all off."

"Does he have that much money?" Doreen asked.

"Enough to buy off people here. Nobody is after millions. They just want enough money to go away and to live their lives."

"Right," Doreen muttered. "Okay, so does anybody know anything about the death of Iris's fifth child and what may have happened?"

Immediately everyone shook their heads.

Madelyn asked, "Is that the case you're working on? That child was dead and buried decades ago."

"Right," Doreen confirmed, "but sometimes things that get buried are uncovered."

That drew gasps from various people, and they looked at her intently.

"I can't say much, but I can tell you that we are looking into various people around here. ... Do you know if anybody else lost a child back then? Anybody else even in the Winters family?"

There was quiet pondering about that question.

"I seem to remember an infant death," Madelyn offered, "but who was that? I think that was ... Claudia's firstborn. I know she was absolutely devastated by it, but there wasn't anything suspicious about it."

Doreen nodded but wrote it down anyway. "Any idea how long ago that would have been?"

"Oh, years and years and years, maybe decades ago. Claudia's been gone over ten years now. So, how can you go after any of these cases when nobody is alive to even deal with?"

"That's part of the problem," Doreen admitted. "If nothing else I still want to at least get some closure for the family."

"There's no family left to get closure for," Corrine piped up.

"Maybe, but I have a toddler's body who I want to bury with her legal name," Doreen shared.

That raised eyebrows, as everybody turned and looked at each other.

A bit smugly Nan asked, "Anybody else have other information that would help? Anything about other children?"

"How old of a child?" the nurse asked, turning to look at Doreen. "That might help."

"Eighteen months," Doreen replied.

"Ooh, ouch, that's so hard. That's past that first flush when anybody would expect an issue or would potentially have an issue. So you would think you're well and truly past that stage."

"Exactly," Doreen agreed. "Yet this child didn't die of natural causes." All around her, the silence was so loud, she could practically hear her heart beating.

Chapter 23

AFTER THE MEETING ended, Doreen wrote up the little bits of notes she had gathered—plus names and contact information on the new women Doreen had talked to today. It was still wide open as to what had gone on—or what could have gone on with Baby Jane—but, hey, Doreen was getting somewhere.

And yet, as Nan frowned afterward, she muttered, "I'm not sure that was any help."

"It gave us information, and it did confirm that Iris had lost an infant," Doreen noted.

"You're really thinking Iris would have killed her own child?" Nan asked, looking at her.

"No, I'm not saying that at all."

"Not saying anything is close to it," Richie muttered off to the side, but she could tell that it had pained him to sit in on these conversations. He looked over at Doreen and asked, "Did you tell your grandmother?"

"No, I didn't," she said. "I thought that was for you to do, if you chose to."

He groaned and nodded, now facing Nan. "Doreen took my DNA, and she's uploading it to the genealogy site," he shared. "I figured that maybe, at this stage in my life, I should find out the truth."

Nan sat down beside him, reached for his hand, and nodded. "If nothing else, knowing the truth might help you put it to rest."

"But what if the child was mine?" he asked, looking at Nan with a haunted expression.

"Then we'll deal with it," Nan declared. "Not a one of us has a closet free of ghosts, and, in your case, it's not as if you were welcome to stay around."

"No, I sure wasn't," he said, "but then I sometimes think I was less of a man for not having stayed around anyway."

"What would you have done back then?" Nan asked.

Richie shrugged. "Old Buck is still alive and kicking, still making threats," he pointed out. "Maybe if I had stood up to him all those years ago, he wouldn't still be bullying people around." Nan stared at him, and he shrugged. "He was looking at coming here, living at Rosemoor. Then he saw me and made some comment about losers and things like that." He shook his head, then added, "I just went on by, but it's obvious that Buck wouldn't move into Rosemoor because I was here."

"If he had a choice," Doreen shared, "then that's good for him, but it wasn't your fault. Even if it was, maybe we should buy you coffee as a thank-you for keeping him away from here."

He smiled at her. "You do have a kind heart."

She chuckled. "I don't know about a kind heart. Mack would probably call it a foolish heart."

"No," Richie argued, "you're one of those good people we need more of."

"Maybe," she conceded. "In the meantime, let's not worry about what's going on in that corner of your world. We can come up with enough trouble elsewhere."

"You got that right," he muttered. "I keep hoping we'll get answers sooner than later though."

"We'll get them when they're ready," Doreen stated, "and not until then. So no point in worrying."

He groaned. "I know that. I just didn't want to hear about it."

She nodded. "It's all good."

"Says you," he muttered. "There could be so much else going on now."

"There's a lot going on, and I'm getting bits and pieces, but nothing is left to be done right now."

"So Iris is confirmed as the mother of Baby Jane, right?" Nan asked Doreen.

Doreen nodded. "It's a match to Iris's DNA. But Buck's DNA is in the database, and it's not his child." At that, Richie straightened and stared at her in shock. She shrugged. "At least I haven't been told it was his yet."

Richie slumped. "But that could just mean they haven't gone through everything in the database yet."

"Maybe," Doreen agreed. "Again, this will take time, even though I know that's not what you want to hear."

"It's never what any of us wants to hear," Nan muttered. "Time is the one thing we don't have."

Doreen turned to her grandmother. "Does anybody know the receptionist over at Riverdale?"

"I probably do, if it's the same one," Nan replied. "Why are you asking? They tried to get me to move over there at one point in time."

"The receptionist I spoke to had a name tag that read *Tabitha*."

"Yes, I know Tabitha. Why? What do you want to know?" Nan asked, looking at her with bright curiosity.

"When Lilybeth died, I was on my way over to see her. She had left the letter at the front desk, and I want to know if anybody else went to see Lilybeth on the day she died."

"Ooh," Nan muttered, frowning at her. "So, you think maybe somebody visited her and knocked her off then." She rubbed her hands together.

"I'm just saying," Doreen began, "that we need to eliminate that possibility. If Lilybeth had a visitor, we would then know that much. It was early in the morning because I was trying to get down there quickly. So, it was quite possible it was somebody who was already there."

"Ha, old Buck's there," Richie noted. When she turned and looked at him, he nodded. "And, if he thought Lilybeth would tattle, believe me that he would have had no problem popping her."

She frowned at that as Nan shrugged. Doreen admitted, "I'm biased, I know, but he's the one with the record."

"And it's that record that's interesting to me too," Nan added, "because I would have thought that he had enough money to buy his way out of that."

"It wasn't the first time he had hit Iris though—or some other woman."

"It wasn't his first time?" Nan asked.

"Nope, it sure wasn't, but I'm not sure anybody else ever pressed charges."

"And, of course, if they don't press charges, it won't be classified as his first time," Nan pointed out.

"Maybe, but that doesn't mean that he didn't deserve everything they threw at him."

"Sure, but it doesn't sound as if he had to pay very much

for what he did either."

"No, I don't think so. It was just after his wife died. The court or the authorities or whoever put it all down to trauma and grief, so he was given a pretty light sentence, and he didn't go to jail or prison or whatever. He served time at home. It's not as if he served any hard time or anything."

"And since then, any idea what he's been up to?"

"Trouble," Richie claimed and then groaned. "As you can tell, I just might have an issue with him."

"Ya think?" Doreen teased, smiling at him. "*Just might have an issue* is a whole different story than going balls to the wall into an issue, so let's just stick with the facts."

"You are starting to sound so much like Mack," Nan declared proudly.

Doreen winced. "The trouble is, Mack is very heavily involved in a court case right now, and he can't get out to give me a hand on any of this, so I'm flying blind. Yet I did connect with the coroner."

"Ooh," Nan said, looking at her in joy. "That could be such a great connection."

"Could be," Doreen agreed. "As long as I don't push the conspiracy theories too much, and I stick with the facts, we might get along just fine." She smiled at her grandmother.

"Maybe, but I heard she's a pretty-tough cookie though," Richie added.

"I've heard the same. Yet I'm not against her being a tough cookie," Doreen pointed out, "particularly if she's fair."

"No, we need her fair, and we need her tough, and we need her on the ball," Nan stated, clapping her hands.

"Absolutely, so it's all good."

"Yes, it's all good," Nan agreed. "So, what's next?"

"I still haven't necessarily found everything I need. We're still operating blind on so much right now."

"Of course we are, but you're still gathering evidence. You've already got a family link, and you've already got a biological mother for Baby Jane, and what you don't know yet is whether there's been a crime."

"No, I sure don't, but, with any luck, I will get the answers to that question too."

"There has to be a crime, doesn't there?" Richie asked, looking at her. "That poor baby. Buck must have done it."

"Maybe, but remember that it doesn't take a whole lot for a baby to die. They're pretty tender and vulnerable at that age," Doreen explained. "So, you know, one push, one blow to the head, one something is all it takes."

"It's still a crime," Richie declared.

"Absolutely it's still a crime," Doreen agreed, "but I'm also just as concerned as to what could be a recent crime."

"You're thinking about Lilybeth again, aren't you?" Nan asked.

"I am."

"Dear, I think you'll have to leave that be. She was ready to go."

"Maybe so, but I still need to double-check that she didn't have any visitors that morning."

"Fine." Nan reached for her phone and made a call. Doreen heard Nan talking to the receptionist at the Riverdale retirement home. "I was looking at moving over there," Nan said, "but then I heard about Lilybeth."

There was more chatter on the other end.

"I know. I know, and I understand that she was ready to go in so many ways, and she was living as a recluse. That's one of the reasons I wanted to move over there, to be closer to her, so she wouldn't be alone all the time. It's so sad. It would be lovely to know she at least had some contact with people, so she wasn't alone."

Nan listened to the other woman, her eyes lighting up as she nodded. "Oh, that makes me feel so much better, thank you." She disconnected, then turned and looked at Doreen in triumph. "She did have a visitor."

"Who was it?"

"She apparently went to the cafeteria early that morning and spoke with the staff, but she also spoke with a couple men."

"And who were the men?" Doreen asked.

Nan grinned. "Who were the men? Well, just think. They were both from the Winters family. She talked to old Buck, and she also talked to Clarence."

"The politician, Clarence?" Doreen asked, frowning at her grandmother.

"Absolutely, the politician, Clarence."

"And then what?" Doreen asked.

"Then Lilybeth decided she wasn't feeling great, and she went back to her room and collapsed on the way … from a heart attack."

Chapter 24

DOREEN WENT HOME to start dinner but felt the excitement of something starting to break. When the coroner contacted her a little later, she asked, her voice bubbling over with excitement, "Did you find something?"

Elizabeth hesitated. "Wait. Did you find something?"

"Maybe," Doreen replied. "Lilybeth had a visitor—or at least a visit with two of the Winters family."

There was silence at the other end. "And what happened?"

"They both talked to her. One was Buck Winters, who is a resident there, and his son Clarence."

"Clarence, the politician?" she asked, her voice rising.

"Yes, and then Lilybeth supposedly, and that's according to the men, … wasn't feeling very well. So, instead of going for breakfast, she headed back to her room but collapsed on the way. Later it was declared that she had a heart attack."

"Good God," Elizabeth muttered.

"So can any drug bring on a heart attack like that?"

"Of course," the coroner stated. "I haven't got the tox results back though."

"Oh. … I was hoping you had results already."

She laughed. "It takes a little longer than that."

"Right, I keep forgetting. Mack is forever telling me that the process takes time."

"It does take time, but it sounds as if you're right about it."

"So, no results yet, but you must have had a reason for calling me."

"Yeah, I sure did," Elizabeth replied. "I took a look at the two coroner reports on both of the sisters. Neither had been tested for any drugs."

"Really?"

"Yes, really. They weren't tested presumably because, according to the family, that sort of thing runs in the family."

"Right, of course it runs in the family, and, if people are letting it run in the family, that becomes pretty convenient."

"What do you mean?" Elizabeth asked.

"They're saying it runs in the family because of Iris, right?"

"Yes, I understand she had a heart condition."

Doreen asked, "Can you pull her medical records?"

"Why?" Elizabeth asked, the doubt evident in her tone.

"What if she also died of a heart attack that wasn't natural?"

"So, you're saying they set it up as a potential pathway to get rid of the sisters?"

"Exactly, but I would need somebody to take a look at what they gained by all these deaths, but it's possible, isn't it?"

"I suppose it's possible," Elizabeth noted cautiously, "but it certainly isn't something I can put any proof to."

"No, we would have to exhume Iris's body, and that's

not an easy process."

"No, it's definitely not," she agreed.

"It has happened in a couple of my cases," Doreen shared, "but I presume we would get a lot more of an argument because I don't think the three Winters men still living, or at least the three senior men still living would have anything to do with it."

"Right, but now you've really got me wondering. So I'll pull Iris's file and see just what is there."

Doreen asked, "Like right now?"

First came silence, and then Elizabeth laughed. "You definitely are into this, aren't you?"

"With Lilybeth having just passed away, I don't want to take any chances."

"But who else could they possibly be concerned about?"

"The Riverdale receptionist just told Nan this morning that Lilybeth had visitors before her demise, that she spoke to both of those men. So, if they have any idea that Tabitha's talking about it, it only makes sense that she could be in danger too."

"But they could have been seen talking in one of the hallways of Riverdale," Elizabeth suggested. "There's no reason for them to be worried about that getting out."

"Yet, if they had something to do with Lilybeth's death, then Buck and Clarence will act as natural and as calm as they can. On the other hand, sometimes these killers get cocky. At other times they start to worry and think they're better off just dealing with potential issues by tying up loose ends."

"And, if Tabitha had a heart attack, that would be a little too obvious. She would need to have a condition that carried the possibility of a heart attack at the very least."

"But it could also be just a car accident."

There was silence at first, then Elizabeth added, "And some people think I'm disturbed in my thinking."

Doreen winced. "I understand," she muttered, her tone low. "I think a lot of people wonder about me too."

"It's just the way your mind works," Elizabeth stated.

"It certainly is now. I didn't use to be like this, connecting various stuff. However, after seeing so many people and what they do and how far they're willing to go to keep things quiet, well, it's just the way I think now."

Elizabeth sighed. "Let me take a look at things, and I'll get back to you." And, with that, she disconnected.

As that was all Doreen would get out of the coroner for now, Doreen had to be satisfied, at least for the moment. It did bother her to think that Iris may have had a little bit of help along the way getting to her death too. Plus, Iris didn't seem to be a very happy person at any time in her life. What a sad commentary of her existence.

As Doreen scanned through the Winters family list, she realized that each of the siblings had only ever had one child each, so the two sisters had left behind one daughter each.

Frowning, Doreen picked up the phone book and searched for a number for either of them. As soon as she found something that might be one of them, she contacted her. When an woman answered the phone, her voice quivering and tired, Doreen winced and began, "Hello, I'm looking for Sandra."

"Yes, you found her," she replied. "Who's this?"

"I'm Doreen. I'm looking into a case that's come up locally."

Sandra asked, "What case?" There was no accusation in her tone but almost a sense of resignation.

"I'm pretty sure you have an idea," Doreen said, without sharing very much.

Then Sandra started to cry. "Oh my God, I knew this day would come."

"That depends on if we're talking about the same case," Doreen stated, not at all sure she should be talking to Sandra over the phone like this. "Do you want me to come down so we can talk about it in person?"

"I don't know you," she replied. "But, ever since my mother passed away, I always figured this day would come."

"Okay, do you want to tell me what it is that you think this day will bring?"

"I think my mother was murdered," she declared.

Doreen winced. "Right, that is on my list here."

"Of course it is." Sandra was still sobbing. "My beautiful mother, … she loved everybody."

"And maybe loved somebody a little too much?"

"I don't know about loving someone too much, but she was certainly inquisitive and questioning a lot of things."

"Like the death of your grandmother?"

Sandra gasped. "Oh, my goodness, you do know."

"I know some of it, but I am missing a few key things."

"Oh my," Sandra noted, her voice shaking. "This day should have come while my mother was alive."

"Maybe, and yet maybe it's something we can do now. At least then her death wouldn't have been in vain."

As Sandra sobbed heavily, Doreen frowned and asked, "Why don't I come visit, so we can talk? No pressure, no worries, just a nice quiet little conversation about some of the things that have been so wrong for such a long time that have caused you so much torment."

Sandra sobbed and sobbed.

Doreen tried again. "Let me come visit you, and we can go over this together. Are you okay with that?" Doreen asked again and then again.

Sandra never answered.

"I won't come down if you don't want me to," Doreen added, "but you and I both know it's past time."

"Yes," Sandra whispered. "It's past time."

"Then I can come?" Doreen asked.

The woman sobbed and sobbed and sobbed.

Doreen waited and waited but knew that she needed to get something clear. "I really do need an answer from you."

"Yes," she finally said. "Come." And then she whispered, "But don't tell anybody." And, with that, she disconnected.

Doreen stared down at the phone and realized she hadn't confirmed the address. And that might be a bit of an issue. She checked the address she had and decided to go with it. If nothing else, she could always phone Sandra and ask for clarity about where she was, if need be. Doreen quickly grabbed the animals, thinking that maybe today of all days Mugs could work his charm on this woman, who was so distraught and who apparently also believed her mother had been murdered.

As an afterthought, she gave Elizabeth Harley a quick phone call back. Elizabeth sounded almost annoyed. "I know I'm being persistent," Doreen stated. "I'm just calling to tell you that I'm heading down to visit Sandra, Claudia's daughter. She was almost incoherent on the phone, but she did give me the impression that it was time and that she believes her mother and her grandmother were both murdered."

A shocked gasp came from Elizabeth on the other end. "Good God."

"Yeah, so I'm heading down there. Since Mack is at a trial, I don't have him as my backup, and I can't even tell him where I'm going," she shared, with a half laugh. "So, if the captain calls or gets after me, at least I told somebody."

"Wait, what do you want me to do?" Elizabeth cried out. "This is really not my field."

"Maybe contact the captain and just tell him."

"Yeah, okay. I can do that," Elizabeth agreed and then went off on another tirade. "Are you sure you should be going there?"

"Yes, I am sure I should go. I don't know how long the window is open for Sandra to discuss what's going on," Doreen explained. "But what I do find is that often the window closes very rapidly, as soon as the family finds out what's happening, so I need to go now. I just don't know what I'll find." And, with that, she ended the call.

With the animals in tow, Doreen raced out to her car. As soon as she got down to the right neighborhood, she stopped and realized that either the house had changed or something was off on the address. She phoned Sandra, then waited and waited until finally the woman answered. "I'm trying to find your house," Doreen said.

"Oh, I'm in the carriage house in the back."

She gave the address, which was exactly where Doreen was.

"But you have to drive around to the section behind the main house," she shared. "There's a carriage house in the back, and I live there."

Chapter 25

DOREEN FOLLOWED THE instructions, and, sure enough, she found a small carriage house. She hopped out with the animals in tow and looked around. The door opened, and there stood a woman. She appeared far older than she should have been, at least by Doreen's quick estimate. But then Sandra was still shaking and bawling. "I'm so sorry," Doreen muttered, as she walked closer.

Mugs walked toward Sandra and shoved his face up against her knees and just rubbed on her.

She bent down and pet him. "Oh my, I didn't know you had animals."

"I do, indeed." Doreen smiled down at them.

"Come in, come in," Sandra murmured. She sniffled several times, pulled a tissue from her pocket, blew her nose, and then did it again and again. She looked back at Doreen. "I probably shouldn't even be talking to you."

Doreen sighed. "If we need to bring something to light because of a miscarriage of justice," she pointed out, "I'm the one to talk to."

Sandra nodded. "The family will be so angry with me."

"Which ones?" Doreen asked.

The woman looked at her and said, "My uncles."

"Ah, yeah, there is them to worry about, isn't there?"

"Yes," she agreed. "They've always been very dominant, and we could never get out from under them."

"Meaning you and your mother?"

"Yeah, my mother," she confirmed, scoffing. "She wanted to leave town dozens of times and even tried a couple times. It wasn't so much that she got forced back, but circumstances were never very helpful to getting out on a permanent basis. They didn't want her to be independent. They didn't want her having a life on her own. It was all about keeping control of the narrative."

Doreen nodded. "I understand. I was married to somebody like that." When Sandra eyed her in surprise, Doreen nodded. "It's not an easy way to go through life."

"No, no, it's not. My mother hated it. And then she just gave up, as if she couldn't fight anymore. So she settled into life here, but she was never the same. She was never happy. She was never … I don't even know how to explain it, but she was just marking time and waiting to die."

Doreen frowned at her in surprise. "It was that bad?"

"Oh yeah. … It was definitely that bad. She made her bid for freedom, lost it, and wouldn't do it again. It's as if every ounce of effort she had available to her died almost immediately."

"I'm so sorry. That would have been tough."

"It was tough. And it was so very sad to see, since she was always so depressed. If they had told me that she had committed suicide, I would have believed it. But a heart attack? No way."

"And why is that?"

"She'd just gone in for a physical, including a full cardiac workup. I convinced her to do that, so, if she did have heart problems, we could address them. If she didn't, … well, we would address that too."

"So, your doctor confirmed everything was normal?"

"Everything was fine, no heart murmur, no arrhythmia. … There was nothing."

Doreen nodded. "And I suppose everybody just said that, because of your grandmother's health issue, it was an inherited issue in the family and could happen anytime."

Sandra nodded. "Wow. How did you figure that out?"

"People gaslight others all the time," Doreen declared, "and I had the misfortune to become somebody who did it to myself as well."

Sandra winced. "I'm so sorry. I hope you aren't as bad as my mother."

"No, not at all," Doreen replied, with a gentle smile.

"It was a shock at the time, but I moved on, and I try to have a completely different life now," Sandra shared.

"After a loss, you tend to think that there's no life afterward."

"Right, and, for some people, there isn't life afterward. Still, for others, it's important for them to find a way to make a life, and that's where the problem comes in. In order to do that, you have to be left alone to heal, to figure out what to do in your life," Sandra explained. "My grandfather refused to allow me that time."

"What about your father?" she asked.

She shrugged. "I don't even know who he was or what happened to him. My mother got *in the family way*, and we all paid for it."

"Including you?"

"Of course including me," she snapped, staring at her.

"It doesn't matter who got my mother pregnant. It's always the mothers and the children, the ones left behind, who have to pay the penalty."

"That's hardly fair," Doreen muttered.

"It's not fair. It's not fair at all," Sandra cried out passionately. "I barely had a life. If I had a boyfriend, all I heard about was that I was a strumpet, just like my mother."

"Oh, good Lord." Doreen stared at her. "And why didn't you leave?"

Sandra's shoulders sagged. "I couldn't leave my mother. She seemed so fragile and heartbroken over everything."

"But your mother has been gone for ten years now, hasn't she?"

She nodded. "Yes, and still I'm sitting here. You're right. I should have left. Maybe I still should leave. But where would I go? What would I do? I don't have any money. I'm not sure I could find work, but—"

"What about another partner?"

"I've never had a partner," Sandra admitted. "It's not as if the men in this family would allow me to have a normal life. Every male has to be vetted."

She nodded slowly. "And they won't let anybody pass muster, will they?"

"Even if they did, my grandfather and my uncles always mention something about my being a *bad seed*." When Doreen just stared at her, Sandra shrugged. "They criticize me constantly, to where you feel that something is very wrong with you, and you can't ever get over it. You try hard, but—"

"Got it." Doreen nodded. "I understand that completely."

"I really think maybe you do," Sandra replied.

Doreen smiled. "I was married, and my husband re-placed me with a much younger woman, and I got nothing when he kicked me out, except for my twenty-year-old car and my dog, Mugs. I was lost and didn't know even the basics of so many life skills," she shared, then shrugged. "So, it was a really tough time for me, but I found a whole new lease on life by moving here. My grandmother has been an absolute godsend, and, since then, I found Mack and eventually got engaged."

Sandra shook her head. "I never had that serendipitous event," she said. "So, for me, life has been a series of never-ending close calls, but never anything really good."

"Is somebody out there you would like to spend time with?"

Sandra flushed and then nodded. "His wife passed away a couple years ago."

"Have you thought about maybe bucking the system and spending some time with him?"

"My uncle Clarence told me that it wouldn't be appro-priate."

"Appropriate?"

"Yeah, he's not wealthy, so he's not anybody special, I guess. He's not somebody who could move the family's careers forward," she muttered in disgust.

"Right, and, of course, that's the only thing that matters to them."

"Exactly," she agreed.

Knowing that time could run away on them and that Sandra may or may not continue to speak with her, Doreen got down to the matter at hand. "Why do you think your mother was murdered?"

"Because I'd only just had her checked out by a doctor,"

she stated, staring at her. "And she'd also warned me that if something happened to her, to look to the uncles." Doreen raised her eyebrows at that, and Sandra nodded. "What was I supposed to say? What was I supposed to do? I can't talk to them. It's not as if I get to speak," she explained. "They talk *at* me."

"Right," Doreen muttered, nodding. "I've had that happen a few times as well."

"Exactly, and I don't really have any leg to stand on. If I did anything to stand up to them in any way, I couldn't live here anymore."

"So, who lives here right now?"

"It's my carriage house," she stated, doing air quotes. "Yet it's not mine really. Apparently it's all part of the family trust, and, if I leave, I leave it behind, with no place to live and no money to live on."

"So, you have no way to support yourself. You have no personal money, correct?"

Sandra nodded.

"Which is what these kind of controlling men do, and this is how they keep you from becoming independent," Doreen noted.

Sandra stared at her, and once again tears filled her eyes. "I just wanted to have a life, just something better than what my mother had."

"But your mother made what, in their minds, was that one big mistake, and now you've paid for it all your life."

She nodded. "And so did my mother. After the birth, I think they were secretly hoping that either she would die in childbirth or I wouldn't make it," she muttered. "After that, she told me how the men just kept it quiet."

"Do you know of any children in the family who passed on?"

"Yes, there was one," Sandra noted. "It's always been hush-hush, and I don't really know very much about it."

"So, whose child was it?"

Sandra stared at her and said, "It was a long time ago."

"I know," Doreen stated, "but you need to tell me whose child it was."

"Don't you know?"

"I think I do, yeah, but again I need more than that."

"Right, it was Grandma Iris's," Sandra replied. "I don't know the details, but sometimes pregnancies go the way we want them to, and sometimes they don't."

"Of course," Doreen agreed, "and sometimes children are born, and then they die as toddlers."

"Yeah, you know there might have been something about that. I don't know the details. I wasn't privy to any information, and you can bet my grandmother never mentioned anything."

"Do you think the details bothered her?"

Sandra nodded. "I think they really bothered her. At least, that's what my mother said. She told me that there were all kinds of secrets in this family, and none of them were good."

"Secrets have a tendency to be that way," Doreen replied, with a smile. "People tend to get away with an awful lot of things because they think nobody will ever tell. But what I've found with the work I've been doing is that time runs out very quickly, and, while many people want to tell, some of the truth will die with them because all too many go to the grave, refusing to talk."

"That would be because of old Buck," Sandra muttered. "It would be a whole different story if he wasn't around."

"You're still afraid of him, aren't you?"

Sandra nodded, as a visible shudder ran through her body.

Doreen sighed. "He's in a retirement home, but you're still afraid of him."

"Yes," she cried out, "you don't understand. He's just mean."

Doreen nodded. "Do you think he ever hurt Iris?"

"I know he did. But I also heard the sons had a talk with Buck, and apparently they got him to stop somehow."

"Do you think they did that because they care?"

She shook her head. "No, they did it because they didn't want anybody getting caught. I don't think they particularly cared about their mother. She was nothing, just a doormat. I think they were more concerned about their father getting caught for something."

"You don't think they cared about their mother?"

"No, I don't. She did something that seemed to … somehow ostracize her from the family."

"As in had an affair?"

Sandra nodded slowly.

Doreen continued. "Did that result in a child, who might have died?"

Sandra stared at her. "I've never thought of that." She then shivered. "And that's not something I really want to think about now either," she declared, looking sick all of a sudden.

"If you think about something that would ostracize your grandmother from not only her husband but her sons as well, it would need to be something along that line. I don't know how strong of a faith they have, but—"

"It's a convenient faith," Sandra declared. "We pull it out and put it on display when we want to use it for something specific."

Doreen filed away that phrase in her mind because it was so true of some people, and she hadn't ever really considered it in that light before. "And, if your grandmother did have an affair, what do you think would have happened to her?"

"I would be surprised if she was still alive afterward."

"But she isn't though, is she?" Doreen asked. "How much do you know about the family?"

"I don't know anything," she muttered, "and honestly, I think, from their point of view, … I'm barely family at all."

"Right. Do you have any idea who your father is?"

Sandra shook her head. "No, I don't. I often thought that it might help me to adjust to my lot in life if I knew, but my mother went to great pains to keep it from me."

"Did she tell you that she just didn't want you to know, or did she tell you that she had no idea?"

Sandra frowned. "I'm not exactly sure. You're scaring me a little."

Doreen asked her, "Why?"

"Because I hadn't considered all these dark thoughts in terms of my family."

"Of course not," Doreen said, with a gentle smile. "None of us want to ever think of things in those terms."

"Do you have any family living?"

"I have a grandmother at Rosemoor."

"Ah." Sandra nodded. "Old Buck is at the other place, Riverdale."

"Yes, I haven't spoken to him, but I did understand he was there."

"You don't want to speak to him," Sandra declared. "He's very scary."

"Okay, I'll keep that in mind in case I ever do have to talk with him. Does he ever leave the home?"

"Not now. He's getting much too frail."

"Does it make you feel better to know that he'll be gone soon?"

Sandra winced. "Karma could get me for saying this, but, yes, absolutely. The thing is, it's not enough. Those two sons of his, my uncles, they're just as scary."

"I don't think I've ever met the one, but I did meet the other."

"Yeah? You would have met the politician, Clarence," she said, with an eye roll. "He thinks that he's some gift to the people. And that's women and men alike."

"Oh, interesting." Doreen smiled. "That's always a *fun* man."

"No, it's not," Sandra argued, staring at her. "You need to avoid them."

"And why is that?" she asked.

"Because they're really not the kind you can make accusations about and then walk away."

"Interesting, and I will keep that in mind. What is it that you think your mother did that got her killed?"

"She wanted to leave," Sandra stated. "They all had this huge family fight, and she planned to leave. She told them that she was done, that she was fed up, and that they couldn't force her to stay any longer. I hadn't even realized how much she was being forced to stay. At least in her mind."

Doreen waited and listened. "How soon after that did she pass on?"

"The next day," Sandra stated, "and, of course, from their point of view, it was a heart attack brought on by the stress of the argument. At least that's what they told me," she muttered, turning to face Doreen.

"And your mother was buried?"

"Cremated and then buried. I figured that was so nobody could find evidence."

"That's quite possible, yes," Doreen agreed. "I'm not sure about how drug detection tests work on ashes. I will have to ask an expert."

"You would think that the intense fire would burn everything."

"Maybe," Doreen replied, "but, every year, technology improves. And speaking of technology, you could always take a DNA sample and upload it to the genealogy database, and maybe eventually find out who your father is."

"Maybe," she conceded. "I've wondered about that every once in a while, but then I'm afraid to."

"Afraid, why?"

Sandra snorted. "You've got to understand my uncles and old Buck."

"Meaning that they wouldn't like it if you found out?"

"Something like that."

But she was very cagey about it, and Doreen had a terrible thought. "Or are you thinking that one of them could be your father?"

She winced and shuddered. "I would hope not," she gasped, white as sheet. "Dear God, I hope not."

"Did your mother ever say anything about sexual assault within the family?"

"No, she never did, and I would hope that wasn't it."

"If you did find out the truth, it would put a lot of these worries to rest."

"But what if it's the worst possible truth?"

"Maybe it is," Doreen replied, "but we tend to build up all this in our mind so much that it becomes very difficult to find out the truth because our fears are so prevalent."

"Maybe," Sandra said, then shuddered once more.

"How often do you see your family?"

"I don't. I live in this little carriage house, and they pretend that I just don't exist."

"I'm sorry. That's a tough way to live."

"Maybe. But maybe it doesn't matter anymore," she muttered.

"But you're not all that old yourself."

"I'm old enough," she muttered, "and I'm okay to end this life too."

"But what if you could have a life with this man who you like?"

She smiled at Doreen. "I'm not against that, but I'm pretty sure the family would never allow it."

"What if the family doesn't have any say in it?" she asked. "You two could move away and could have a life of your own."

She shook her head. "You have no idea what a stranglehold the family has on me."

"Even if Buck was out of the picture?"

"Maybe," she muttered. "I don't know."

Doreen left it for the moment. "If you ever want help doing the DNA, you just let me know. I just did it for a resident at the home, at Rosemoor."

"And which resident is that?" Sandra asked, looking at her.

"Richie," Doreen replied.

Sandra's eyes widened. "Richie? As in ninety-years-old Richie?"

"Yeah," Doreen confirmed. "Do you know him?"

"My mother mentioned something about him."

"That your grandmother Iris had an affair with him? Because that is something I do know."

"Good God, I'm surprised he's still alive, if Buck knows."

"Maybe that was something Buck and Iris fought about all the time, and maybe that was one of the reasons she stayed with old Buck."

"If she stayed and it was because of that, she would have stayed to keep Richie safe."

"I don't think Richie and Iris had a relationship for very long," Doreen shared, gazing at Sandra closely. "But I could be wrong."

"I do remember that name though," she muttered. "And the story was that Buck had quite a snit over it all, and then seemed to be quite calm about it. As if something had blown over, and the best man won or something. He apparently never seemed to worry about it afterward."

Doreen nodded. "We've got all kinds of tests running right now. So, I'm sure the truth will come out at some point in time."

"You really got Richie's DNA?"

"We really did." Doreen smiled. "We've been doing it with lots of other cases as well."

"Right." Sandra frowned at Doreen. "I feel as if you're trying to tell me something."

"I'm wondering about the sense of telling you more," Doreen admitted. "In the coroner's office is a box of bones. The bones are that of an approximately eighteen-month-old child, found thirty-five years ago in southeast Kelowna."

Sandra's eyes widened. "Good God." She stuttered and sputtered. "What's that got to do with us?"

"The child's body was broken, as in beaten," Doreen

shared, "or run over, or something equally catastrophic. The child was not buried in a coffin, was not buried in a formal funeral setting. She was tossed in a pillowcase and buried in a garden, only to be discovered years later, when someone dug up that garden in order to plant yams."

Sandra shook her head. "That poor baby," she cried out.

Doreen nodded. "The thing is, we uploaded the DNA from the bones to one of the genealogy sites," she explained, "and it came back as a match to your family."

Chapter 26

AFTER DOREEN SHARED that info, Sandra had been beside herself, not able to talk very much. So Doreen had quickly taken her leave, adding that she would call her in the morning—which may not be an optimal solution to this mess either. But Doreen needed answers, and Sandra seemed to quite possibly be the best place to get them from, at least for the moment.

As Doreen walked out to her car with the animals, Mugs sniffed the air and started to growl. She turned and looked around but couldn't see anything wrong. "What's the matter, sweetie?"

He was still not happy, but he got into the vehicle willingly enough. Not sure what that was all about, but not willing to stick around to see if something would jump out of the shadows, Doreen intended to head home but instead pulled up to Riverdale, the other senior home. She sat in her vehicle for a long time, wondering just what had caused her to stop here. Getting out, she turned, looked at the animals, and said, "I'll be back in a few minutes."

Mugs didn't like that at all. He barked and barked, jumping up against the window glass. She frowned. "Okay, fine. I don't know what this is all about, or why you're so upset, but I'll take you. I guess you all might as well come along."

And as soon as she put him on the leash, he calmed down, and Doreen led the way to the receptionist and frowned. "Are you Tabitha?"

The woman nodded. "Yes."

"I'm Doreen. You look a little different today."

Tabitha laughed. "I had my hair done."

"Oh my, I'm so sorry, I should have recognized you right away."

"No, I'm quite happy that you didn't," she replied, looking around carefully. "I was attempting to change my whole look."

"You certainly did that, and you succeeded quite nicely," Doreen said, with a bright smile.

"What can I do for you?" Tabitha asked in a formal tone of voice.

"I heard that Lilybeth spoke to a couple people the same morning she died."

"I think it was, jeez, who was it? … I think it was old Buck. Did you want to talk to him?"

"I don't know. Do I?" Doreen asked.

"Probably not," Tabitha replied, with a laugh. "He's definitely one of our crankier inmates."

She rolled her eyes at her. "*Inmates, huh*?"

"Ooh, ouch." Tabitha laughed at the instinctive term. "I shouldn't have said that," she muttered. "But I've got to tell you, in his case, he's definitely one of the crankier people we have."

"Of course," Doreen agreed. "Where would he happen to be just now, do you know?"

"He's around terrorizing somebody I'm sure," she said, with a smile. "Let me take a look and see if he wants to visit with you. I presume it's about Lilybeth's death?"

"I would certainly appreciate talking to somebody about it."

"Of course. I hadn't realized you were such a close family friend."

"And, even then, I wonder how close I was."

"That's the way of family," she noted.

"And the way of friends," Doreen muttered.

As Tabitha rang Buck's room from the receptionist's deck, Tabitha frowned and shook her head. "He's not answering."

"Okay, that's fine," Doreen replied, casually looking around the empty hall. "It's not as if I was expecting to see him."

"Maybe not, but I'm sure if he knew you were here, he would talk to you."

"Oh? And why is that?"

"Because he prides himself on being a detective himself. He mentioned that he should talk to the police about something."

"Now that is interesting. A confession?"

She burst out laughing. "Oh no, he's not the kind to confess on his own, but he is the kind to make other people pay for stuff," she muttered, with a shake of her head.

"That doesn't sound good."

"No, he's not the easiest person to get along with. We've certainly had that discussion with him about multiple issues in the past."

"Ah, well, I wouldn't want to set him off."

"No, I don't think you would, but he was spouting long

and loud about the fact that, being where he is, where all of them are, makes him quite vulnerable, and he was using Lilybeth as an example." Doreen frowned at her, and Tabitha nodded. "Of course we all know she died of a heart attack, but he was still carrying on about it."

"And is he carrying on as someone who got away with murder, or does he sincerely believe he needs protection, and somebody should be doing more about it?"

"That's also fascinating because it was more of the second way."

Doreen just stared at her, stumped.

Tabitha nodded. "I know, right? Almost everybody in this home would have thought it would be as you first said, but he was seemingly much more upset that she was gone."

"So, maybe he had a little soft spot in his heart for her."

"Maybe," Tabitha conceded, "but I don't think she had a soft spot in her heart for him."

"Ooh, ouch."

"Exactly. That's the reaction from all the women here."

"So maybe Lilybeth spoiled his advances, and hers may not have been so nice of a rejection either."

"I think she probably did," Tabitha nodded, with a smile. "And there's nothing you can do about any of it."

"Maybe not," Doreen admitted, "but I definitely want to speak with him."

"Let me try him again." This time someone came on the other end. Tabitha explained that Doreen was here. Then Tabitha nodded and hung up. "He's ready to see you." Tabitha gave Doreen the room number and simple directions on how to find him.

Doreen moved past the front desk, and Tabitha didn't say anything about the animals, which was also fascinating and a little difficult. She looked down at Mugs, trotting at her side, seemingly without a care in the world. Goliath was a different story. He was slinking along, not happy to be here at all. But the smells in the home were definitely not ones that she would expect him to be very comfortable with either, although they weren't any different from Rosemoor.

Buck's room was not very far away, and, as she knocked, a voice called out, "Come in."

She opened the door to see an old man, but the grin on his face revealed absolutely nothing good about him. She left the door open, and, stepping inside, she nodded. "Hi, I'm Doreen."

"I know who you are," he stated, with a wave of his hand. "You're the one who killed my lady."

She stared at him, nonplussed. "I'm what?"

"You're the one who killed Lilybeth."

"And how do you figure that?" she asked, staring at him in shock. "I wasn't even here when she died."

"Maybe not, but she was devastated that it was all about to come out."

"Interesting, and was she really *your* lady?" she asked him. "Because, according to one of the people I talked to, you didn't have a lady friend, and Lilybeth in particular had rejected you."

"Oh, she didn't say no," he argued. "She was just playing hard to get. They all play hard to get." He shrugged. "Everybody does, and they don't mean it, but that's just the way they act. Women, they're really useless."

Then he gave Doreen that same smile, and she had to admit it almost terrorized her, and she didn't even know the old man. "So, that's what you do? You just terrorize people here?" she asked, staring at him. "You've got nothing better to do?"

"Been doing it all my life, so why would I stop now?" He snorted, as he glared at her. "And who are you to tell me what to do?"

"Nobody, apparently," she said. "I was under the impression that you are the one who killed Lilybeth."

He stared at her in shock, and she watched as a foaming spittle formed at the corners of his mouth. "I would never," he roared.

And she had to admit, based on his reaction and the way he spoke, she believed him. So, if not him, who did?

Chapter 27

DOREEN LUCKILY DODGED whatever Buck had reached for and then tossed at her. She stepped out into the hallway and slammed the door shut behind her, as something—maybe a shoe—hit hard against the door.

Two women, walking down the hallway, noted the room number, and chuckled. "At least you got out. He hit the last lady who went in there."

Doreen shook her head. "Wow, no wonder he's not popular."

The two older ladies laughed. "You've got to keep your distance from him. He's got gropey hands."

"That's not good," Doreen said. "You should be safe in this place."

"We should be, and now that he's in rough shape, we are safe. Before, when he could get around better, not so much. I actually left Riverdale for a bit but had to return because I just couldn't handle being on my own. However, I came back under the condition that I had nothing to do with him and that I was at the opposite end of the home."

"And yet you still have to go past his room," Doreen noted.

"I can now because he can't move very quickly anymore. Regardless he would persist and persist and persist."

"I hope nobody gives in to him," Doreen noted, frowning at the women. "That's abuse, pure and simple."

"The family donates a lot to Riverdale, so I don't think anybody here is in a position to complain about his behavior."

Doreen just stared at them and finally nodded.

One of the women added, "It's just a bad deal for a lot of people."

Doreen frowned. "But still, you shouldn't have to deal with that. Neither should the staff, for that matter."

The women smiled. "Thank you, dear, for caring, but you can't stop it by words alone."

Doreen winced and nodded. "You're right." Then something else hit the door.

The two women laughed. "The fact that he's still throwing a temper tantrum is also a delight," said one of the women.

The other one also seemed delighted, as she noted, "He does this all the time, and we're always so sad when somebody can't quite avoid him. But now that he's incapacitated to the point that he can't run the hallways as he used to do, it's a whole lot better in here. We'll stay in Riverdale now just because he can't bother us as much as he used to do."

"What exactly did he do?" Doreen asked in shock.

"Chase us down the hallway, chase us into our rooms. If we didn't make it there in time to lock him out, we had to call for help multiple times. I don't know if everybody escaped him though," the one woman shared, turning to look at her companion.

The other woman winced. "I don't know either, but

heaven help them if they didn't."

"And was he that … *active*, even if he was rejected?"

"Yes, he was," they declared shortly. "He either black-mailed people, or—" They looked at each other and stopped.

Doreen asked cautiously, "Or?"

"Some of the people here don't have a ton of money," one woman explained. "So I think there may have been some financial arrangements made."

Doreen sighed. "There's no way to say this nicely, but I guess men are still being men, aren't they?" At that, one of the women laughed. "That is one of the things we really struggled with ourselves when we moved in because we thought for sure that was not a thing now. Yet apparently it's not only still a thing but it's a big thing."

Doreen winced and nodded. "Well, ladies, thank you very much for telling me."

"No problem, and I can tell you that none of the people out front will be honest with you about him."

"So, what then? Does he just stay in his room until they let him out?"

"Oh, he's not locked in. And, if we tell them when we go down there that he was throwing things at you, they just threaten to lock him in, but nothing would really happen."

"I suppose at some point in time he's considered dangerous, hopefully?"

"*Nah*. I don't see it happening. I think he puts too much money into Riverdale," one of the women stated. "He is dangerous, but he always has been. Now he's mostly just a pain in my backside."

And, with that, still laughing and knowing that their laughter was loud enough that Buck could hear them, they walked down the hallway, almost singing. As Doreen stared at the door, another object hit the door hard. Maybe he got angrier because he couldn't even get out of his room to do more.

She hurried down to the front door and outside. She caught sight of the receptionist, who had a smug look on her face. When she stopped and stared, the woman wiped the smile off her face and buried her head, picking up the phone, trying to make it look as if she had no clue what was going on. For the first time Doreen realized that maybe Tabitha had a whole lot more going on here than others realized.

As soon as Doreen got back home again, she phoned Sandra and asked, "Do you know Tabitha from the Riverdale home?"

"Of course I do. She's my cousin."

"*Right*, that makes total sense."

"In what way does that make sense?" Sandra asked.

"Something about a look on her face."

"If she let you in to see Buck, you can bet she was smirking in the hallway."

"And why is that?"

"She hates him with a passion."

"Really?"

"Yeah, really," Sandra confirmed, "but then I don't know who doesn't." And, with that, she disconnected.

Chapter 28

DOREEN MADE HERSELF a bowl of soup and a sandwich for lunch, while she pondered the events of the morning. When the phone rang, it was Sandra again.

"You asked about Tabitha earlier?"

"Yes, I did."

"I understand old Buck had a very bad morning."

"I imagine he did. And, when you say she doesn't like him, is there a particular reason?"

"It's not so much that she doesn't like him as much as she's determined to get whatever inheritance is coming her way early, so she can get out of town."

"Do you think she'll get any inheritance?"

"I'm not sure. Her father is a powerful man in town, and the family has quite a few businesses, but working for the family is not anything she's ever wanted to do."

"*Hmm,* yet maybe she would be good at it."

An odd sound came from the other end. "Sounds as if you didn't hit it off."

"Something in her gaze showed me a different side of her."

"Oh, yes, indeed. She's her father's daughter," Sandra

declared bitterly. "If we're downtown or outside, and she sees me, she'll cross the street to get away from me."

"That's just rude."

"Not only that, Tabitha's been known to make up tales about my mother and spread them."

"I'm sorry. That's not a very nice family."

"No, it isn't."

"Do you know what training Tabitha had to work at a retirement home?"

"She was a nurse of some kind, and then there was this big hullabaloo about it. Now she's just working at the front desk, while there's an investigation of some kind."

"Interesting. As in doing something wrong maybe?"

"I don't know," Sandra replied. "Honestly, I stay away from the whole family."

"So, is Tabitha the daughter of Clarence or Carl?"

"She's Clarence's daughter."

"Interesting. I haven't even met Carl yet."

"He's always traveling all over the place, doing his big business deals," she muttered. "He doesn't really make much time for anybody here. The two brothers don't get along that well." She let out a big sigh. "Honestly, I think he stays away to avoid Clarence."

"And yet Clarence thinks he's that big, magnanimous, very popular guy."

"That's what he wants you to think," she said, "but, the truth is, most people don't like him. And he's known for his shady business dealings."

"You really need to get away from this family, don't you?" Doreen noted.

"Yeah, I do, but it's not quite so easy."

"Maybe you can start by picking up the phone and contacting the widower you know because, although it might need to start from him, from his perspective, he's not likely in a position to do anything as long as the family has that same hold on you that it had before."

"I'll think about it," Sandra said. When she went to hang up, she added, "You need to be careful."

"I know. I need to be more than careful now."

"Has anything else happened?"

"Yeah, I made the mistake of seeing old Buck. He threw a fit, throwing all kinds of things at the door."

"But he didn't hit you?" she asked anxiously.

"No, he didn't hit me, not to mention that I had the animals with me."

"Did he hit them? Because he really hates them."

"No, he didn't hit them either," she replied, with a gentle smile, even though the other woman couldn't see it over the phone. "That's definitely not something Mugs would take kindly to."

"No, but if Buck had his way, he would set it up so your dog bit him, and he would make sure that the pound got involved, and you would have to shoot him," Sandra explained. "Buck wants everything his way, and, if he can take away something that's precious and special, he will."

And, with that, she was gone.

Chapter 29

DOREEN THOUGHT ABOUT Sandra's words long afterward. It revealed so much about who old Buck was that he would try to take away something that somebody cared for and about. Was that what happened to Baby Jane? Had he done it more—not because of Richie or whoever the father may be—to spite the mother and to keep Iris under his control?

Thinking about the old Buck character Doreen had met, the look in his eyes, and what she'd heard about him, she realized that one element of Buck's personality made the most sense, more than anything else.

She picked up the phone and called Elizabeth.

"And again you call," the coroner muttered in exasperation.

Doreen winced. "Sorry, I keep forgetting you have a job."

"I do have a job, and it keeps me quite busy," she spat. "What did you find?"

"Ha," Doreen replied. "I'll call you back in a few days when you've got time."

"Oh no you don't," she snapped. "You've already distracted me, so spit it out."

"I wanted to ask you something about the bones."

"What about them?" she asked.

"Would those breaks have all happened around the same time?"

"Meaning?"

"Apparently old Buck Winters likes to control people and will do anything necessary to make that happen." Then she explained what Sandra had shared, using Mugs as an example. Doreen finally realized what Richie had been telling her all along.

"Ah, one of those guys, is he?" Elizabeth groaned.

"Plus, as I left his apartment, he threw at least four objects at the door and not in quick succession. His anger lingers."

"So, what are you thinking?"

"I'm wondering if he would have killed the child in order to keep his wife under control, to keep her terrified, to keep her there as part of his life, even if he didn't want her."

"That would be a real bad move."

"Particularly if the child wasn't his," she pointed out. "He could disassociate completely from any sense of emotion about the child."

"It's still a bad move."

"I'm not arguing that at all. Apparently this guy is very much that kind of person. So I could see him taking his frustration out on that child, long after she died even."

"Oh boy," Elizabeth muttered. "I'll take another look at the toddler's bones. I don't remember all the details on that particular case, but it's definitely possible."

"I'm thinking maybe one beating killed the child, potentially right in front of Iris—maybe more than one. And, if

Buck wanted to terrorize Iris further, he would just toss Baby Jane in a pillowcase and chuck her out in the garden."

"And did they own that property way back when?"

"I'm still going through all the county records, but it looks to be one of their rental properties."

"So, he could have just walked from wherever they lived at the time and dumped it on a nearby rental land."

"That's what I was thinking," Doreen stated, "and of course I don't want to think that, but ..."

"But it's hard not to, isn't it?"

"It absolutely is hard not to. Considering Buck was *that kind of guy*, it wouldn't surprise me in the least."

"He shouldn't get to sail through life without paying for that," Elizabeth declared, the fury evident in her tone.

"And we don't know that for sure, and I can only do so much until we get more DNA results."

"Right, and you think he would prefer to do that to the mother, as versus, say, making the father pay?"

"I think he terrified the father enough early on that he was satisfied the man would never be around Iris again. Maybe he figured that was punishment enough and that no other man would come sniffing around again either. I don't really know."

"What do you mean, you don't know?" Elizabeth quipped with half a sigh, now rummaging through something. "It seems as if you have ferreted out quite a bit already."

"I have ferreted out quite a bit, but I haven't got it all yet, and there's so much more that I need to sort out."

"Of course." More sounds were heard from her end. "But, in answer to your question, yes, it's quite possible that all these bones were broken at the same time."

Armed with that information, Doreen pondered what was going on and how she could prove it because Elizabeth was right. Without any evidence, Buck would get away with it. What Doreen didn't know was whether anybody else had been involved in the toddler's death. It was too horrific to even contemplate, yet usually so much more motivated people to do these heinous acts that she couldn't just write off the chance that one of the sons wasn't involved somehow as well. She considered whether it was truly just the massive ego of Buck that had done nothing but terrorize this town. If that were the case, why was he even in a retirement home? She wished she could find some more information on that and decided to call Sandra back again.

"Now what?" Sandra asked reluctantly.

"The home where Buck is—Riverdale—does your family own it?"

"Not anymore," she said. "I don't think so. There was a time when I think they did, and a big company from back east bought it out, but a condition of the sale was that Buck gets to stay there."

"Ah, so he *wants* to be there."

"Sure, he does. He's king of the castle there, isn't he?" she muttered, with a bitterness that seemed to surprise even Sandra herself.

"Understood," Doreen murmured. "I guess I was trying to figure out whether your cousin Tabitha had something to do with it."

"I don't think so, although I think she's … I don't want to say she's *learning* from him because I think she already learned everything quite well."

"You really don't have anything to do with them, do you?"

"No, and I don't want to, and believe me that they don't want me to either. Now, if you don't mind, this is exhausting, and I really just want to forget about it for a while."

After she disconnected, Doreen contemplated Sandra's reaction and realized it was a perfectly natural response on her part. A lot of upsetting family issues and a lot of potential issues were involved in all this, but still, one question remained.

"If her mother, Claudia, had been murdered, why?" Doreen asked out loud. "Was it because she was asking questions that nobody wanted asked, or was it something else entirely?"

Knowing that she would piss off Sandra, but needing to find out for sure, Doreen called her back, and when she answered, her voice trembling with fatigue, Sandra muttered, "Please stop."

"I know. I know, and believe me that I want to stop as well, but I do have to ask you another question." Then she barreled on, not giving Sandra a chance to refuse. "What was the gain for somebody killing your mother?"

Then came dead silence. Finally Sandra said, "You haven't figured it out yet?"

"I've figured out all kinds of stuff, but figuring out people who are so very twisted means there can be multiple reasons. So was Claudia killed just because she asked questions about her mother, that she wanted to leave the area, or was there something else?"

"I think it was her asking questions, but she also found a baby book my grandmother had hung on to, and I guess nobody had seen it or had found it to throw it away. And that's when my mother really started asking questions."

"Which baby book was this?"

"I don't know for certain, but I presume it had to do with the toddler in the coroner's office."

"How would Claudia know about that?"

"Because she was alive at that time, and so was my grandmother. My mother told me that my grandmother had a really bad time over it all and almost had a complete collapse."

"Ah," Doreen muttered, "which just lends more credence to the child being your blood relative and also to your family wanting to put a stop to Claudia's questions."

"Exactly. My grandmother was hysterical, and she had to be put on medication. Claudia kept the secret until my grandmother had passed away, but once Iris was gone, that's when my mother started asking questions."

Doreen winced.

"I don't know what else it would be," Sandra said. "That's why I'm telling you that you need to be careful. Whatever they're trying to keep from you, they won't just tell you to leave and hope you go away. They'll be very clear-cut about it all."

"Oh, I get it," Doreen replied. "Still, if that little girl was murdered, somebody knows about it. And, with the burial done out back of one of the family rental properties, that's just beyond cold."

"Is that where she was found?" Sandra asked, getting choked up with tears in her throat. "I knew it was someplace in southeast Kelowna, but I hadn't really figured out where and hadn't put too much effort into finding out more," she admitted. "There's only so much pain anybody can handle. Now please let me get a little rest and distance before you call me back again," she suggested. "I know I went down this pathway today, but it's not an easy one to be on. And I really, really don't want to face the family. If they put me out on the street, I have no place to go."

Chapter 30

LATER THAT NIGHT Doreen was warming up the leftover pasta from the previous evening when Mack arrived. She smiled up at him as he walked over and gave her a big hug.

"You okay?" he asked Doreen.

She winced at the fatigue in his expression. "Hard day?"

"Yeah," he said. "Sometimes court can be the worst part of the job, but, with any luck, it's over now."

"That would be nice," she agreed.

"How have you been doing?"

"Getting into trouble by just asking questions," she admitted, followed by a shrug. "Something I seem to do quite naturally."

"That you do," he confirmed. "So, what happened now?" So, she explained the information she had ferreted out. "Good Lord."

She nodded. "I know. It's kind of shocking, kind of scary, kind of mean," she muttered. "And people all over the place are terrified of that old man."

"Interesting," he murmured, as he sat down and tucked into the leftovers with her. He didn't say a whole lot while they were eating, but, when he pushed away his empty plate, he asked, "Do you want me to go talk to the old man?"

"I don't know if it'll do any good," she replied. "He certainly seems to think he's above the law or he can bypass the law. He apparently can't get kicked out of Riverdale because of the agreement with the current owners and the amount of money the Winters family donates to Riverdale and things like that."

"And yet it wouldn't matter what agreement he had with the owners if any of the women filed a formal complaint. He would be dealt with, by lawyers and the court."

"But then the women would have been kicked out of their homes, and I'm sure he made them very much aware of that eventuality."

"Of course," Mack muttered in disgust. "It sure doesn't make him look very good, does it?"

"Not only him but I'm still questioning the involvement of his sons."

"And that's a whole different kettle of fish."

"I know. Believe me, … I know."

"The question is, how do we find out if they were involved? And, if they were, the only way we'll find out is through a confession."

"Even if you got the old man talking, he would recant anyway," she declared, with a wave of her hand. "He's just that kind of a guy."

Mack burst out laughing. "You really don't like him, do you?"

"You should have seen him," she stated. "That sense of power gone wrong, … that sense of righteous arrogance, while doing whatever he wanted, knowing that nobody had any way to stop him." She shook her head. "You wouldn't like him at all."

"No, I can tell I wouldn't," he agreed with a smile, as he looked at her. "And it's obvious you don't either."

"No, I don't," she stated. "It's hard to like anybody like that, but at least he's kind of contained where he's at right now."

"So, what are you thinking?"

"I think Buck killed Iris's child from her lover," she declared. "I think Buck buried it in the garden of some nearby rental place, told her what he'd done, then used it against her all the time to keep her with him. At this point, I'm not sure that Iris was killed, now that I see how this all played out. She may very well have committed suicide, which they may have covered up because of the church's teachings."

"Are they a church-going family?"

"They were at one time, but I suspect Buck probably figures he's better than God and may have left the church."

"Right," Mack noted, "or it could be that Buck still is part of the church."

"Maybe, but I don't know which church would have him."

Mack chuckled. "No, and I could get into trouble for saying this, but you know when you tithe, and you tithe a lot, that money is something a lot of people will protect."

"It's still wrong though," she pointed out. "There is nothing nice about this man."

"So, a lot of people would say he needed the church even more then. Somebody needed to save his soul."

She shrugged. "Or we could just toss him out and let the devil deal with him."

He burst out laughing. "You do know that many would take umbrage against you for that."

"I know, and I don't mean it the wrong way," she added. "But say Buck did this, say he killed an innocent child, because it was a child Iris absolutely adored, and, if Buck found out something about the child, such as its not being his, that's a reason why he would have killed the child. And then he would have held it over Iris's head from then on, and I'm sure that would have just worn her down."

"And the death of Sandra's mother, Claudia?"

"Apparently, after Iris's death, Claudia started asking questions that made people angry. I guess when the child was killed, Iris went to pieces, was put on drugs, and everybody kept it quiet. However, Claudia suspected something more was involved that nobody was talking about. She had also found a baby book but didn't really investigate that child until after her mother passed away, as it upset Iris so much."

"Of course, nobody was talking about the dead child," he stated, staring at her, "particularly back in those days."

"It's not even about *those days*," Doreen clarified. "It's about that family, the Winters family, right? And the minute it involves *family*, everything goes bad."

"We'll have to work on your concept of family," he muttered.

"It's certainly getting a twisted view in this case when it comes to the Winters family," she acknowledged.

"Anybody mention a name for this child?"

"No, but now that you mentioned it, I didn't ask either."

"I wonder if there's any letter or anything from her grandmother that may be still around, something that would give some credence to this whole story."

"You mean, the proof that I need?" she asked, looking at him. "Like maybe a baby book with the birth certificate and a photo of the child, hopefully?"

"Considering I've spent however many days it's been in court, trying to back up all these charges with proof and more proof," he shared, rolling his eyes, "yeah, that would help."

"It is a question I'll have to ask Sandra tomorrow," Doreen noted. "I did promise to leave her alone for the rest of today. I guess I pushed it and was calling her a little too much with more questions."

He nodded. "You can really badger people when you get going."

She winced. "I'm not trying to," she wailed soulfully. "I'm just trying to find answers."

"And because you're trying to find answers, and you're a bit of a terror when you're bothered," he noted, "you tend to badger people." She glared at him, and he chuckled. "Some people don't mind. For other people, like this Sandra, it's opening up wounds," he pointed out. "You've got to remember that she is a victim too."

"I know," Doreen muttered. "And it's really sad listening to her talk about the family, about what her life is like. Although she didn't really share much, it's obvious it's been painful and not something she is really prepared to go into too much detail about."

"You wouldn't want to either," Mack said, "so let's give her a little bit of privacy."

"I will, but you know what it's like when you've got questions you need answered, and I can't just … stop."

He grinned. "I do know exactly what that's like," he stated, "but also remember that they are not obligated to talk to you at all. So you've really done pretty well, getting as much as you have from her."

"I know." Doreen groaned. "It's just so frustrating when people keep all these secrets inside. If they would just answer the questions, then I'll be happy to go away."

"Except you don't. You don't go away," he said, with a big smile. "You come back with more questions."

She stared at him, and her shoulders sagged. "You're right. I do, but it's because I haven't gotten to the bottom of it yet."

"And, for Sandra, it's something that she's had to live with for a long time, and she's successfully blocked it out. She has pushed it to the absolute limit of what she can handle, and now you're opening it all back up again."

"And yet it's her mother, and it's her grandmother, and it's potentially her half-aunt. All these things should matter."

"Oh, it matters," Mack said. "Absolutely it matters, but these people also need time. They need time to process."

"And what if there isn't any time?" she asked, staring at him. "I raced to Riverdale to talk to Lilybeth because I just had that feeling, and yet I was already too late."

"But you don't know for sure that her death was murder. She may have just had a heart attack."

"I know, and I'm still waiting for the tox screen from Elizabeth."

He asked, "You're on a first-name basis with the coroner already?"

She nodded. "Yeah, she's been very good at answering my questions today."

He stared at her and shook his head. "I wouldn't have thought that was possible. She's generally not considered to be all that friendly."

"No, probably not." Doreen shrugged. "Once I explained the whys and what questions I was asking, I think

Elizabeth got just as involved in the outcome as I did." Doreen laughed. "Honestly, I wouldn't be surprised if she doesn't call me next."

"Oh, that's interesting," Mack muttered. "I hadn't considered a possible friendship for you in that direction, but you know, maybe …"

"The captain said we were two peas in a pod, but I don't think we have any similarities at all. What we do have in common is how our minds work, with all that delving, probing, and our insistent need to figure things out."

"You absolutely do." He smiled. "And, in that regard, I would agree. You do have a lot in common."

"I don't know," she muttered. "She was getting a little irritated with me today too."

He burst out laughing. "She does have a job, you know?"

"I know. I know, and I did apologize," she shared, with a grin in his direction. "Elizabeth didn't seem to be too upset."

"No, believe me, if she wanted you to buzz off, she would just tell you to buzz off," he stated. "Now, can we turn our attention to something not work related?"

"Sure," she replied.

As they got up and took their tea to the living room, he began, "I would bring up the wedding as a topic, but it's probably a little too early."

"It is a little too early."

"Okay, well, maybe you could at least give me some idea of what quarter of the year you want to do it."

"Fourth," she replied instantly. When he looked at her, she shrugged. "That was instinctive."

"Instinctive why?" he asked.

She groaned. "Because it gives me the most amount of time to adjust to the idea."

He searched her face and then agreed. "And, because I know where you're coming from, I'm fine with that."

"Are you sure?" she asked, raising her eyebrows.

"Yes, I'm fine with it. The last thing I want is for you to feel pressured into this." She looked at him, and her lips twitched. Mack groaned and added, "Okay, I don't want you to feel pressured into this because I don't want you to back out."

"I don't break promises," she declared. "I just need time. It's not been all that long for me, and I don't want to get married again if I'm not ready."

"Okay," he said, but he looked a little worried.

"Do you think I should talk to a therapist?" she asked.

He now looked surprised and then shrugged. "If you want to, absolutely. If it'll help you get over Mathew, I'm all for it. I keep forgetting that he was your husband for a long time and your marriage to him sucked, plus the manner of his death and the way the whole thing played out has to be added stress too."

"The marriage itself was stressful enough," she shared, "but a part of me says I'm still making too much of it."

"No," he disagreed. "If you need to talk to somebody about Mathew, then you should talk to them about it. I'm fine with that."

She smiled. "I forget how reasonable you are."

"How can you possibly forget that?" he teased, with a laugh. "I tell you all the time."

She burst out laughing and agreed. "That you do, and I appreciate it." Just then her phone rang. She looked down at it and laughed. "It's Elizabeth." He stared at her, and she answered the phone. "Hi, Elizabeth."

"Hey, so—" And then she stopped.

"Problems?"

"I'm in a conundrum as to whether I should be talking to you or directly to the police."

"As it turns out, Mack's right here, so how about I put you on Speakerphone?"

"Oh, that'll be perfect," she replied. "Mack, how are you doing?"

"Been in court for too many days," he grumbled.

"Oh, ouch. Sorry about that."

"Thanks. I know it's a necessary part of the job, and sometimes it's a breeze, but then there are other days," he muttered. "So, what have you found?"

"I'm calling to let you know that I found traces of a poison that can bring on a heart attack in Lilybeth's system." She took another moment to add, "It's pretty rare, but it's something that just a pinprick can bring on."

"And how fast acting is it?"

"Lilybeth was very small, barely one hundred pounds from what I could see. Now, I didn't weigh her, but considering her very slight stature, it would have happened very quickly."

"As in her making her way back to her apartment maybe? Considering they were in the same building, or is that too fast?"

"I'm not an expert on toxicology," she noted, "but I will say that was certainly within the realm of possibility."

"That's just very depressing," he said, then shook his head. "You've released the body, correct?"

"I have," she confirmed, "and honestly only because of Doreen did I take the samples that I did. I didn't do an autopsy, but, when she brought this up, I decided to take samples for further testing, and sure enough she was right."

There was such a note of admiration in Elizabeth's tone that Mack rolled his eyes as he looked over at Doreen, who beamed at him. "I don't know how, and I don't know why," he admitted, chuckling, "but, darn it, … she often is correct."

Elizabeth laughed. "I don't have to tell you that we can't use her methods for our court cases, but it sure helps to point us in the right direction."

He agreed, "Yeah, that sums up my life with her."

At that, Elizabeth replied, "You guys need to tell me how you want to proceed. I'll be changing the cause of death because of this, and I will inform the family tomorrow."

"Is there any family?" Doreen asked. "I thought Lilybeth was the last of her line, or near enough."

"Right. So I have a representative noted, a nurse, who apparently works at the home, at Riverdale."

"Oh no," Doreen muttered. "Are you by any chance talking about Tabitha?"

"Hang on. Yes, I am. Why? Do you know her?"

"Yes, because Tabitha works at Riverdale and is part of the Winters family."

Chapter 31

MACK WAS BACK at work. He'd phoned the captain last night from her house and then headed straight back to the office. She'd protested about not wanting to send him off to work in the evening, but he just shrugged it off and stated that it was a completely different story now. He needed to go in and to confirm people were on top of this purported death by murder of Lilybeth.

Doreen nodded and didn't say anything else.

When he turned back to her, she groaned and held up her hand. "I know. I know. It's an active case now," she stated in a mimicking tone.

"I would usually say that, yes, but now I'm not so sure, just because you are already involved in it."

"I didn't create this mess," she declared, with a gasp.

"No, I didn't mean it like that," he said, taking her hand. "I'm just thinking about how much involvement we need you to have."

"You need to go talk to Buck Winters and his sons, Clarence and Carl. They are all rotten, so that won't be any fun. Expect to have things thrown at you." When he frowned at her, she winced. "Yeah, I didn't get a chance to tell you about that part." And she proceeded to tell him about her visit with Buck at the home.

"Good heavens."

"Yeah, and apparently the family used to own Riverdale, and they sold out to a bigger company—at least that's what I was told. I guess a large company was buying retirement homes across the province," she added. "So, … anyway, the agreement with the new Riverdale owner was that Buck got to stay there for life. So, he pretty much just terrorizes everybody else there."

"Sounds as if they bought him a spot to hide him away."

"Sure, but it's also government-subsidized for people who have income issues, and I believe that a lot of the women there don't feel as if they can escape Buck, where he is free to be *him*."

He stared at her, shaking his head as he walked out. Then he called back, "Lock the door."

She locked the door, then didn't hear him leave. So she opened her front door and stepped out onto the porch to see him talking on the phone inside his vehicle. He honked at her and then he put away his phone and drove off. She went to step back inside when she noted Richard was out on his front step, watching her. "Everything okay?" she asked him.

His eyebrows shot up. "Everything is okay with me. Is everything okay with you?" he asked, and concern filled his tone.

She smiled at him mistily. "It's another one of those cases where I was hoping it wouldn't pan out as I fear it will."

He rolled his eyes at that. "In other words, you're up to your usual tricks."

"Maybe," she agreed, "but I was really hoping to be wrong in this case."

"But you weren't?"

She shook her head. "No, I wasn't. And that's really sad."

"What's it about?"

"Some lady at the old folks' home was murdered, and everybody thought she just had a heart attack."

He stared at her. "Down at Rosemoor?" he cried out.

"No, over at Riverdale."

He frowned at her. "I did hear something about that." He pondered it for a moment. "That was Lilybeth."

"Yes, did you know her?"

"No, I didn't know her personally, but my mother knew that lot." He gave a shudder. "Lilybeth was a midwife or something."

"That's exactly right. But, if you didn't have children, you might never get to know her."

"No," he agreed, with a snort. "Not sure I would want to either."

"Do you want to explain that?"

He shrugged. "Everybody knows. … Okay, so I don't know that *everybody* knows this, but back then apparently Lilybeth would stay quiet for a price tag."

Doreen's shoulders sagged. "Ah, at the end of the day, that is probably why she was murdered."

Richard stared at her.

"She talked to me before she died. As a matter of fact, she left me a letter, a half-garbled explanation."

"If she was close to dying," he suggested, "she was probably trying to clear her conscience."

"Maybe. I was supposed to meet with her and went down there, more like raced down to talk to her, and she had just passed away. I was there, and the ambulance was literally right there too."

He just stared at her.

"I didn't like the way she was talking about leaving me this letter, but I felt this urgency, that, if I didn't get down there immediately, she might have pulled the letter, and I wouldn't have gotten it. But I also wanted to talk to her about the contents of the letter because she seemed to be having second thoughts."

"Of course, so are you thinking that somebody heard you?"

"Maybe heard us, maybe heard about the letter, I don't know," she replied.

"Yeah, but did anybody find out that you were the one who was there? That alone is enough to make anybody upset these days."

She stared at him. "What do you mean?"

"Everybody knows how heavily involved with the police you are, and that's just a death sentence if you're a criminal." He chuckled. "It's kind of nice actually. The streets feel quite safe these days."

"Weren't they always?" she asked.

He pondered that and then nodded. "I guess you're right. They always were kind of safe. But it's a different feeling now. It's helped people care."

"Then that's good," she said. "I'm glad you approve."

"I don't approve of your methods, and I surely don't approve of the mess you bring down on me," he noted, "but, every once in a while"—and it's obvious he was thinking about his brother and all that his brother had been through—"every once in a while, you do good work." And, with that faint praise, he stepped back into his house and slammed the door on her.

She walked back inside her own house and waited until she thought Mack was done driving. Then she called him.

"You miss me already?" he asked in a teasing tone. "I'm about to take a look at our deceased's room."

"Is it even still her room?" Doreen asked ignoring his teasing but it did put a smile on her face. "I wouldn't be shocked if these people may have cleaned it out already."

"They shouldn't have touched it, at least not until the next of kin did something with it."

"Yeah, well, we already know who the appointed representative is, and she works at the front desk."

He sighed, then asked, "You want to come along?"

"I absolutely do want to come along," she cried out in delight, and then she froze. "Can I bring the animals?"

"Is there a particular reason?"

"Yeah, you have no idea what that old man is like. He was kind of terrifying."

He asked, "You found him terrifying?"

"Yeah, I sure did. He's really mean, old, and crabby, but more than that there was just that … You'll laugh at this, but he gave me that sleazy serial-killer vibe."

There was dead silence on the other end. "Bring Mugs," he stated, "and I'll meet you there in five."

And, with that, he disconnected.

Chapter 32

DOREEN DROVE DOWN to Riverdale and parked, then walked into the front of the building, happy to see a completely different receptionist. She smiled at her as she brought the animals in. The woman looked at her, raised her eyebrows, and stated, "Sorry, no animals allowed."

But Mack was right behind her.

"We need them," he stated briskly, as he held up his badge.

The woman frowned at him, then eyed the badge and nodded. "You're looking for Lilybeth's room, is that correct?"

"Yes."

"And you're not going anywhere else, right?"

"No, we're not going anywhere else," Doreen confirmed.

She frowned and added, "Could you at least take the animals outside and enter through the patio then? At least that will keep the hair away from the residents who might have allergies."

As that was a reasonable request, Doreen nodded. "I can do that."

The receptionist led Mack away, while Doreen headed

back outside, trying to figure out in her mind exactly where Lilybeth's room was. When one of the patio side doors opened as she was out searching for Lilybeth's room, she was relieved to see Mack and raced over to him. As she stepped into the room, she looked at him and stated, "That was a reasonable request on her part, wasn't it?"

He nodded. "I wouldn't cause any issue over it, but come on in. Let's take a look around."

As it was, Lilybeth's room was clean, neat, and tidy.

Mack noted, "I did ask the receptionist about the turnover rate, and she stated that it was being rented at the end of the month, which is in another ten days," he noted. "And although Lilybeth's representative has been informed, as far as the receptionist understood, nobody had been to clean it out yet."

"That makes sense," Doreen muttered. "She did just pass on."

He looked at her and nodded. "Did you say that Lilybeth had no living next of kin but had appointed a representative for her estate, a nurse, someone who works here?"

"Yes, Tabitha, the other receptionist, who is part of the Winters family," Doreen noted. "I'm surprised this receptionist didn't say that."

"She might not know, and, if you think about it, there would be some benefits to having a nurse, working in this place, as your designated agent."

"I don't think Lilybeth got any benefits for having Tabitha as her representative. I think Tabitha got perks because she was blackmailing people," she shared.

He shook his head. "You do know how to find the buried secrets."

"I didn't mean to though," she wailed.

"I know," he said, "and that's the funny thing with you. It seems as if it just happens naturally."

Focusing on the room, Doreen looked around and pointed out, "It's almost as if it's unlived in."

"It is unlived in now."

"You know what I mean." She turned around the room. "It's as if no personality is here."

"What was Lilybeth like?"

"*Um.*" Doreen frowned, as she thought about it. "Tabitha called her *militant.* Lilybeth definitely had a personality, but maybe not necessarily a nice one."

He nodded and swept one hand about the room. "And this is what was left. Nothing at the end of the day. So, if she was blackmailing anybody, it was probably more to keep her spot here, so she wouldn't get put out on the street."

"The government would have found her a home, I'm sure," Doreen noted.

"And maybe the home was trying not to get into trouble over her."

"Maybe, but there are rules, and, if you break them, they will send you off to some other place, and that could be all that Lilybeth was trying to do—just live out the last of her days here. I think when I saw her, she was feeling … defensive, very much as if she'd made a lot of mistakes in life, and this was just one more."

"Oh, that's possible," Mack agreed, "absolutely possible. If she was having second thoughts, maybe she mentioned something to somebody."

"Maybe," she murmured.

They quickly searched the bed and the dresser and a small closet and a bathroom. By the time she was done,

Mack was just coming out of the little kitchenette area.

She frowned, looked back at the bed, and said, "That bed's got to have more storage in it."

He looked at her and nodded. "Let's take another look."

He quickly lifted up the mattresses, one by one, and only when they got down to the very bottom did Doreen cry out, "Aha." As he peered under the mattress, still holding it up with his big arms, she pulled out an envelope from underneath and lifted it up for him to see. Mugs sniffed it and started barking.

Mack took a smell of it and sighed.

"What is it?" Doreen asked.

"Smells like weed, but I can't be sure."

And, indeed, the envelope had a little bit of powdery stuff in the bottom. "She can't have that in here though, even if it's legal in Kelowna."

"I think it's just the remnants in the envelope." A note was inside, which Mack pulled out and began to read. "*If you find this envelope, it's not mine. It belongs to somebody who's made so many errors in this life, so many mistakes. He has caused so much pain that I hope he gets everything that's coming to him when he finally hits the afterlife. I may not deserve to go to heaven myself because I have also made many mistakes.*"

The letter went on and on, and Mack sighed. "It's like the ramblings of a very tired mind."

"Right, but does she actually say who she is talking about?"

As he continued to read, he stopped and read out loud again. "*And, in case you're wondering who I'm talking about, it's old Buck. That man has caused so much pain and so much terror, and I swear to God he's killed at least four people. That's what happens when you keep secrets. Once you keep one, you have to keep them all because people find out, and they black-mail you. I gave him a dose of his own medicine to come and stay here because I can't stand the thought of being alone out on the street. I don't know what would happen to me if I wasn't here.*

"I'm pretty sure he killed a child, his wife, and both his daughters, in that order. And, if it wasn't him alone, it was him and his sons. Not one of them respects women. Not one of them sees any point in sharing a mother lode of inheritances if they don't have to. I do worry about the younger generation and how they seem to think they'll get something out of this. Something will happen to them, and it'll happen to them way before they expect, and it'll just be sadness all around. But I can't stop it, as I can't even help myself. Dear God, I just hope I'm not around when it happens."

Mack shrugged, turning to her. "It's hardly a confession."

"Maybe not," she muttered, "but it's a heck of an accusation."

He nodded. "And you know what accusations are too."

"Right," she muttered, scratching her nose. "They are worthless unless we have proof. Are you telling me there isn't anything in here we can use?"

"We can try, but, once the family gets wind of what's here, there'll be a bloodbath."

"Maybe, but what about the receptionist, Tabitha? She's family, and the younger family are all about looking to get a windfall and then getting out of town. At least according to Sandra."

He turned and frowned at Doreen. "That's Tabitha then, the receptionist here, the *younger generation* mentioned in this letter? The legal representative for Lilybeth?"

"Yeah, that would be Tabitha," Doreen confirmed. "And, according to this letter, I presume she could be the next one to get into trouble."

"But the old man won't kill her, right?" Mack asked.

"No," she said, turning to look at him, "but that just means it'll be up to one of the two brothers."

"Clarence, the politician?"

"Or Carl, the big businessman," she noted. "And, if we can't prove which one, we won't prove it at all."

"I know," he muttered, studying her. "But I'm really glad you appear to have picked up some Criminal 101 stuff."

She smiled at him. "You're a good teacher."

He laughed, and then the door opened, as old Buck sat there in his wheelchair, with Clarence at his side.

"Look at that," Buck began, staring at them. "What are you doing here?"

Mack held up his badge. "We're investigating a murder," he replied. "And you two are the ones we want to talk to."

Clarence started to bluster. "What are you talking about? I didn't have anything to do with this, and I won't stand here and allow that kind of talk. That kind of talk can destroy careers."

"It can also destroy lives," Doreen noted, with half a smile.

"Where's your brother?" Mack asked Clarence.

"Last I heard, he was off in China doing something," Clarence replied.

She stared at him for a long moment. "When was the last time you talked to your brother, Mr. Winters?"

He frowned at her. "It's been a while. We haven't been close."

"Maybe not," she noted, "but I really need to know

when you last saw him."

Mack stepped up beside her and reached out a hand. She grabbed his hand and squeezed hard.

Doreen continued. "It occurs to me that he's been missing, and he's been missing for quite a while."

Clarence glared at her. "If he's missing, we would have heard from his office, and there would be an investigation. But it wouldn't be happening here because he wasn't here when he went missing."

"*When* he went missing?" Doreen repeated.

"*If* he went missing," Clarence immediately clarified.

She stared at him and nodded. "I guess a fair bit of money would be involved in an inheritance, wouldn't there?" Clarence did his best to look innocent and shocked that she would even ask the question, but she was on to him now. "I wondered which one of the two of you it would be. Then I realized I had never even seen Carl. He's not in town, and everybody just says he's off on business. How long has he been missing?"

When Clarence refused to answer her questions, she turned and looked at the old man. "And you're really okay with that, *huh*? You're okay with one son taking out the other, so Clarence gets everything he wants, while everybody else just dies off?" She stared at Buck. "So how on earth are you okay with that?"

The old man stared at her for a long moment, then slowly turned to look at Clarence. "I don't know what she's talking about, Clarence, but where is your brother?"

"Heck if I know," Clarence stated cheerfully. But there was an edge to his tone as he glared at Mack and Doreen. "You still need to explain what you're doing here."

"I don't have to explain anything at all," Mack declared.

"However, we do want some answers, and you can start with that question."

Buck Winters slowly turned, looking at Clarence again. "Where is your brother?"

"I don't know where he is," Clarence snarled. "If I knew, I would tell you."

Buck studied him for a long moment. "I haven't talked to Carl in a very long time."

"Neither have I. And I told you that."

"You told me that you had a bit of an argument and that he took off."

"What was that argument about?" Doreen asked. "I want to know, but I'm already pretty darn sure the argument was all about money—all about money for your political career, all about money to push your agenda into politics, right?" she asked. "It takes a lot of money to do that. But Carl wasn't into that, was he? He wasn't into your wasting money on running for a political position, was he?"

"He only cared about business," Clarence stated, staring at her. "And he's entitled to care about what he wants to care about."

"He is," she agreed, with a nod. "The thing is, I don't know where he is, and, until you can bring him forward so we can talk with him, I'm wondering if you didn't follow in your father's footsteps and do something to Carl."

For the moment, as Clarence glared at her, he hadn't really registered the insult about his father. But, when he did, he turned to look down at the old man, then back at her and asked, "What are you talking about?"

She smirked at old Buck. "You didn't tell him?" she asked in a mocking tone. "You didn't tell him that you murdered his mother? You didn't tell him that you murdered his sisters? Why is that?" she asked. "I thought this was all about togetherness, the two of you."

Clarence turned and frowned at his father, as the old man continued to glare at Doreen.

Doreen continued. "But you're okay if he murdered your son, right?"

"He did not murder my son," Buck declared in a harsh tone. Then he turned to Clarence. "Please tell me that you didn't kill your brother. Dear God, please no." Clarence just stared at him, and the old man started to rant and rave. "Good God. How could you do that? We need him. Don't you understand? He's the only one who ever understood the business. He's the only one who kept the company afloat. Without him, we're nothing. How could you do that?"

She took a step back as the two of them started in, insults flying like crazy, and she realized that Mack had his phone out, recording it all. She beamed as she watched the chaos she'd created take the place by storm.

Finally the men fell silent, and Clarence glared at her and Mack. "You repeat this, and it's clearly hearsay. None of that will ever get even close to being allowed in court," he stated in a smooth tone.

"Of course not," Doreen said. "Do you really think the court cares about the fact that you murdered your brother for the inheritance or the fact that your old man killed his wife and killed his daughters, even his illegitimate one?"

Then she turned to Buck and smiled. "The little one you killed wasn't your blood daughter." Then she turned her attention back to Clarence. "So maybe Clarence murdered his sisters. Maybe that was all about you."

He just stared at her, his jaw working.

She nodded. "After all, why would you share an inheritance like that? It would have been all yours, and all you needed was your brother to agree to your political career," she suggested, with a smile.

"You need to just shut up," Clarence snapped.

But the old man turned and grabbed Clarence's hand and repeated, "Tell me that you didn't kill your brother."

"You don't even care about the rest of the family, do you?" Clarence asked, turning on Buck. "It was always all about Carl."

"It was always all about Carl because Carl actually understood business," Buck snapped. "Carl kept us going when things got bad. Carl bailed us out, remember?"

"I wanted to go into politics," Clarence stated. "I wanted to be somebody."

"You didn't need to kill Carl to *be somebody*," Buck snapped.

"He didn't want to spend the money on my political campaign. He said it was a waste of time and energy."

"And it was," Buck agreed, staring at Clarence, then Buck slumped in his wheelchair. "I can't believe you killed my boy," he muttered, tears in his eyes.

"Yeah? What about me? I'm your boy too."

"Yeah, you're my boy all right—in more ways than one." He turned to Doreen. "How did you figure all that out?"

"All because of the bones that you buried in the garden all those years ago," she began. "That little girl had a story to tell, and we finally have the technology to catch up and to tell it."

"That little girl," he muttered, "wouldn't stop crying."

"She just wanted her mother, but you decided her mother needed to be taught a lesson. And that lesson was that you were in control, right? That it was all about you. That everything was about you," she explained, staring at him. She could see Mugs wanting to get closer and closer to old Buck. She tried to call Mugs back, but he wasn't interested.

Buck looked down at the dog as it came closer and declared, "I'll kill it, you know? You let it get anywhere close to me, and I will kill that dog," he vowed. "And I'll watch your face and smile while I'm doing it."

"You might," she conceded, "but then again you might not. He might get you first."

Chapter 33

MACK STEPPED FORWARD just then. "Nobody will kill the dog," he declared in an authoritative tone. "And obviously we still have a few issues to work out."

"There aren't any issues to work out," Clarence argued, glaring at the old man. "Did you really kill Mom?"

Buck shrugged. "She was fading away to nothing anyway. It was a bloody kindness, what I did," he muttered.

"Why? So, you could go bang other women?"

"I don't care about other women, and you know that," he stated, glaring at him. "Iris was so whiny at the end. So angry over the child. The woman just couldn't ever get over it."

"But that's exactly why you killed your daughter Claudia, right?" Doreen asked. "Because she heard all about it from Iris. And eventually Claudia got suspicious too, and she wouldn't let it go. She wanted to know the truth, didn't she?"

He glared at her. "She should have kept her mouth shut too. What do they think? That I'm made of money? Meredith did that, and suddenly she died. That and Iris dying should have been enough for Claudia, but obviously not.

Women are such hardheaded fools."

"And you needed your boy Carl alive because you *weren't* made of money, right?" Doreen asked. "Somebody to take over the mess you've made out of all the family businesses, somebody with an actual head for business, not like you. Not like Clarence." Buck and Clarence both glared at her, and she nodded. "All the things that you worked for, Buck, and yet here you've got Clarence, busy killing his brother because Carl wouldn't agree to fund Clarence's political career."

At that, Buck turned on his only living child. "That was just stupid, Clarence."

"Really?" Clarence asked, staring at him. "I'm still stuck on the fact that you killed my mother."

"Well, get over it. It was the same with her. She was just whining there at the end. Ungrateful is what she was."

Clarence thought about it and nodded. "She was pretty bad, I have to admit."

"So mourning the death of her fifth child is a reason to kill Iris?" Doreen asked, staring at these men in shock.

"No, of course not," Clarence replied defensively. "I was trying to figure out what was wrong with her back then."

"What was wrong with her was your father," Doreen snapped. "And you should have figured that out by now, since you guys are two peas in a pod."

Clarence glared at her. "I didn't kill my mother."

"Yeah, but what about your sisters?"

"I didn't kill my sisters either," he cried out. "You heard him, right?"

"Sure. He's the one who killed Claudia. But which one of you killed Meredith?" Doreen asked.

"You've been talking to that old good-for-nothing gossip

Sandra," the old man snapped, glaring at her. Mugs crept closer, until the old man tried to kick her dog, but Mugs was just out of range.

"I told you that I'll kill him," Buck yelled, "and I'll watch you cry."

"Is that what you did all those years ago? Kill an innocent child, then watch while your wife cried in devastation?"

He stared at her and shrugged. "She needed to be taught a lesson."

At that, Clarence turned and looked at him. "Good God," he muttered, now with apprehension. "You killed a child? Why would you do that?"

"Because it wasn't my child. It was your mother's child."

Clarence stared at him. "What? She had an affair? That kid wasn't yours?"

Doreen snorted. "They were separated at the time. Buck didn't want Iris, and, while they were separated, somebody else decided they wanted her. He wanted her in a big way, didn't he?" she asked, staring at Buck. "But you couldn't let them be happy, could you?"

"You don't know anything," Buck roared, glaring at her. "She needed to be taught a lesson. Just because I told her that she could go play doesn't mean she was allowed to go play for real."

"Ah, only you are allowed to do that," she noted, with a nod of her head. "That's pretty funny, considering how you treated her and your daughters."

"If Claudia hadn't made a point of asking me about that little girl, it wouldn't have been yan issue," he declared, sneering at Doreen. "But she wouldn't let it go either."

"So, she got the same treatment as her mother."

"Yeah."

"And what about poor Lilybeth?" Doreen asked.

"*Poor* Lilybeth, nothing. Lilybeth was anything but poor. All she did was blackmail me constantly."

At that, Clarence turned and stared at him in shock. "That old woman was blackmailing you? Why?" he cried out.

"Because she found out, probably from your mother, and that old woman just wouldn't lay off. Lilybeth kept hassling me about killing a child, and finally I had to bring her in here and give her a space to stay until she died."

"I'm surprised you didn't knock her off earlier," Doreen noted, staring at Buck. "I can't imagine what it was like, facing her every day."

"She said she had proof."

"She did have proof, and she left a letter."

He stared at her in shock, so irate that he tried to get out of his wheelchair. When he fell back into his seat, he slammed his hand on the handlebar of the wheelchair, roaring, "That stupid woman."

"Yeah, and, whether she was right or wrong to do what she did," Doreen added, "obviously she knew what you would be like to deal with."

"She should. … I had an affair with her many years ago. She didn't think much of my breaking up with her then. I think that's when she got her claws into my wife."

"And that's possible, but, of course, you were allowed to have an affair, but your wife wasn't?"

"No, she wasn't," he snapped. "She was mine."

"And yet you didn't want her."

"Whether I wanted her or not had nothing to do with it. She wasn't allowed to let somebody else touch her," he declared, "and, once I got that through her head, she was fine again. But every time I looked at that little girl, I saw *him*."

"You don't even know who the father was," Doreen said. "You've probably wondered all these years, but you don't know for sure."

"I sure didn't care either, not once that kid was dead," Buck said. "She snapped like a little twig. Honestly, I didn't even realize what I was doing. I was just so angry. She just broke in my hands." He stared down at his hands. "Once it was done, nothing I could do about it. The kid was gone. Besides, it was a perfect teaching moment for your mother," Buck declared, turning to glare at Clarence, who stared at him in shock.

Clarence looked over at the others. "I didn't have anything to do with that."

"No, I'm sure you didn't," Mack said, "although you might have been old enough to understand what was going on."

"Not really, but Mom changed at some point. She became somebody else in a way. She just hid away and wasn't happy anymore."

"Yeah, look at what *she* did," Buck yelled.

Doreen nodded. "Iris found somebody else, after your father told her to get lost and that he wouldn't take her outbursts anymore. So Iris found somebody else, and then Buck forced her back into his life and got rid of the other guy." She turned on him and asked coolly, "Did you kill him too?" His gaze narrowed to slits, and she nodded. "Yeah, well, we'll need the location of that body too," she stated calmly and then turned back to Clarence. "Buck probably killed Iris's lover right in front of her, and then the child, who Buck couldn't be sure was his or not," she added. "So,

Clarence, you killing your brother is just a *chip off the old block* thing."

Clarence started to tremble and collapsed. "But I didn't mean to," he wailed. "It was an accident."

Doreen shook her head. "It might have been an accident, but you sure didn't get help for Carl, did you? You didn't let anybody know there was a problem. I'm guessing you ended up burying him somewhere close by, so you can keep an eye on him, just like your father here. He buried that little girl in a garden on one of his rental properties. And guess what? They dug up the child's bones while trying to plant a patch of yams."

"Yams?" Clarence asked, blinking.

"Yeah, yams," she confirmed. "They were turning over the bed, and they pulled up this shredded pillowcase with the bones of a toddler inside. No proper funeral, just, you know, a tiny body dumped in the middle of nowhere," Doreen shared. "What was her name?" she asked, turning to look at Buck.

When he glared at her, she shrugged. "That's okay. We'll put something descriptive on her gravestone. Maybe *the lovechild Buck Winters murdered* or something of that nature. We need to let everyone know exactly what you did."

"I don't care what anybody says. I had every right to get rid of that thing. It wasn't mine, and I shouldn't have to raise it."

"You don't know if she was yours or not," Doreen pointed out. "What I can tell you is that we've already run the child's DNA, and it definitely came back as your wife's."

"I told you that already," Buck replied, with a sneer, "and you don't get to tell me anything else."

"I can if I want to," Doreen said, giving him a hint of a

smile. "I just don't particularly care to." She then turned to Clarence and then back at Buck. "Which one of you took out Lilybeth?"

Clarence shook his head, furious. "We aren't murderers. We don't just turn around and kill off people we don't want in our lives."

She looked at him, and a smile clicked onto her face. "Really? Have you looked at your dad lately?"

Clarence stared down at his father and asked, "Dad, you didn't do something to Lilybeth, did you?"

"She was blackmailing me. Then she told me that she wouldn't take my secrets to her grave, and she figured she might know someone who could help her."

"Who?" Clarence asked, staring at Buck in shock. "What are you talking about?"

"She was talking about me," Doreen acknowledged. "I'm the one who would help her reveal the truth."

Clarence turned and looked at her. "I don't even know who you are. I don't even know what you're doing here."

"I'm the one who'll see that you go to prison for murdering your brother, and I'm the one who'll show up in court every day to confirm that Buck lives long enough to go to prison himself. Then all of that precious inheritance money will go to the victims' families," she said. "And not a penny will go to that lovely little daughter of yours, Clarence. Tabitha was complicit in murdering Lilybeth."

The old man's gaze widened. "How do you know that?"

"Because you weren't capable," she stated. "Tabitha set you up though. She let us know that you spoke to Lilybeth last. Tabitha was sure to let us know that, if we looked at anybody, it was likely to be you, Buck." When his eyes opened wide, she nodded. "You seem to have created a whole lineage of people just like you. What I want to know is where you got the drugs."

He shrugged and didn't say anything.

"Did you use the same drug on all of them? But why would you change though?" she asked, with a nod. "How many people did you kill with the heart-attack-inducing drug? Iris's child you just broke like a doll," she noted, "but you drugged the four women and then, of course, the child's father."

"He deserved to die," Buck declared in a shaky voice.

"Right, and tell me exactly why? Just because he touched what you considered to be yours?"

"That's right, and, if you think that doesn't matter, you're wrong."

"I'm sure it matters to you," she stated in a calm voice. "Absolutely it matters, but I don't think it'll matter to the jury, not when they take a look at what you did and who you did it to."

He just glared at her. "I won't live long enough to care."

"No, maybe not," she agreed, with a smile. "But I can tell you that all those people you murdered, they will all be there waiting for you."

"Let them wait," he roared, with a sneer on his face. "I lived and they didn't. That's how the law of the land works."

"Apparently that's what you taught your son Clarence too," Doreen said, with a nod. She looked over at Clarence. "Kind of sad though. You'll spend the rest of your life in prison for what you did to your brother. But your father? He got to live out his life, despite all his crimes. However, Tabitha, that daughter of yours, Buck's granddaughter, she'll be in purgatory there right beside you two."

Clarence shook his head, "She wouldn't have had anything to do with this."

"Really?" the old man laughed. "She's more like you than you know. She's the one who approached me about it. She told me that Lilybeth had been talking to this crazy detective lady in town, the one with the huge success record on solving cold cases. Tabitha told me how she was afraid that, if I had anything to hide, it would be a problem."

"What did you do?" Clarence wailed.

"I told her that I did have a few things I would prefer to keep quiet. She's the one who told me Lilybeth had been talking all of a sudden. My agreement with Lilybeth was that she kept her mouth shut," he snapped, glaring at Doreen, "and she broke that confidence with you."

"Yes, she did. Like many people facing their own mortality, Lilybeth realized that she needed to clear her own conscience, if she was to spend her final days in any sort of peace."

"She shouldn't have blackmailed me then, should she?" Buck snapped.

Just then Mugs came up beside him, and the old man swung down to try and cuff him. Mugs jumped back, but he had something in his mouth. He raced over to Doreen, the old man frantically trying to wheel himself closer. As Mugs reached her, she saw that he had a small vial in his mouth. She snagged it up, then nodded and handed it to Mack. "That's the poison he likes to use," she stated. "Did you just kill your granddaughter too?"

At that, Buck stared at her in shock. Beside him, Clarence gasped. "No, no, no, he would never do that. He loves Tabitha."

"Buck loves her until they become partners in crime, and then," Doreen noted, "all bets are off. I didn't see her on my way in."

At that, Clarence bolted out of the room and headed to the front desk.

Doreen looked over at Mack.

He sighed. "I've already got the police out front. Do you really think Buck killed Tabitha?"

"No, I think she's smarter than he is."

The old man sputtered, but a woman spoke from the doorway. "Thank you for that much at least."

And there was Tabitha, Buck's granddaughter, with a gun in her hand. The old man looked at her and cackled. "There you go," he said in a fit of laughter. "I wondered if you had the guts for it."

"Oh, I've got the guts for it," she stated calmly, "and that's because I want to get the heck out of here. And now that I know Dad killed off the only golden goose in the family, I want to take the money that's left and run."

Doreen shook her head. "You can run, but you can't hide."

Tabitha laughed. "You don't know anything. *I* did though, and I pegged you right from the start. The minute you walked through that door, I knew you were trouble, and it didn't take me very long to get it out of Lilybeth," she admitted, "and I took care of her right quick."

"And yet you gave me the letter."

"I wasn't sure what to do at that point, and I hadn't even had a chance to read it, so I figured it didn't matter. Lilybeth was dead, and a letter from an old biddy wouldn't make any difference." Tabitha raised her gun.

Doreen immediately checked for her animals, noting that Goliath was nowhere to be found. She looked around, twisting and turning.

"What are you doing?" Tabitha asked in exasperation.

"Do you not realize I'm holding a gun on you?"

"You might be," Doreen replied, "but you could also end up in really bad straits yourself in just a few seconds."

"What are you talking about?" Tabitha cried out, staring at Doreen. "What is wrong with you? You come in here, and you act completely confident, and nothing seems to faze you. You don't even care that I'm holding a gun on you."

"Why would I?" Doreen asked, turning to her. "Seriously, why would I?" The woman just blinked, and Doreen nodded. "You people have already killed so many others, and you don't have a clue what you're up against, and here you are, acting as if you're something special."

Fury twisted Tabitha's face as Doreen went on.

"You've already admitted to killing Lilybeth, and here your grandfather has admitted to killing your mother, your aunt, and your grandmother."

Tabitha stopped, turned to the old man, and asked, "What's she saying? You killed my mom?"

"No, I didn't say I killed your mother," he said, turning to Doreen. "Can't you keep it straight?"

"My apologies, he killed your aunt Claudia. By the way, do you know what happened to your mother? I would certainly think that bears looking into as well."

Tabitha frowned, a horrified expression on her face, then looked at the old man and asked, "Did you have anything to do with it?"

"No, of course not," he snapped, "but you could ask your father, seeing as I've just learned that he's apparently killed your uncle," he muttered.

"The whole lot of you are nuts," Doreen announced.

The gun turned her way again, as Tabitha sneered at her. "You really shouldn't talk to people who hold guns on you, at least not with such disrespect."

"*Right*," Doreen muttered, looking at Tabitha with a bored expression on her face. "You know what I am? I'm tired of people telling me what I should and shouldn't do. I'm tired of people wielding guns, thinking it makes them all powerful. You know what's better than any of that?"

"What?" Tabitha snapped, glaring at her.

"It's called loyalty."

At that, Goliath jumped up onto Tabitha's back. He dug in his claws and slowly dragged his way down, with her screaming and flailing all the while, the gun firing off in all directions, but Doreen and Mack were well and truly hidden behind the bed. When the firing stopped, Doreen looked up to see Tabitha screaming at the cat, who was nowhere to be found.

She was still frantically firing a now-empty gun, which kept clicking and clicking.

Doreen looked over at the old man, who stared at his granddaughter.

"You idiot, you could have killed me," Buck roared.

She turned to him and shared, "That was the plan anyway. You would be next."

He stared at her in dumbfounded shock. "You would kill me?" he cried out.

"Why not?" she snapped. "You may want to sit around here, waiting until you die of old age, but I don't. I've waited long enough. You're done for." She lifted the gun and went to fire at him.

"I think it's empty, dear," Doreen noted helpfully. "You might need to reload first."

Tabitha blinked at her and muttered, "You are so done."

"I don't think so." Then Doreen shrugged. "However, I

could be wrong."

Tabitha just looked at her and asked, "Why aren't you scared?"

"Because that was my cat who attacked you," she said. "And you have no idea what'll happen if you come after me again."

"If I see that cat again, I'll shoot it," she bellowed, "and I'll shoot the dratted dog too."

"I wouldn't do that either," Doreen warned. "They get really upset if you target them. I get that you're angry and all, but it's probably a good idea to call it a day."

Tabitha glared at her, then at Mack, almost helplessly resigned. "Can't you shut her up?"

"No," he replied. "I've tried, believe me, but she doesn't listen to a word."

"You're not kidding," Tabitha snapped. "So I'll make her listen." Then she lifted the gun again, but got nothing but another harmless *click*. Mack then stepped toward her, and she tried to avoid his grasp. "No, no, no."

"Yes, yes, yes," Doreen said, with a bright cheerful smile.

Tabitha went to throw a punch, and, just as she did so, Mugs stepped up against her, clipping her back leg, dropping her to the floor, so she knelt in front of him. "No," she cried out.

Mack quickly grabbed her, twisted her arms behind her back, and snapped his cuffs on her.

"What about me?" Buck asked, glaring at Doreen. "You think I'm not somebody you have to worry about?"

"I've got your vial of poison," she noted calmly.

"Yeah, but what about my handgun?" he asked, as he lifted his own incredibly tiny gun.

She looked at it and smiled. "Wow, is that a derringer?"

Seeing the gun brought back memories for her.

He stared at her and shrugged. "I don't know, and I don't care. Why do you care?"

"I don't really," she admitted. "My husband used to collect weapons like that. Honestly, I just thought they were for show since they looked more like a toy."

"It's not a toy," he declared, as he pointed it at her. "Now, you'll take me out to the vehicle and help me get to the airport, so I can get a private plane out of here."

She shook her head at him. "That's not happening."

"Of course it'll happen. I'm the one holding the gun."

"You might be holding the gun, but you won't get to use it."

Just then Thaddeus popped out of her hair and crowed, "Thaddeus is here. Thaddeus is here. Thaddeus is here." Then he flew out, batting his wings hard in the old man's face, forcing him to cover his eyes. Thaddeus grabbed the gun in his beak and basically dumped it to the ground. It went off harmlessly, setting off more cries from the spectators gathered in the hallway, all peering through the open doorway, staring at the goings-on.

Mack groaned, then walked over and checked the old man for more weapons. As he looked at Doreen, he asked, "Are you done now?"

"It's not just me," she clarified. "The animals get to play their parts too, you know?"

He rolled his eyes, looked at Thaddeus, and asked, "Are you happy now?" He preened several times and then walked onto Mack's shoulder, as if it was a higher and much better place for a bird of his importance.

Doreen sighed. "Of course he's happy. Thanks, Thaddeus."

He laughed. "*He-he-he.*" Then he nuzzled up to Mack. "Thaddeus is here. Thaddeus is here."

"I know, buddy. Thanks for your help," Mack said.

Mack looked over at the door, now full of curiosity seekers and his constables, trying to make their way inside the room.

When Arnold entered and looked around, he nodded. "I guess Doreen's on the case, *huh*?"

Mack groaned and nodded. "Isn't she always?"

Arnold grinned. "I gotta say that it's nice to have her as part of the team though, you know?"

"Sure." Mack groaned. "But you know what would also be nice? If the team was doing the job they were supposed to be doing."

"Hey, you can't blame us for this one," Arnold said, raising his hands. "The captain asked Doreen to look into it."

"I know," Mack grumbled. "The captain will be thrilled because we've solved the cold case, and I don't even want to know how many other murders."

"But just think," Doreen said, giving him a cheeky grin. "I waited for you to show up for the pistol-waving action part this time." He just looked at her and sighed. She wrapped her arms around him and gave him a great big hug. "I'm really glad you're back and done with court."

"Me too," he replied. "Are you done causing chaos for tonight?"

"I am." Then she yawned and nodded. "I think I can confidently leave you guys to clean up the mess."

At that, everybody at the doorway cheered and laughed.

She smiled, kissed Mack on the cheek, and added, "Really glad to have you back on the team again."

"I'm not part of your team," he muttered.

"Nope, I know. You *are* the team. … I'll just gather up the animals and get them out of here. You'll update the coroner, won't you?"

"Elizabeth will love you."

Doreen grinned. "Maybe. At least she can now get the bones off her shelf after all these years."

"But you didn't get a name."

She turned, walked back to the old man, and asked him, "What was the name of the baby you killed?" He glared at her, and she shrugged. "I can tell everybody what a jerk you were, but I could also tell them of all the things you did accomplish in life, and it wouldn't be a complete loss," she muttered. "But killing that baby? That's the one murder that'll get to everybody. Especially if she was laid to rest without a name."

He stared at her. "Her name was Mary," he muttered in a heavy voice.

"And her father?"

He shrugged, glanced around the room, and added, "Nobody cares about the father."

"Oh, I think somebody cares about the father."

Buck sighed. "It was a guy from Vancouver. He was up for some geological study. Anyway, they met when she was out walking, and somehow it ended up being this big hot and heavy affair. I don't know anything more."

"Yeah, you do. You know his name. No way you would have killed him without at least knowing his name."

He glared at her. "It doesn't matter."

"It does matter," she stated, "because somewhere is a family who doesn't know what happened to their son, so a name and the location of the body *now*." And heck if he didn't start spilling.

By the time it was done, Arnold just shook his head. "Another family will be happy to have some closure."

"And yet not happy," Doreen corrected, as she straightened up to face Arnold. "Of all the stupid reasons to get killed."

He nodded. "And yet, if they've been waiting for him to come home all these years, at least now they might get some answers too." He patted Doreen on the shoulder. "You look a little tired, Doreen. Take the critters and run along. We've got this." And he hitched up his pants, turned to Mack, and muttered, "Please tell me that you've got a recording of all that."

Mack held up his phone.

Arnold grinned and rubbed his hands together. "Boy, this will be another feather in the cap for us." He was chuckling now. "And a video recording to boot." He turned to Doreen. "Go on. Get lost. We'll handle this."

Mack nodded. "You've done all the hard work, Doreen. We can do the rest."

And, with that, she smiled. "I think I'll take you up on that."

"Just don't expect me home anytime soon," Mack added.

"No, I won't." She gave him a bright smile, knowing that today, whether people were happy about it or not, it was still a good day. As she headed out, she found the coroner coming in, scrambling to get past the crowd.

Elizabeth glared as she entered the room and asked, "Now what is going on here? If I listened to the gossips, it's all kinds of craziness. There are animals, shootings, dead bodies, all kinds of stuff. What is going on?"

Mack turned to her and smiled. "See? This is the problem with having Doreen on a case."

"Doreen?" Elizabeth turned to look at her.

Doreen smiled at her. "Mary, … the child's name is Mary," she said. "Her father's name was Pierce Masdine, and her mother's name was Iris Winters. That little girl, her name was Mary."

At that, even the coroner's eyes teared up. She opened her arms and wrapped up Doreen in a great big hug. And then she pushed her back off to the side. "Go, go, go," she snapped. "We have work to do." Elizabeth looked around and asked, "Who's dead?"

Mack smiled. "No one."

Elizabeth blinked. "Who called for me then?" she cried out, glaring at him.

He shook his head. "I have no idea. It's been a bit of a nightmare for the last little bit."

"Ya think?" she quipped. "About time you got back to work, Mack. That fiancée of yours, she had to work really hard to get this done. You really should make her a deputy."

At that, Arnold started to laugh. "Oh my God, can you imagine how bad it would be if she was official?"

Darren, who stood at the doorway, cried out, "Please, no, there's no way I could handle my grandpa if Doreen was official."

Arnold grinned. "You've got a point there."

And they all burst out laughing.

Epilogue

DOREEN SLEPT IN the next morning, only to wake up to find Mack standing in her bedroom doorway, grinning at her. She blinked several times and groaned. "What time is it?"

"It's eight."

"In the morning?" she asked, sitting up.

"Yes. I've been up most of the night. I slept for a few hours, but now I'm heading over to the office. I just thought I would pop in to check on you and to have a cup of coffee."

Still yawning, she grabbed her robe and headed down to the kitchen behind him.

He quickly set up the coffeepot and looked over at her. "For somebody who churns up all the chaos you cause," he muttered, "you should look a whole lot more exhausted, but instead you look absolutely beautiful." He leaned over, gave her a searing kiss, and muttered, "Come on. Move up the wedding date already, will ya?" She blinked several times as he placed a cup of coffee in front of her. Just then his phone rang, and he listened for a minute, quickly responded, then disconnected and groaned. "See? Now look what you've done."

"What have I done?" she asked.

"Everybody is bringing up all their own questions from other matters all over town and beyond, now that you've solved this case. They're looking for help for everything. Remember that envelope from under Lilybeth's bed?"

"You mean, the letter inside?"

"Yeah, and some pictures too?"

"Right, but I didn't get much chance to look at them before the chaos happened."

"Yeah, well, we blew up the photos, and one of the men knew where the garden was from one of those pictures, and they headed over there to see if they were right. They were supposed to finish up and to go home but couldn't leave it alone. They argued about the garden."

"What? Where was it?"

"I don't know, and I really don't have a clue why I should even tell you," Mack added in exasperation. "Nor do I have a clue what inspired them to grab a shovel and to dig around. But they did …"

"You better tell me. I found the photos, after all."

"You may have found them," Mack noted, "but Darren thought he knew where the pictures were taken from."

"And then they went and dug in that area?"

"Yeah, they did, mostly because Arnold was bugging him about it, saying he was wrong and didn't know. So, true to form, they made some ridiculous bet out of it, but anyway it didn't take Darren very long, and they dug up something."

"What was buried there?"

"Old X-rays."

"X-rays?"

"Yeah, but the old hard kind that they used way back when."

"Okay, if you say so. What difference does that make?"

"I don't know." Mack raised both hands. Then his phone buzzed, and he read the text message and groaned. "Well, now I do," he said, with a sigh.

"What is it?"

"Apparently they found a bone with the X-rays."

She started to grin.

"No," he ordered in exasperation, but she just cackled. "Our hands are full right now," Mack declared.

"That's good. Maybe by the time you're caught up, I'll have the X-ray mystery solved. By the way, what was planted in that garden?"

"I don't know. Do you want me to find out?"

"Yep, I do, indeed."

Several texts later, Mack groaned. "I don't know what these are." He pointed at them, as he held up his phone to show Doreen the image of a flower.

She looked at them and nodded. "They seem to be part of the chrysanthemum family."

"Maybe." He shrugged. "See? It doesn't work. You can't do an alliteration for this one. Besides, it won't be your case. It'll be mine."

"Really?" she asked, checking out the photos. "Looks to be an old bone."

He frowned as he pulled the picture back, realizing that the bone was there.

"It's part of a jawbone," she noted. He raised an eyebrow at her, and she nodded. "Elizabeth will love this one."

"No, she won't. Besides, you can't make an alliteration out of it. So you don't get to have anything to do with it."

She looked at him and smiled. "*X-ray in the Xanth*."

"What's a *xanth*?" he asked in confusion.

"Mums."

"Mums?"

"Yeah, chrysanthemums," she explained, with a beaming smile. "So, that's next."

"I don't care if it's next or not. That bone has been there for a very long time, so it and the X-ray can lay there for a little longer. I have to go finish up the mess from last night."

"Okay." She gave him a hug. "Now at least I know what's next on my list."

"Doesn't have to be," he protested. "You need to rest. You told me that you needed a rest before getting married."

"I do," she agreed, but then she grinned. "I just don't need a super big rest."

"Right," he muttered, with an eye roll, "as if I'll believe that."

"You should because now"—she rubbed her hands together—"we have *X-ray in the Xanth*."

He leaned over, kissed her hard, and announced, "I'm going to work, and maybe that's just self-defense on my part."

"Call it what you want, but I've got my next cold case to work on."

"You do that. Just remember to get some rest, as you've got a wedding to plan." And, when the smile fell off her face, he laughed and laughed. "No pressure."

She smiled and nodded. "I really do appreciate you."

He gazed at her and nodded. "And I really appreciate you."

This concludes Book 2 of Lovely Lethal Gardens Rewind:
Yipped in the Yams.

Read about X-Ray in the Xanth: Lovely Lethal Gardens
Rewind, Book 3

Lovely Lethal Gardens Rewind:
X-Ray in the Xanth
(Book 3)

Something in Doreen's last case sends Chester and Darren out with shovels to a location she'd never seen before. When she finds out why, she's all in—particularly when they find a body. She hates to be delighted with a new case, as that always sounds macabre, … but it's a new case, and that's always exciting to her.

Yet nothing is ever simple when Doreen gets into the mix. As she slowly unravels this new mystery, the case bends and twists in several different directions, with more deaths adding to the mess. She even gets blamed once or twice for causing extra work.

By the time she's thoroughly embedded herself into this cold case and Mack's related current case, the puzzle is as confusing as any case she's ever solved. And no happy conclusion is in sight …

Find X-Ray in the Xanth here!
To find out more visit Dale Mayer's website.
https://geni.us/DMSXRay

Author's Note

Thank you for reading Yipped in the Yams: Lovely Lethal Gardens Rewind, Book 2! If you enjoyed the book, please take a moment and leave a short review.

Dear reader,

I love to hear from readers, and you can contact me at my website: www.dalemayer.com or at my Facebook author page. To be informed of new releases and special offers, sign up for my newsletter or follow me on BookBub. And if you are interested in joining Dale Mayer's Reader Group, here is the Facebook sign up page.
http://geni.us/DaleMayerFBGroup

Cheers,
Dale Mayer

About the Author

Dale Mayer is a *USA Today* best-selling author, best known for her SEALs military romances, her Psychic Visions series, and her Lovely Lethal Garden cozy series. Her contemporary romances are raw and full of passion and emotion (Broken But … Mending, Hathaway House series). Her thrillers will keep you guessing (Kate Morgan, By Death series), and her romantic comedies will keep you giggling (*It's a Dog's Life*, a stand-alone novella; and the Broken Protocols series, starring Charming Marvin, the cat).

Dale honors the stories that come to her—and some of them are crazy, break all the rules and cross multiple genres!

To go with her fiction, she also writes nonfiction in many different fields, with books available on résumé writing, companion gardening, and the US mortgage system. All her books are available in print and ebook format.

Connect with Dale Mayer Online

Dale's Website – www.dalemayer.com
Twitter – @DaleMayer
Facebook Page – geni.us/DaleMayerFBFanPage
Facebook Group – geni.us/DaleMayerFBGroup
BookBub – geni.us/DaleMayerBookbub
Instagram – geni.us/DaleMayerInstagram
Goodreads – geni.us/DaleMayerGoodreads
Newsletter – geni.us/DaleNews

YU CHENG
AUTHOR
*03
Falling
Via Lactea

Falling

An imprint of Via Lactea Ltd.

Author: Yu Cheng
Translators: Arien; Yun; Hobbitsflower
Editor: Moca
Proofreader: OWL
Layout Designer: Ayan

CONTACT:
Customer Support: info@vialactea.ca
Wholesale & Distribution: market@vialactea.ca
Other Cooperation: https://vialactea.ca/pages/cooperation
Discord Channel: https://discord.gg/vialactea

Follow us on X/Instagram/Facebook: @ViaLactea_Ltd
Official Website: www.vialactea.ca

ISBN 978-1-77408-522-6 (pbk)
Printed in Canada

LOCATION:
Shops At Waterloo Town Square
#27, 75 King Street South, Waterloo, ON
Canada
N2J 1P2

Via Lactea